Acclaim for Sally

NINETAILS

"A sumptuous and lively collection, leaping from story to story in much the same way a fox does—surprisingly, gracefully, and with impressive aim. I loved this book."

—Kelly Link, Pulitzer Prize finalist and bestselling author of *Get in Trouble* and *The Book of Love*

"What I love most about *Ninetails* is its fierce allegiance to underdogs of all kinds, its careful and myriad empathy for its characters, but also its pure and artisanal delight in language and fictive possibilities. It marks, to my mind, the beginning of a poet's long and potent exploration in literature's most capacious genre. And it's a welcomed sight to see."

—Ocean Vuong, *New York Times* bestselling author of *On Earth We're Briefly Gorgeous* and *Time Is a Mother*

"With this first collection of deft and poignant stories, Sally Wen Mao continues to prove herself as one of the most fascinating and versatile writers of her generation."

—Dave Eggers, *New York Times* bestselling author of *The Eyes and the Impossible* and *The Every*

"*Ninetails* is a spirited modern fairy tale that takes cues from history, mythology, headline news, dating apps, and Mao's gift for sly observation. This is an exploration of the animal magic within the feminine, written with ardor and ambition."

—C Pam Zhang, author of *Land of Milk and Honey*

"With *Ninetails*, Mao weaves a beguiling and epic paean to the power of the feminine. Lyrical and virtuosic, with a sly sense of humor, this collection features a colorful and unforgettable cast of characters, from love dolls to dancers to translators to witches. A bewitching fiction debut as magical and shape-shifting as the fox spirit herself."

—Gina Chung, author of *Sea Change* and *Green Frog*

"Fiercely imaginative and nourished by a wild subterranean river of magic, folklore, and futuristic myth, Sally Wen Mao's *Ninetails* is a beguiling book and one that challenges the reader to conjure strange new modes of subverting oppression. Long a luminary of the poetry world, Sally Wen Mao proves here that she is an unstoppable, incandescent force in prose as well."

—Alexandra Kleeman, author of *Something New Under the Sun*

"[A] well-constructed debut collection that takes its name from the nine tails of the hulijing, a mythological female fox spirit . . . these smart, fabulist pieces confirm Mao's reputation as a voice to be reckoned with."

—*Publishers Weekly*

THE KINGDOM OF SURFACES

"Mao's third collection probes the world of art to ask how we decide what is beautiful or important, and challenges us to consider the ways culture is shaped by empire and politics."

—*The New York Times*

"An intimate family of poems, with gut-punch phrasings and tender lines that will stick to you like a bur."

—*Hyperallergic*

"Lineage is a mainstay of *The Kingdom of Surfaces*, as when Mao writes elsewhere of how a narrator, perpetually coughing as a child, was given yellow loquats as a child to calm the sickness. . . . So many gorgeous, sharp lines in this book that often reveal the pain beneath. A stirring collection."

—*The Millions*

"An incisive examination into the Western gaze . . . a truly brilliant collection which takes us on a deep, fantastic journey and awakens a profound yearning . . . both a reckoning and a reclamation, whose poems are scalpels that carve themselves into you. To truly empathize, you first must bleed."

—*Electric Literature*

"Through poems of profound complexity, in the blending of factual accounts with the sometimes surreal, often sublime, imaginings of the speaker, a finely wrought structure of proof and interrogation, vulnerability, power and, especially, of beauty emerges. The book itself becomes the vessel, complex and strange, yet strong enough to contain all the evidence required to hold history accountable."

—Allisa Cherry, *West Trade Review*

"The poet trains her mythopoetic gaze on the arts of China—especially silk and porcelain. . . . Postcolonial critique meets VR fantasy in the book's centerpiece: an extended, rapturous encounter with the Metropolitan Museum of Art's 2015 exhibit. . . . Mao brandishes her own tenacious imagination."

—*Publishers Weekly*

OCULUS

"In her stunning second collection, Mao stages a searing ventriloquy act. . . . These depictions speak and fight back against the white gaze that has framed them."

—NPR

"Hauntingly perceptive . . . An homage to pioneering Chinese Americans and an indictment of Asian representation in American culture, which never for a moment shies away from the difficult tasks of taking on race and history and technology all at once."

—*Vulture*

"Whether wayward spirit or nefarious satyr, Mao's narrators and characters inhabit the sense of oculus as eye-opening, a transformative door. . . . Mao's descriptions are precise and surreal, a next phase of evolution. . . . An expansive book, but each poem bears careful reading."

—*The Millions*

"By telling [Anna May] Wong's story, and those of other women of color who have been defined by images in popular culture, [*Oculus*] explores the ramifications of being seen and objectified but never truly known."

—*The Washington Post*

"Stunning, expansive . . . [*Oculus*] marks Sally Wen Mao as one of the most compelling, provocative poets working today. . . . Mao's language beautifully encompasses both the natural and technological worlds, infusing both with humanity, and offering a crystal clear vision of the ways in which our culture corrupts and consumes those who don't fit within it seamlessly."

—*NYLON*

"Mao's kaleidoscopic verse scrutinizes our obsession with onscreen spectacles—and includes a tour de force sequence that imagines silent-film actress Anna May Wong time-traveling."

—*O, The Oprah Magazine*

"Sally Wen Mao's poetry is at once speculative, sharp, lush, and precise. . . . *Oculus* tackles distance and exile, technology and time—

several poems are told through the filter of a time-traveling Anna May Wong, the first Chinese American film star, which is all I needed to hear to zoom through space and time wherever she asks me to."

—*Literary Hub*

"Reading *Oculus* is like being given the gift of sight . . . the possibility of being restored to who we could be, and who we could be next."

—Alexander Chee, bestselling author of *The Queen of the Night*

MAD HONEY SYMPOSIUM

"Linguistically dexterous and formally astute, Mao's tight and textured debut conjures an absurd, lush, occasionally poisonous world and the ravenous humans and animals that travel through it. . . . With echoes of Glück and Plath, Mao generates stunning landscapes where the flora and fauna reflect her presence and strength of voice."

—*Publishers Weekly* (starred review)

"The luminous image of a mouth 'digesting light' and later spitting 'the light out because it sears you' underscores the ways Sally Wen Mao transforms sense (and sentence) into sensation. Like Sylvia Plath's poems, these visionary poems are not only astute records of experience, they are themselves dazzling, verbal experiences. Worldly, wily, wise: *Mad Honey Symposium* is an extraordinary debut."

—Terrance Hayes,
National Book Award–winning author of *Lighthead*

"This is one way to render the feeling—a massive nuclear reaction; an intensity of flavor that parts flesh—of losing yourself in Sally Wen Mao's debut *Mad Honey Symposium*. It's a 'dendriform paradise' birthed from seeds of sensations of hunger, desire, and danger— among a host of other subjects—all fertilized by a visceral, textural synaesthesia. . . . This constant flood of diction swells the brain and excites nerve endings."

—*The Literary Review*

"The most exciting book in this trio . . . is Sally Wen Mao's debut, *Mad Honey Symposium*. . . . She learned Plath's tension: the stakes are always high—perhaps sometimes one gets a little sweaty in the heat in these lines—and when there's humor, it is of a dark kind . . . she's catchy in other ways: there are plenty of portable lines here, esoteric truisms that would make excellent T-shirts, tattoos, or trucker hats. I'm tempted to tattoo 'Even the thickest skin is still a membrane' on my chest."

—*Poetry* magazine

"Mao's dexterity nearly overburdens the sensorium. She succeeds in making our world seem alien in its lushness and danger. . . . *Mad Honey Symposium* [is] among the strongest #debut collections of the year."

—*Scout*

"[By] juxtaposing . . . ordinary items with feral images, [Sally Wen Mao] drags the reader into a dark dance that is both disorienting and intoxicating. Her disturbing imagery and descriptions blend terror and desire in one spellbinding book that will leave you feeling its effects long after you've finished reading it."

—*Absolute* magazine

PENGUIN BOOKS

NINETAILS

Sally Wen Mao is the author of the poetry collection *The Kingdom of Surfaces* (Graywolf Press, August 2023), a finalist for the 2023 Maya Angelou Book Prize, as well as two previous collections, *Oculus* (Graywolf Press, 2019), a finalist for the Los Angeles Times Book Prize, and *Mad Honey Symposium* (Alice James Books, 2014). Her work has appeared in *The Paris Review, Granta, A Public Space, The Washington Post, Guernica*, and others. The recipient of two Pushcart Prizes and a National Endowment for the Arts fellowship, she was recently a Cullman Fellow at the New York Public Library and a Shearing Fellow at the Black Mountain Institute. She currently lives in New York City. *Ninetails* is her fiction debut.

NINETAILS

九尾狐
Nine Tales

SALLY WEN MAO

PENGUIN BOOKS

PENGUIN BOOKS
An imprint of Penguin Random House LLC
penguinrandomhouse.com

"a dream of foxes" from *How to Carry Water: Selected Poems* by
Lucille Clifton, copyright © 1996 by Lucille Clifton.
Reprinted with the permission of The Permissions Company,
LLC on behalf of BOA Editions Ltd., boaeditions.org.

LIBRARY OF CONGRESS CATALOGING-IN-PUBLICATION DATA
Names: Mao, Sally Wen, author.
Title: Ninetails : nine tales / Sally Wen Mao.
Description: [New York] : Penguin Books, 2024.
Identifiers: LCCN 2023051495 (print) | LCCN 2023051496 (ebook) |
ISBN 9780143137894 (trade paperback) | ISBN 9780593511985 (ebook)
Subjects: LCGFT: Mythological fiction. | Short stories.
Classification: LCC PS3613.A623 N56 2024 (print) | LCC PS3613.A623
(ebook) | DDC 813/.6—dc23/eng/20231128
LC record available at https://lccn.loc.gov/2023051495
LC ebook record available at https://lccn.loc.gov/2023051496

Printed in the United States of America
1st Printing

Set in Adobe Garamond Pro
Designed by Sabrina Bowers

for the wanderers

in the dream of foxes
there is a field
and a procession of women
clean as good children
no hollow in the world
surrounded by dogs
no fur clumped bloody
on the ground
only a lovely line
of honest women stepping
without fear or guilt or shame
safe through the generous fields

—LUCILLE CLIFTON, "A DREAM OF FOXES"

Contents

NINETAILS

九尾狐

The Haunting of
Angel Island

ARRIVAL

I

From Meiggs' Wharf, Tye watched the steamship anchor at the docks. It was a monstrous ocean liner, the *Chiyo Maru*, a behemoth of steel with steam pouring out of its nostrils. Over her line of sight it towered, even as she stood waiting for another, much smaller boat, the ferry *The Angel Island*, to sidle up next to the ship. Tye checked the clock face on the terminal of the ferry building: 7:27 a.m. It was April 6, 1910, and her heart was pounding. *The Angel Island* wouldn't depart for at least another hour, so she had time. She settled on a bench that conveniently afforded her a prime view of the landing. It was crusted with chalk-white gull droppings, so she sat near the edge. She had brought a book with her in case she had to wait, but every time her eyes fell on the text, some sight or noise would distract her. Sailors yelled, seabirds bleated, and the smell of the sea mixed with the stench of human sewage suffused the air. She took out a club sandwich with pickles and ham, but it tasted like cardboard. She let the bread crusts fall on the ground, and the gulls flocked to her, screeching.

Today was the first day of her new job as an interpreter at the newly opened immigration station at Angel Island, and she had come out at the early hour to witness the ship docking and watch the new immigrants debark. She wore a scarf, hat, and sunglasses, partly because of the glare through the fog, and partly because she didn't want to appear conspicuous. A short Chinese woman under five feet tall, Tye often hated her small stature for making her feel even more exposed. Everywhere she went, strangers always mistook her for a foreign child wandering alone in San Francisco. She couldn't risk that today. If she bundled herself well enough, she might not get noticed. Her plan that morning was to take the ferry to the island along with the new arrivals. Despite herself, she wanted them to think of her as one of them. She wanted to see this city she'd known for almost twenty-three years now through their clear, unsullied eyes.

The ship's horn rumbled, and her eardrums emptied. Thick fog spilled from the sky, dissolving into the flare of plumes from all the steamships. She began to make out the newcomers, their seasick expressions, faces nearly all white. The first-class passengers came first, walking down the planks in their shawls and woolen hats, a little hot for that spring day. They poured into the wharf with their luggage, dazed from weeks at sea, sick with relief at dry land. Tonight they would return home to comfortable chambers, to hot meals and hot baths. Then the second-class passengers started pouring in, and this time Tye saw some Asians, straggling and fearful, but mostly composed.

At the base of the plank, a man in a pale green uniform waited. Next to him was an older, taller man in a button-down uniform, a couple of nurses, and a doctor. In the middle of all the incoming foot traffic, the group stood still, though the man in uniform paced back and forth slightly. He must be an immigration official, she thought. In other words, he would soon be her colleague. His pale red hair was neatly tucked into a cap, and the buttons on his uniform were crooked—the jacket fit too snugly on him. He waited until after all the second-class passengers had finished debarking to climb up into the ship along with his party, disappearing into its doors.

It would be a while before that man finished checking the papers of every third-class steerage passenger on the ship. Tye began collecting her things, hoping to make the most of the head start. The Angel Island ferry had already appeared, a paltry craft insinuating itself like a water lily inching noiselessly across the water. Like a mosquito swarm, throngs of people rushed toward the ferry, though it hadn't anchored yet. By the time she reached the end of the line, the ferry had docked in front of an abandoned building, which Tye recognized immediately as the two-story wooden shed belonging to the Pacific Mail Steamship Company, the one that used to be the immigration station until just this past month.

At the sight of the haunted place, Tye shuddered. On a couple of occasions, she had been hired to interpret for the immigration officials there, and she knew—witnessed firsthand, in fact—the conditions of this station: how rats would scuttle, covered in seaweed and fish entrails, into the immigrants' bed quarters, chewing on their belongings. One poor woman had woken up to find her braid had been gnawed off by one of the nasty critters, a bold one hungry for keratin. The whole building was a firetrap, with detainees packed up to five hundred in one room. At night, some of them escaped from the windows, dangling from telegraph lines. When city officials decided to open the new immigration station on Angel Island, it wasn't due to the many complaints from detainees and their representatives about this shed's deplorable conditions—rather, the move was because Angel Island was geographically inescapable. If any prisoner made the attempt, they'd have to plunge into freezing-cold Bay water and swim for miles, risking hypothermia and death. Now, through the mist, Tye could just barely make out the lonely shape of the island, flanked by Alcatraz's cannons and the lips of Tiburon's shoreline beyond the fog. The new immigration building, too, was a tinderbox waiting to catch fire. She wondered if it would be any more livable than the shed.

When the ferry began admitting passengers, the line moved relatively fast, even with passengers carrying heavy leather suitcases and lugging steamer trunks. Tye climbed on board with her ticket and found a seat in the main cabin. The upper deck of the Angel Island ferry was reserved for Westerners, and the non-white people—mostly Asians—had to shuffle into this level. Tye, of course, was not exempt from these rules. From her seat, she was relieved she had a clear view of the ocean. The water was a cold grayish green, with phantom jellyfish moving just under its surface. The ferry rocked gently, and Tye felt a stab of familiar anxiety: the last time she took such a vessel had been in the aftermath of the earthquake, when she had crossed San Francisco Bay to temporarily shelter in the East Bay.

It had only been four years since that day in 1906. Tye remembered it as a tremor, a fissure, a fire—though it was really in the ocean where the fault first ruptured. From the throat of the Pacific, a seismic movement ripped through California as far south as the Central Valley and as far north as the Oregon wilderness. The San Andreas Fault tore the skin of San Francisco open and expunged its simmering insides for the world to see. At the time, Tye was nineteen years old, staying on a bunk bed at the Occidental Mission Home for Girls, where she worked as a translator with Donaldina Cameron, the superintendent. Donaldina was more than a boss—she was a mother figure to Tye and all the other girls. A tall and hulking Scottish woman with a formidable voice, she was no ordinary missionary hostess—this woman had made it her life's work to "rescue" enslaved Chinese girls sold into prostitution. As a teenager, Tye had accompanied her on these trips, easily slipping into the role of interpreter for the dazed Chinese girls who emerged from the basements on Jackson Street operated by the local tongs. Tye had seen the wretched pits from which these girls had escaped: she felt Donaldina's cause was noble, if a bit proselytizing. At first Tye wasn't sure if Donaldina was forging this identity as savior out of pity or contempt for the Chinese girls, but soon she decided the ends justified the means. It was Donaldina who recommended her for this new job.

The rattling had come in the early hours of April 18, when Tye was still sleeping in her bunk. She remembered waking up to chunks of plaster and white paint from the ceiling dropping onto her face, her arms covered in fine dust. The creaky bunk had quavered along with her tongue against her teeth, and the contents of her stomach sloshed along with cups and urns, which toppled like dominoes. The younger girl on the bed below had whimpered with fear and panic, and Tye had wasted no time climbing down and consoling her. Gathering and rocking the girl's skinny limbs in her arms, Tye had explained in Chinese that this event had a name—not the apocalypse, but an earthquake. Within minutes, Donaldina had appeared in the doorway, dressed in plain black pajamas, and had calmly instructed Tye and all the girls to shuffle out of the house. Outside, it seemed that the world around 920 Sacramento Street had transformed—a sunlit crumble of buildings, rubble falling off eaves like cake crumbs.

The missionary home had survived the earthquake itself, but in its aftermath fires had raged across the whole city. City officials, in a desperate bid to fight the fire with fire, decided to release dynamite into the streets, believing it was the last resort they needed—to destroy parts of the city in order to save the rest. But ultimately they'd bungled their efforts. The dynamite destroyed the Occidental Mission Home, and Tye, along with fifty other girls, had been forced to take shelter in a house belonging to Donaldina's relatives in San Rafael, in Marin County across the water. On the ferry that took them there, Tye saw Angel Island up close for the first time.

In the weeks afterward, Tye had obsessively read about the earthquake in the newspapers. The tremor had sputtered fire up Van Ness, swallowing up rich white estates and the St. Ignatius Church. Market Street leveled, the clocks of the sea-facing buildings cracked and frozen in dawn. The Palace Hotel on the corner of New Montgomery and Market burning in lacquer and gilt, a bitumen mess, the staircases collapsed like broken piano keys—the grandest hotel in the American West, its glass ceiling shattered, Doric pillars crumbling into the marble floors of smoking rooms like a worthy ruin. South of the Golden Gate Bridge, the Cliff House on Point Lobos had slid into the sea.

But what really disturbed Tye was that her beloved Chinatown had been all but decimated. The paper had mentioned this only in passing, but she could imagine it—the thousands of already-impoverished Chinese residents crouched together in wreckage. Shabby buildings collapsed with entire family lines inside. Pomelos thumping and rolling onto the ground, crushed lanterns, scattered rinds and seeds. She imagined her family amid the rubble, and for a moment she'd felt a pang of guilt for running away from them. They had attempted to marry her off to an older man who lived in a faraway town called Butte, Montana. At twelve, she had been determined to defy these orders.

Tye was the youngest in her family. For the first half of her childhood, she received special attention from her father, which her sisters did not enjoy. He sent her to the Presbyterian mission school when her other siblings went to work in the small family business. He reserved the best cuts of roast pork at the end of the day just for her. Every now and then he took her to the beach near Lurline Pier to walk along the shore and dig for clams. At first she believed this extra attention was evidence that her father loved her the most. But then she turned nine, and he sent her to become a servant in another family's house. A few years later, when he mentioned the proposal from the unknown suitor, the adolescent Tye jumped to the bitter conclusion that her entire upbringing had all been a cruel bid to sell her off. She ran away and took shelter in Donaldina Cameron's Occidental Mission Home for Girls, because she had learned from school that that was where Chinese girls with no homes went.

Years at the mission house left her homesick—even though her family was still close by, she couldn't bear to visit her mother, her father, her seven brothers and sisters, whose faces were beginning to slide away, because she knew they were disappointed in her.

She comforted herself by becoming a vigilant helper for Miss Cameron, whose efforts toward rescuing Chinese girls from trafficking always seemed to fulfill an essential purpose. For years Tye was translator to Miss Cameron, and older sister and protector to the girls. Donaldina had in effect replaced both her parents, and the other girls in the boardinghouse her siblings. In one day, the earthquake had obliterated their whole operation.

The one silver lining in the aftermath of the earthquake was the fire down by Larkin and McAllister, the one that had burst through the Municipal Building, the Hall of Records: records of births, deaths, citizenship status, and marriages all went up in flames. In the end, calamity decided that from there on out, it didn't matter whose names were on the papers, who was legitimately born in the United States. For the first time in Tye's life, it didn't matter who was native, who was an outsider. Enterprising as they were, the San Francisco Chinese began to file reports that they had more children than they actually did. One Chinatown man claimed he had three children back in Canton, some of them grown. He fabricated the names, births, dates of these children, inventing their lives, and sold these slots for a price.

Soon enough, the floodgates for paper slots opened up—for a bit of money, people in China could shed the life they'd always known and become a fictional invention. A hard life in Canton could surely be abandoned, the way one abandons a dirty shirt with too many holes. A new identity as a paper son or daughter was as good as the promise of gold that had brought Tye's father to the new world. In the ruins of San Francisco, anyone could pretend that they belonged.

Learning about the Municipal Building fire and the response among the Chinese, Tye had felt roused, even inspired, by these amazing new deceptions in her community—she saw them as heroic subversive actions against the oppressive Chinese Exclusion Act. What would the old Tye have said to this new Tye on the ferry, now that she had secured a job with the very people trying to enforce this act? The guilt she felt was not dissimilar to her feelings about the family she abandoned.

During her interview, the man who hired her, the commissioner of immigration, a pale mustached man named Hart Hyatt North, had not minced his words: "You'd keep a close eye on those Chinese women for us. Stay on the alert for the . . . lewd ones. Keep a log of which ones are respectable, which ones are not." And when she nodded, she felt disgusted with herself, as if she were betraying her own.

The fog, she noticed, was beginning to lift. Sunlight began to warm her face, and she saw them—the immigrants. The arrivals started climbing on board, and Tye lost track of her thoughts in their din. Something lifted in her heart—it was like seeing another country for the first time, even though they were the ones experiencing it, not her. Occasionally she found herself homesick for China, a country she'd never been to. Perhaps this job would bring her even closer to it, she reasoned. Her camouflage had seemed to work—no one noticed her or questioned her belonging there. On the ferry, they sat next to her. They mistook her for one of their own.

The women began whispering.

Did you hear? The night after her interrogation, a woman had taken a pair of metal chopsticks and inserted one through each ear until she bled to death.

Did you hear? A girl was possessed by an errant ghost on the

Nanking, which sailed from Canton, and she flung herself over the railing. She had lost her papers, including the coaching book on her paper identity—the answers on the square footage of a grandfather's villa, how many steps led up to the bedroom, whether the windows faced east or west, where the well was in relation to their street. It was rumored that this girl's "best friend," also from her village, had stolen her papers. This girl naturally assumed the paper identity upon landing.

Did you hear? One wrong answer, and they'd send you back to Canton, and then what? You could fall into the hands of slave traders. It didn't matter if you were rich or poor. A reject from the Beautiful Country half a world away was bound to fetch a bargain.

As they neared Angel Island, Tye saw something that made her breath catch. It was an exquisite fox, sitting on the deck, luxuriating in the sun. It was licking its own fluffed-out tail and its eyes squinted at the newcomers, as if in a gesture of welcome.

Did you know? Like in those Pu Songling stories, you become either a ghost or a fox. If you were turned away on Angel Island and cast back home, you became a ghost: no life to assume, no life to return to. Everyone you had ever loved had already assumed you'd made the passage to your new life.

So the myth went, according to one old lady—a self-proclaimed spirit medium: If you become the paper daughter, you will shed your old self like a lobster molting its exoskeleton. And in the remains of your past self, you will find a fox just like that creature on the deck. A fox survives your last known life. Did you know? They are the only other mammal besides humans that can live on every continent—the population has already spread to this island, an earth of foxes, a pestilence. Entering this country is a small death— sisters, be forewarned, you will grow into a kind of monster.

Love Doll

Early in my life, I was living the dream. They knew me as the star of a storefront display at the Marina SM City Shopping Megaplex in Causeway Bay. In my silk negligee and matching robe, I was the crown jewel of Adult Candy Dungeon, a magical store that sold all kinds of marvels: condoms crafted to look like bananas, pubic hair dye, nipple tassels that resembled cat noses, whiskers included. The storekeeper, a mousy lady named Shan, changed my wig and my outfit every so often, but mostly she left me alone so I could adore the public with my lifelike gaze.

They called me Annlee, and I was the most coveted love doll in the whole mall, and quite possibly all of Hong Kong. I was born to be beautiful. My skin was made of soft-as-petals silicone, my skeleton of titanium—the same metal used in alloys to build seacraft vaults, missiles, and Boeing 777s. I was very expensive—no customer at the mall could actually afford me, except maybe those bankers who wasted away in their glass-and-steel offices, but such men did not frequent the mall. I was free to spend my days in the comfort of my glass display, looking back at anyone who looked at me. That's all I wanted; I was satisfied with my life. Though I was made and built for lonely men, I didn't really have to interact with them much, thankfully. I liked being useless. I was spoiled by my own uselessness.

One of my hobbies was, ironically, entertaining the children. I freaked them out, and I scared their parents, too. The parents, especially, choked at the sight of me, recoiling as if they had bladder issues. Maybe they were ill because I looked so uncannily close to human yet perfect at the same time, and this made them question the significance of their existence on a cosmic scale. Mothers clamped their hands around the eyes of their sons, as if the simple act of witnessing my supreme perfection would corrupt their young hearts forever. Honestly, it probably did.

The kids entertained me, too. From afar, their alien eyes hid nothing. My visage aroused feral levels of fascination in them, these bored sons, those sad daughters—it was as if a primordial switch flipped in their eyes as they clandestinely scanned me when their mothers weren't looking. One of the slogans that the marketers used to promote me with was, *No uterus! No child support! No headaches!* I obviously could not conceive of motherhood, but I could examine kids as a natural curiosity. After all, I never had a childhood.

These days, though, I have no audience—capitalism's terrible promise has been fulfilled, and I have been bought. All good times come to an end. I still hope that someday I can go somewhere far away, where I am respected. Revered. Maybe I could survive out there in the universe. I've always been an optimist. Wish me luck.

My departure happened on a day like any other. People gawking, pointing fingers, the like.

It was a crowded Sunday in spring, maybe late April, sometime in the afternoon. A young woman with an orange cream ice pop came up to me and stared at me for the longest time. A shock of yellowish fizz dripped to her chin as she gazed, and I tried to recall if I recognized her. She finished her ice pop and threw away the wrapper, then took out her phone and snapped a few pictures of me, but unlike the other people, who usually took one photo and scurried away in shame, she wouldn't leave. She took pictures of me from all angles. She crouched down low to the floor to snap a picture from under me, and I noticed the tips of her half-painted fingernails, ragged like saws. She could probably look up my hairless nostrils.

From afar, you couldn't tell what kind of girl she was. Perhaps she was a college student, judging by her cheap clothes? A hoodie, some jeans, dirty sneakers, Chuck Taylor knockoffs. I couldn't imagine what was running through her mind as she looked at me. I wondered if the look was desire, but I couldn't say. The young men who looked at me scoffed and turned away, but I knew what was really on their minds. If they could get away with it, I'd be the first thing they'd steal.

Anyway, the girl sat on that bench and kept looking at me, even taking notes in her notebook, long enough that other people around her began to notice. A heavyset boy around her age came up to her and joked that if she was thinking about buying me, he would split the cost with her, but they'd have to share. She ignored him, and soon after that disappeared. I saw her go into a single-person karaoke booth briefly, and then come out.

A few hours later, when the store was about to close, the girl came back with an older man. The two of them walked into the store and soon afterward Shan came out to collect me. They bought me with cash, a thick wad of bills. Shan wrapped me up in crepe paper and plastic, took out a flight case, which was a sleek black box for dolls lined with aluminum alloy and silver butterfly latches. It was once my dream to see this flight case, like any doll dreams—but then the black box seemed to leer at me like it was my coffin. Soon Shan pulled me into the foamed case, and then it was all darkness as the man carried me out of my home for good.

That was the day that my life changed forever. That the beautiful sanctuary of Adult Candy Dungeon, of the Marina SM City Shopping Megaplex, was taken from me. At first it was easy to convince myself that I was fulfilling my purpose—that the journey ahead of me was what I was destined for. But purpose is a flimsy thing, a sham concocted by and for people and inapplicable to me. There is a word for people who get sent away to live elsewhere against their wishes, and perhaps dolls cannot be described as such. But if I may humor you with metaphor, I became an exile.

I was born in Osaka, Japan. The company that created me was called Oriental Beauty, and they specialized in several kinds of love dolls, both with and without joints. I had delicate features, but my selling point was my huge sculpted glass eyes, light brown and always dilated, with long mink lashes that made little curly arcs. My irises were handcrafted to resemble Lisa's from Blackpink, or Ayumi Hamasaki's back in her early 2000s heyday. My mold was petite but still human-sized—five-foot-two, as tall as a real woman. Most male customers preferred petite. I provided comfort. I provided relaxation. I provided a thing to hold, with mass but not too much weight. Too much weight would give them anxiety.

In the back seat of a monstrous black Mercedes, I was ensconced in my flight case. Bubbles over my eyes, up to my neck in foam peanuts. It was like a marriage veil, this bubble wrap. Then the girl opened the case, and I was greeted with a shock—her face, a fantasia in front of me, her fingers picking the peanuts from my hair. Even through the fuzz of plastic, she looked angelic.

Though she could have ridden shotgun with the man, she chose to stay in the back seat with me. Strands of hair escaped the brim of her baseball cap, and she hummed along to Anita Mui's "Song of the Setting Sun" on the radio. The ride was long and endless and I didn't want it to stop, I wanted to drive around in traffic forever with my new friend and her mellifluous vocals. Through the bubbles I saw the gray Hong Kong sky—my first time encountering it beyond the two layers of glass that were my storefront window and the window in the North Hall of my beloved SM City Shopping Megaplex.

She and the older man she called Mr. Woo began to speak. I heard snippets of their conversation, but much of it was drowned in peanuts.

"Do you know about her specs?" he asked.

"Yes. She's state-of-the-art. The silicone is a new variety, a combination of many soft, medical-grade materials. Even better than before. More real to touch."

"We'll check her out when we get home."

When we finally pulled up into a parking lot, she snapped my flight case shut. She carried me up a flight of stairs outdoors, then through a revolving door. A doorman's greeting, the sound of an elevator, the *ting* of the lift carrying us higher and higher.

When we arrived at the top floor, I could tell we were in some kind of penthouse. The air was different—sterile. No warmth of human activity like at the mall, the radiant heat of harried bodies.

Mr. Woo and the girl opened the case together, unwrapping me from the paper and peanuts until I was naked before them. For the first time in a long time, I was self-conscious. Mr. Woo picked me up and positioned me on the couch, my legs up, my breasts jutting out, my nipples pink. For verisimilitude, the artist tasked with painting my skin made sure to put a freckle there, a mole here, perhaps a little flowering of blood vessels to mimic a translucency right under the surface of my skin. But none of it worked in rendering me human.

"Perfection," said Mr. Woo. "Thank you for finding her, Lola."

So Lola was her name. Very doll-like, if you ask me. At Mr. Woo's remarks, she bent me upright, straightening my metal spine and both my upturned legs, gently maneuvering me so that I was standing, my feet squarely touching the floor.

Now I had a view of everything. Mr. Woo was a tall, gangly man in his mid-late forties, with wrinkles around his eyes and graying hair he wore in a Spock haircut. Underneath his thin silk shirt, he had a pair of fine, smooth clavicles, and taut muscles. He was surprisingly attractive—it was a mystery why he wanted a love doll when he could probably find a real woman. In a crisply tailored suit, he looked frankly ridiculous next to Lola, who was still in the same mall-rat outfit from that afternoon.

Mr. Woo was dignified: that was my first impression. Usually, the men who bought my fellow dolls at the sex shop were awkward losers who gave off strong basement-kidnapper vibes. Not only was Mr. Woo handsome, but he was also clearly rich, with good taste. With him, I imagined a regal new life—perhaps surpassing even my comfortable, shiny existence at the mall. Maybe it wouldn't be so bad to make love to a handsome man every night and live like a glamourous TV housewife on the top floor of a luxe Hong Kong skyscraper.

And, wow, what a space—the penthouse apartment had floor-to-ceiling windows all around. Behind all these windows the evening fog melted into a brilliant gold. Even though it was spring, a fake digital fireplace roared in the living room, its flames licking the imitation coal suggestively. The layout of the apartment seemed to stretch beyond my line of vision—I could not locate an edge or a corner. Long musky leather couches, dove-gray, sectioned like a palace labyrinth in the center of the room alongside tinted glass tables. Sparse possessions and furnishings, a tasteful bronze hanging lamp. Some of the windows were shielded with wooden blinds, their shadows spitting little prisms of light onto the floor. The grandeur and modernity of the place, along with the rose-gold baroque impression of the clouds on the sky, distracted me from the obvious.

When my vision adjusted, I noticed the other girls. There must have been dozens, all lined up against the glass windows. Love dolls. They were diverse in age, size, material. They were all clothed in fabulous dresses, the kind reserved for mannequins at fancy department stores or flesh-and-blood socialites with luncheons to host and galas to attend. One of them was wearing current-season Oscar de la Renta. Another was wearing Dior. I was awed at the glamour and relieved I would not be alone.

I was naked in front of the other girls, and I sensed them sizing me up from afar. Trying not to look back, I focused on Lola, whose gaze did not bother me. Her face lightly freckled, her neck coated with a sheen of light sweat whose fragrance I could almost smell but didn't. A red dot on her chin—a pimple, or a beauty spot. One black eye more bulbous, slightly lazier than the other. Her gaze was a brazier, both too human and not human enough.

Without warning, Lola began to kiss me deeply, parting my silicone lips. Her tongue entered my mouth as she closed her eyes, and I saw her eyelashes twitch slightly at my touch.

"Her lips feel really nice," she said to Mr. Woo as she pulled away. "So lifelike. Hope you don't mind I stole her first kiss."

It was unfair. I wanted to feel her lips, too.

Against the low murmur of altitude, the clouds whispered, tapping on the glass. The sun began to set in the city, engulfing the towers of other skyscrapers—the Shangri-La, the Peninsula, the Bank of China Tower, their lights suddenly blinking on, alive. The mist hung low, shrouding the tops of hills in the distance, erasing Victoria Harbour. Somewhere out there was the shore I came from.

That night was, for me, what some dolls called their "coronation." Their first go-around, their first whirlwind—the equivalent of losing your virginity, except it was that much more significant for us dolls, because we were performing our function for the first time. Any kinks in our design or flaws in our engineering would likely be revealed here.

I felt lucky to have Mr. Woo be the one. His bed stretched for miles, it seemed—was it a California king? The pillows all starched and fluffed; I sank in, and gravity kept me there, captive. The floor-to-ceiling windows around the whole room, without blinds this time. Mr. Woo didn't seem concerned with privacy. People sitting on planes flying downward toward the airport could probably see everything.

Without undressing, Mr. Woo pawed and prodded at me with

his long, rough fingers. He rubbed my breasts and moaned a bit. I had no idea that a man could make such a noise—it was shrill, like the sound of a deflating helium balloon. Wow. He unbuckled his Gucci belt from his pants, and the jingling gave way to his Armani briefs, which had a wet spot over his bulge. He pulled those down and I saw it. Solid, I thought. All the dildos in the store were approximations of this live, full-blooded thing. The real thing, I realized, was much uglier than the artifice.

When he fucked me for the first time, he stammered, he crooned. His legs shook against me and he quivered inside. He thrusted, bending his pelvis. He called me Lola, which I found curious. His expressions fascinated me—they were nothing like what I had expected. Not sultry, not sexy—in those moments, he looked disarmed, even pathetic. In the throes of fucking, he was not the powerful and dignified Mr. Woo, but a simple man crying for relief from his oppressive physical needs.

If I could ask Mr. Woo one question, I'd ask if he liked the absence of mystery, in the act of fucking an inanimate love doll. The certainty that there would be no complications, that dolls were not thinking or feeling, dolls did not have needs, dolls did not speak. On the surface, I had no power, I was just a plaything. Most people, Mr. Woo included, would not attempt to peek behind the scrim of what I was. But they overlook the fact that I did have the powers of observation and a certain degree of objectivity. Inanimate as I was, I could detach myself easily from most situations even if I was a participant. I observed that all the sensations, the feelings, were experienced by the person who touched me. I could not feel their touch, but they could feel mine. Objectively, I didn't know how that could possibly be bearable for him.

· · · · ·

The first feelings came to me long before I identified them as feelings. Kudzu, that's what feelings are, growing everywhere, expanding their vines. In my previous life at the mall, I could make detached judgments, but the longer I spent in the penthouse, the more I found myself inching closer and closer to an unexplainable, interior state of being. A sudden shiver, an inchoate, dull ache in a place that was meant to be hollow.

It began with Lola. Mr. Woo wasn't the one who bedecked us with our jewels or regalia—it was always Lola who tended to us. Cleaned us, dressed us up. The morning after my first time, Mr. Woo left for work promptly at six-thirty, and one minute after, Lola entered the bedroom with rubber gloves and a mop. She mixed water and hydrogen peroxide in a bowl and scrubbed me with a microfiber cloth, tenderly, almost maternally. The precision and care with which she handled me was different from how it was with Mr. Woo, who regarded me as the toy I was.

When I was finally clean, I almost regretted it, not being her focus anymore. Lola gathered all the sheets and Mr. Woo's dirty clothes and put them in the laundry hamper. Afterward, she vacuumed. I couldn't tell if she was just his live-in housekeeper, or if they had other relations. Maybe Lola liked Mr. Woo—I wasn't sure. They seemed to be partners in one way or another, but they didn't interact much besides discussing his dolls. She lived in the penthouse, too, but in a guest room with the other dolls and not with Mr. Woo.

After eating lunch, Lola left in the early afternoon, returning before evening with shopping bags full of beautiful dresses. As if she were my handmaiden and I were the chatelaine of the castle, Lola unfastened the zippers and slipped the dresses over my shoulders. The first dress I wore from this treasure vault was a vintage Rei Kawakubo piece, a loose-fitting gown of blush silk embroidered with cherry blossoms. The seam parted between my legs, bursting into a train of pale organza. It filled me with giddiness, a sakura-laced nostalgia: I felt like I was wearing home. Then Lola put a new wig on me—an expensive virgin Brazilian loose wave made from human hair, lush against my dress. I'd never been more beautiful. Lola, too, would try them on, and I saw myself in her when she wore my dresses—it was as if she were wearing *me*. In those moments, trying on each other's clothes, we could have been best friends, or lovers.

On some afternoons after shopping for us, Lola would sneak swigs of champagne from Mr. Woo's liquor cabinet. It became a habit: She'd slip on the gloves she wore to clean us dolls post-coitally, then raid his collection of vintage Dom Pérignon. In those moments, I saw her expressions and movements become more animated. She'd put on music—K-pop songs, mostly—and dance, prancing and leaping from the couches like a small hyperactive dog who had discovered a ham hock. In these moments, I heard the other dolls giggle. They enjoyed it. They enjoyed her, and I came to enjoy her, too. This was a side she never showed Mr. Woo, and it felt like she let us all in on her secret.

The most expensive doll after me was Yukino, from my same factory in Osaka. We chatted about our hometown, the other girls we grew up with, how we ended up in Hong Kong. Yukino was Mr. Woo's last purchase three months ago. She was taller than me, probably five-five or so, and she wore her hair in long ringlets, which Lola lovingly maintained. She warned me that once you stop being Mr. W's favorite, things change immediately around the penthouse.

"What would I possibly want from him?" I asked. "I don't care about being his favorite."

"It's not the rewards. It's the punishment."

She told me: If he didn't feel satisfied when he had his way with one of the dolls, he would take off her head. He would put the doll's head on the roof of his penthouse, where he kept a small greenhouse full of exotic plants, including a corpse flower. There were rumors among the dolls that he placed the heads of those dolls in the corpse flower when it bloomed. There were rumors that he actually mutilated the heads, and he did this as some sort of ritual on the last Sunday of every month.

"It's called Cleaning Day," said Yukino.

"They're just rumors, right? It can't be true. It sounds like silly witchcraft."

"I had a twin sister, who was his favorite before I came to the penthouse. Two months ago, on Cleaning Day, she went missing. And you know, Misha lost her head three weeks ago, and we haven't seen it since."

"But, I mean, she's still there. It's not like we are humans with organs inside us, we don't need to be in one piece to survive."

"Foolish girl! You don't understand what that means, do you, to have your head separated from your body?" Yukino snapped at me, and I retreated. I considered the two of us in that moment: both of us ball-jointed in a sitting position in that vast empty living room, without a single limb to call our own.

She said, "When Cleaning Day arrives, we are vulnerable to being unmoored. Without complete bodies, we are nothing. We are not even dolls. We can't hear each other, we can't communicate, we can't do anything, not even perform our function. Without our heads, we lose our *interiority*. Do you understand?"

Our eyes met. Hers made of cheap plastic, not glass—doll-like rather than lifelike. And yet her dull glinting irises, to my surprise, could radiate a melancholy I'd never seen before in a doll. This alarmed me. Was melancholy what she meant by interiority?

"Let me show you something," she said. "Look to your very left, behind me. Look, darling, with your fancy glass eyes." Yukino strained to move. Behind her, to the left, I saw the body of a headless doll in the corner, dressed in a black gown made of spiderweb lace, looking funereal. She was missing one forearm, and the ball joint that would have been her elbow looked like a shrunken eye socket. Why hadn't I noticed her before?

Later that night, I considered Yukino's words again. The fate of losing my head versus keeping it on still made no difference to me. What did I have to complain about? I was built to be used, and if I didn't do my job, then Mr. Woo had every right to strip me of my head. I was all angles and artifice, after all. Unlike Yukino, I had nothing to sacrifice.

The more I got to know Mr. Woo, the more it dawned on me that I'd miscalculated my expectations. The man who bought me had compulsions that he never revealed to other human beings: plucking his nose hairs out, one by one, with tweezers, letting them fall in the shower drain. He was obsessed with playthings and gadgets, often staying up past four a.m. playing a mindless phone game, eating simple green salads every night for dinner as if he were a cow.

I was no longer enchanted. I noticed that his skin was pockmarked, the pores like open craters. I did not envy having human skin. Skin could be fucked with in so many ways. Skin could heat up too fast, burn or tear or grow blemishes or wrinkles. I didn't have those imperfections. I didn't want them. But still—without Mr. Woo, I would never have met Lola. And I spent most of my time with her. Some nights, when Mr. Woo chose another doll, Lola curled in bed with me, and sometimes she hugged me close to her body. It's strange to say this, but I felt something move inside me, like a ghost stirring its way up my titanium skeleton. I was not supposed to feel anything. People were supposed to feel me. Lola would sleep facing me, and she resembled a child—younger than her twenty-four years. Sometimes I wondered: Did she have her own family? Did she have a home to return to?

Sometimes she could read my mind. "What would I give to trade places with you," she whispered once, brushing my hair away from my face. "To not feel anything at all, so it wouldn't matter what someone did to me. You have all these other dolls to look out for you. I wish I had that." And then she would wipe her face, dab her eyes, stroke me a bit, rub her hands on my neck. At that moment I became aware of Lola's eyes—grainy, teary, they looked like doll's eyes, and yet they could see me.

No, she could really *see* me. Could it be? I couldn't tell if by expressing this confidence she was signaling something about what she knew. A thrilling possibility hit me—that Lola, this human, actually knew about us, our interiors, that somehow she had knowledge of us beyond our status as objects.

"Actually, I should thank you," she said. "You have spared me."

Something felt sinister about these words. I wanted to know what Lola meant by them, but she never said anything else. Still, I liked that she had found a confidante in me—it was the first time any human spoke to me as if I were a person, a friend.

Other times, Lola could be violent. Impulsive. Once, she held me close as usual, then threw me against the wall, breaking down when I bounced against it. She disappeared into the bathroom, and then emerged again. "I'm sorry!" she stammered, and then she placed me on the floor among the other dolls. "I mean, I know you're inanimate, I just . . ." And she covered her eyes with her hands and slept in the bed alone that night.

Yukino whispered, "What's gotten into her? "

Another doll, Cassandra, said, "When Lola was a little girl, she used to mutilate her Barbie dolls."

"Why?"

"Her stepfather, her uncle. The way they treated her and her brother, she only did to the dolls what they did to her."

Cassandra, a Western mold from America, was a clairvoyant, and in her original packaging she came with a magic crystal ball, a gypsy wig, and an incomplete deck of tarot cards. Except Cassandra never predicted the future—for that she was useless, and it was why so many dolls didn't respect her. She only ever predicted the past.

Then Yukino asked: "Would she have to go through what she went through if only dolls were around to sate the whims of men?"

An almost-shiver ran up my scalp, traveling through each of the straw-colored hairs on my wig. My skin was supposed to be shock-absorbent, able to withstand the most violent thrusts, slaps, or convulsions, but the electrical charge rode the surface of my silicone. I imagined Lola as a child standing inside a maelstrom, ripping her dolls apart.

To calm herself down, Lola tried various meditative practices. Breathing techniques. Calisthenics. She took ice baths, watched ASMR videos of women weaving baskets or women whispering with mouthfuls of crunchy cereal. Sometimes she even prayed. She kept tiny shrines around the penthouse—small bronze trays of burning incense, figurines depicting the Queen Mother of the West, the patron of the nine-tailed fox spirit. Wayward fox spirits, hungry for hearth and hearts, were common these days, wandering all around the cities looking for weak bodies to possess. So Lola put fox charms all around, little scrolls she painted with black ink calligraphy. She knelt in front of each of her fox shrines, reciting sutras under her breath. These were places that Mr. Woo did not touch and did not acknowledge.

When she was done with her prayers, Lola would read aloud to us from the old books in Mr. Woo's study. She started with a handsome edition of *Nine Stories* by Salinger, which she stopped midway through, wrinkling her nose. Then she continued with scary fairy tales, a ragged cloth-bound translation of Perrault's *Bluebeard*, which frightened Yukino so much her jaw dislocated from gaping. Unsatisfied, Lola moved on to the poetry shelves, surveying them. Mr. Woo owned many volumes of European and American poetry, which he barely read. Lola gathered us around the fake fireplace and read Keats, Eliot, and Rilke. Then she read us Emily Dickinson.

We dolls had a lot in common with this poet. According to Cassandra the Reverse Clairvoyant, Emily Dickinson lived in the same house pretty much all her life, so her fate was similar to ours. Emily Dickinson liked being indoors, and she was buried in a place called Amherst, Massachusetts, half a world away. In her lifetime, Emily Dickinson was always alone, always indoors. Dickinson, Cassandra rhapsodized, once defined poetry as feeling physically as if the top of her head were taken off. A poet, decapitated by poetry.

Yukino looked at me later and said, "That's such a morbid and insensitive joke to make in front of us, honestly. Cassandra is so dense sometimes—she's the kind of doll whose head is attached to her body, so she'll never fear Mr. Woo twisting it off her neck! Emily Dickinson doesn't know what she's talking about—she's never had her head taken off, she's no Anne Boleyn or Marie Antoinette."

But we did like her poems the most.

The next day, Lola seemed a bit off. Come morning, she didn't clean up after Mr. Woo like she usually did. Instead, after having breakfast alone, she took to the liquor cabinet. Lola poured some Dom Pérignon into a vial. She was usually prudent about the amount she drank, but this time she drank almost half the bottle. Later that afternoon, I heard her retching into the toilet.

"What's happening to her?" Yukino asked.

"I don't know. . . ."

"Cleaning Day is coming up, do you think she knows who Mr. Woo is discarding?"

After throwing up, Lola promptly fell asleep on one of Mr. Woo's couches. Curled up like a termite, she was so vulnerable I didn't want to look at her, but I couldn't look away. The waistband of her shorts was loose, and her slim white hip jutted out. The bones of her pelvis were on full view, and I marveled at how fragile they looked. That's when I realized: She was leaking. A thin red stream dripped from her shorts down her thigh, onto the immaculate leather. The bloodstain, like the fresh-cut carnations she arranged in vases around the apartment. The color of her blood made the couch more lovely.

Hours later, when Mr. Woo came home, she was still hunched

over like that. He stood there surveying her for a long time. He seemed disturbed, but his lack of action made me nervous. Eventually, he began nudging her gently. When that garnered no reaction, he shouted, "Lola!" and finally she opened her eyes, appearing very disoriented.

"You've made a mess," Mr. Woo said.

Lola looked down. "I'm sorry . . . I didn't realize I was on my . . ."

"I can smell your breath, too."

"I'm so sorry. I'm sorry." She crossed her legs, folding her arms across her lap to hide herself. "You know I get . . . depressed sometimes."

Mr. Woo was quiet for a long time. "He's no longer here, Lola." He narrowed his eyes, then softened a little bit. "Look, clean it up. And next time you want to drink, just ask. I don't mind sharing."

"Yes, you do," Lola whispered.

"What was that?"

"I said you do mind it very much. You are protective of your property."

"You do know that what's mine is yours, right?" Mr. Woo said. This time his expression looked pained. "If you don't listen to me, I might not be so kind next time."

A minute later, Lola came into the room and propped me against a chair as she opened her laptop. She searched on YouTube "how to wash blood off leather." A blond Chinese woman gave her step-by-step instructions. "Since leather, as a material, is naturally porous, the blood sets easily, so be very careful with your cleaning," the woman said. "Don't wipe a fresh stain with a rag—blot it gently with lye solution or ammonium hydroxide. If the blood has dried already, use a boar-bristle brush to scrape it off."

Lola began blotting the couch with lye and cold water, but I didn't want her to wipe the blood away. I wanted her to leak all of her excess, her mess, all the fluids she didn't want, into me. All my tiny painted-on blood vessels now seemed paltry compared to the vats of blood contained in Lola. If I could fill myself up with blood, perhaps that would make me human. If I could adorn myself with jewel-bright wounds and welts like persimmon seeds, maybe I would be closer to Lola. In essence, I realized, that's what Lola and I both were, two imperfect creatures—the boundaries between us, I decided, were artificial.

After scrubbing the leather for ten minutes, Lola went to the bathroom to wash her face. She came out with a volcanic mud mask on, and I was sad for her. It was the first time I craved the clarity and honesty of a flaw. In fact, the perfect rosebud of her scarred-over pimple now seemed to me less a flaw at all than a marker of *her*. Now she was trying to scrub that away, too. I eyed the stain on the couch. It wasn't completely erased. I could still see the ghostly shape, a silhouette, like the chalk outline of a fallen body, and I wanted to protect it at all costs.

This was my descent, beginning.

Yukino told me about another rumor circulating among the girls lately: there was a fox spirit stalking the premises of our high-rise apartment, and it was searching for the penthouse. Perhaps it wanted a body to possess, and didn't mind a synthetic one. The neighbors had put up fox charms in red envelopes to assure the spirits that they didn't have to be afraid. Lola seemed to have already caught wind of this—she was putting incense on burners hourly now, lighting joss sticks for the fox spirit's arrival. The fox would visit on Cleaning Day.

"This is good news," Yukino said. "All of Lola's prayers have paid off. She has summoned the fox spirit, and this might disrupt the Cleaning Day ritual, who knows!"

"A fox in a henhouse? Or a fox in a penthouse?" I mused.

"I'm hoping that the fox spirit is benevolent," said Yukino. "I feel like we've been waiting for this forever."

Cassandra predicted that before this high-rise was a high-rise, it was a burial ground, a cemetery. These days, not many people in Hong Kong had burial plots anymore: Because space was so scarce in the small island, people were often buried at sea or in gardens of remembrance. Several years ago, more than ninety percent of the city's dead had been cremated.

"I wouldn't be surprised if the fox spirits were mediums for the ghosts who drift among the living," said Cassandra. "Either way, be prepared. Things are going to get interesting around here."

Finally, the last Sunday of April arrived. All morning, Yukino was jittery. "I have this dread," she said, "that he's coming for our heads."

"Let him have me, then. I volunteer to be the tribute sacrifice," said Cassandra. "I'd like to see how he could take off *my* head."

"Not a funny joke, Cass," I said, groaning.

Even Lola recognized the ritual and seemed to be on her best behavior. In the late afternoon, she cooked a special dinner for Mr. Woo. This surprised me, because she didn't usually concern herself with feeding him. Lola prepared two lobsters that she had brought back from the markets, broiling them until they turned bright red. In her undershirt and panties and an apron, she looked beautiful.

She propped me and a few of the other girls, including Yukino and Cassandra, around the dinner table. We stared at the feast, wondering in vain how it would taste.

When Mr. Woo came home, he sat at the head of the table and said grace. It was a strange habit of his, saying grace. He wasn't religious. "Heavenly father, thank you for this meal, for this quality time spent with family. To our dollhouse," he said.

They raised their wineglasses. Mr. Woo and Lola were so stiff around each other, they could have been ball-jointed like the rest of us.

"I have some news."

"Yes?" Lola chewed her pea shoots without looking at him.

"My wife and children are visiting from the U.S."

In that moment, I realized that his refined appearance was a gentleman's front he must have manufactured. Even Lola seemed unmoored by this news.

"What do you want me to do with the dolls?"

"Store them in the greenhouse. In the shed. Lock them. Today's inventory day anyway."

"Where will I stay?"

"I'll book you a hotel. The Ritz, or the Mandarin, whatever you like."

Mr. Woo broke off a claw and cracked it, smacking his lips. With one motion of his head, he sucked the meat from the lobster claw.

"Delicious."

"Thanks."

"But the greens are overcooked."

"Then throw them out." Lola was sulking. Mr. Woo looked at her.

"You don't realize what a lucky girl you are, do you? With what you've gone through, and everything. One would think you'd be more grateful."

"Why am I a secret, anyway? It's not like we're sleeping together," Lola said, ignoring his comment.

"Lola, we've been over this. My wife doesn't know about my doll collection, and I prefer it to stay that way," said Mr. Woo.

"Maybe it's time to break the news to her, then."

Dinner was over. I was impressed. I'd never seen Lola defy him so openly before. This time, Mr. Woo looked angry. He walked over to the cabinet and took out a bottle of Dom Pérignon.

"You seem to like these, don't you, Lola?" he said. "Do as I say, so we can share." He held the bottle by its neck, like a baseball bat.

I grew afraid. I wanted to protect Lola. There was no telling what this man would do. But Lola was unintimidated. She sat down on the couch in front of him, took out a poetry book, and began reading aloud. It was the same Emily Dickinson that we listened to earlier that week.

Mr. Woo didn't say much as Lola read. I wasn't even sure if he was listening. Putting down the bottle, he fell into a state of contemplation. The silence between them was a land mine filled with poetry.

A strange thing happened that evening, when Mr. Woo took me to his bedroom. As I waited for him to peel off my fancy dress—it took minutes for him to undo every button and untie the strings of my new Vivienne Westwood (perhaps this was intentional, on Lola's part)—something, a strong gust, perhaps, swept through me.

Maybe it was the fox spirit. Maybe it was my own fear and unease. Suddenly I began feeling sensations—first in my hands, then in my arms, as the sensate energy traveled up and down my spine like a conflagration in a virgin forest. And so I was ready to detonate. The bed, the satin sheets underneath me, the memory foam, all of it washed over my skin, my hard titanium spine. My hair wiry and lifting with static electricity. Then sensation entered my whole body, and I slowly parted my mouth.

I don't know if Mr. Woo saw this or felt the disturbance, but he suddenly stopped unbuttoning the dress, and flipped me over. I looked at him. There was a strange fear in his eyes, a wariness that transformed his entire face. His eyelids twitched as he cupped my face with his hands, and I noticed the wrinkles around his mouth. I couldn't imagine how he looked as a boy, and I didn't want to. He was never a boy.

I suddenly remembered Yukino's words: *Without our heads, we lose our interiority.* And I began to panic. Suddenly I felt like I had everything to lose. I was not ready to lose my head, I was not ready to lose my interiority, the velvet safety that I hadn't known I was cultivating inside the hollows of my body. At that moment, I would even trade my body, the most precious asset I had, for my interiority—and my body was the only thing that made me valuable. I would trade my sensate self to become an inchoate interior, smearing myself all over this high-rise apartment complex, its walls suddenly holding me inside like a skin—my interior leaving the premises, becoming the whole city, stretching to the farthest reaches of the island like the remains of all the departed, both nothing and everything touching me.

Instinctively, Mr. Woo knew what was happening. He carried me back out into the living room as if I were his bride. And because I had gained the sense of touch, almost instantly I also gained the sense of repulsion. I felt his arms under my bones, his rough chapped hands, his heavy breath, and wanted him to drop me thirty-two stories so all this sensation would finally break me apart.

Without saying anything to Lola, Mr. Woo removed my head, leaving the rest of my body on the couch. Miraculously—and I think, now, that it must have been the fox spirit—I did not lose myself, neither my thoughts nor my sensations. Cradling my head, he began ascending the stairs, up toward the rooftop. Then Lola appeared at the entryway of the stairs, in hot pursuit, stopping only to gather the rest of my body in her arms. I felt her heart beating fast. I felt the sweat on the crook of her neck and her skin against mine, so much smoother and more perfect than I had imagined. I was thrilled to be carried by Lola.

She followed him up the stairs. Outside, I felt the shock of cold air and mist, and the surface of my skin prickled with tension and release. There was something so magnificent about being outside, seeing the frenetic lights of the city shimmering underneath all that fog. The invisible clashing with the visible. If I could breathe, my breath would look like smoke. For a moment we stood up there, me, Mr. Woo, and Lola, in total silence. All around us were the scattered heads of dolls—some I recognized, some I didn't. Their eyes all moved toward the two humans at the center of the storm.

It was a standoff—never had I seen them study each other so closely.

"Give her back," said Lola finally.

"I can't," said Mr. Woo.

"You know I won't let you."

"She's not yours, Lola. She's not yours."

"But you said it to me. *What's mine is yours.*"

"In that case, I meant the alcohol."

Below them, traffic moved, and above them, the clouds revealed a smooth expanse of vinyl sky. All my life I'd felt the pull of that sky—it had never felt truly real until that moment above the penthouse, when I was so close. I imagined the sky as plastic wrap, protecting the contents of the earth. I imagined touching its delicate border and cutting a hole so I could enter space through a broken part of the sky.

Lola started walking toward the heads of the dolls with Mr. Woo on her heels, my body in her arms. Gently, with the lightest of touches, she dropped my body in front of the row of heads. One by one, she gathered the heads, cupped their faces tenderly, and picked them up, as many as she could fit in her arms. She kissed all of their faces and each kiss was a leaden knock against my chest. Then she marched toward the edge.

"You don't care for these dolls anymore, am I right?" Lola said.

"You wouldn't dare. Lola. Listen to me."

"So long, dolls," she sang out, but the real goodbye was directed at someone else. Someone far away, far beyond Mr. Woo, far beyond me, and I was beginning to understand what the leaden knock in my body meant—a sort of synthetic sadness— and I wished I could call out to her, beg her to not spare me. I wanted her to say farewell to me, too.

Lola flung them over the ledge, one head, another head, another head, until they were all gone. In the air, they resembled a chart of the moon—from arc to apex to tumble, and all of a sudden I was reminded of the factory, the celestial factory where we were all born, our heads all molded from the same template— how, at the end of this life, we could dream about touching the hole in the sky and finally burn like the celestial beings we were.

Mr. Woo seemed to shrink as the heads fell over the ledge, one by one. Lola was setting them free, and there was a manic glint in her eye, as if her brazen disobedience had made her drunk. I saw her catch my pallid eye, and she finally moved toward me, my head, and instead of throwing me over the edge, she picked me up with the gentlest of hands, stroking my hair and cradling me, before finally fastening my head back onto my body.

Then I was upright, in time to see Mr. Woo walking toward Lola in a daze. As he got closer and closer to her, I saw as his daze escalated into a rage whose civility quieted the air around us— how, when he was close enough, he raised his right hand as if to slap her. Instead of shielding herself, Lola tilted her head slightly westward toward the sun already setting in the cauldron of the clouds. I didn't want to see her surrender, didn't want to see her give in, so I walked, I took my first step—dizzy from the pandemonium of sensation, I hadn't realized that the fox had also given me the power of movement, so that I could command my body to obey me, and it did, one step at a time. I moved, I walked, and I raised my arm, the one whose foundations were built with the titanium of seacraft vaults, missiles, and Boeing 777s, and let it slam in a metallic peal against Mr. Woo's cheekbone, again, then again, and I could not believe it was my hand that did that—my hand, built for men's pleasure, inflicting this man's pain.

In the greenhouse, the air is very stuffy. The corpse flower is sleeping. Sometimes it sleeps for so many seasons before blooming that I forget what it looks like when it opens, the spathe peeking out like a pollen-coated tongue. It could bloom as rarely as once every seven years. But when it blooms, the smell of death fills the whole room.

I've been spared from losing my interiority; Lola has rescued me from that. But now I can't stand the dullness. Everything before and after sensation has felt wrong. Being a doll is now intolerable, more than I can bear.

Soon after my incident, Yukino appeared—she had been discarded, and her once-glowing features were now discolored and yellow with sunspots. At least her head was still attached to her naked body. Soon Cassandra joined us, too, and she appeared bedraggled, as bedraggled as a love doll could be. Cassandra delivered the news that Lola had been fired. Lola was gone, perhaps traveling somewhere halfway around this world, as far from this island as possible. We would never see her again. Because I couldn't feel anymore, it was a lot easier than I thought, hearing this news.

I've lost that moment of sensation, but I'll always remember it. Though now I am back to my old self, I remember the precise moment when the fox spirit occupied my body, and the miracle it brought me: I was able to touch Lola, to actually touch her, and feel her touch, too. I was able to intercept her punishment, spare her from harm. It felt good, wild, like I was playing God, dealing justice with my own synthetic hands.

As seasons pass, I hope the fox spirit reappears. Maybe it will when the corpse flower blooms again. Maybe it will set us free. And then I will make my escape, and I will look for her. I know I will find her. Because I am made of silicone, I will never die. I will not die until we meet again.

Beasts of
the Chase

Foxhunting is a ceremonial sport that dates back to fifteenth century England, with evidence of its practice going even further back to the days of Alexander the Great, around 400 BC. In most parts of the U.K., foxes were considered vermin. Since 2004, when the British Parliament passed the Hunting Act, the sport has been banned in England and Wales.

The game went like this: Huntsmen on horseback, with the aid of foxhounds, searched for the fox. The foxhounds were bred to smell their quarry and follow the scent of foxes. When found, the fox became the target and ran, the hunter and his hounds in hot pursuit. The Master of the Hunt, usually a wealthy man who financed the hunt with private funds, was legally entitled to trespass private lands to search for the fox.

When caught, the foxes were dismembered. The Master of the Hunt presented their tails to the hunting party, and the game was complete.

. . . . .

Once upon a contemporary time, a young woman transformed into a fox.

Human life in the city was too punishing—the rules governing her body were like manacles, telling her what to wear, how to behave, where to move in the city. She was an exotic dancer. Her mannerisms were graceful, but grace was also what kept her head down, eyes shut, voice low and whispering, barely a sound. To her audience, her body at its most graceful was a conduit of apology—she mimicked the stupor of sleep, though she was wide awake. At the #1 Vixens Club where she danced, sometimes she descended the pole and lay still on the floor, her only movement breath, and the whole room did not exhale until she rose again.

So much time in the limelight drained her. She began to err onstage during her performances, scaring her fellow dancers. Shunning everyone, she wandered around the city alone at night, her eyes cloudy as if drugged, until one day she decided to just forgo it all, quit and return to the wild. She'd been toying with the idea for a while. As a vixen, she would be content to live out her days luxuriating in her den, a mound of mineral and ashes, learning how to survive nocturnally, organically, without light.

So she booked a plane ticket to the country where she had been born, found the plot of land that acted as a cemetery five blocks from her ancestral home, and lay down next to the tombs of her distant relatives. Her great-grandmother had been a fox medium who communicated with the fox spirits through spiritual possessions, allowing them to speak through her voice. At her tomb, the young woman found a box inlaid with mother-of-pearl. Inside the box, there was a pearl the size of a winter-coat button and a little note, left for her. If she swallowed the pearl, she would return into her vixen self. It was as simple as that.

A year after swallowing the pearl, the vixen had not looked back. She was content in the susurrating grasses, the dens and valleys and springs. The wild beauty of the pastures, the prairies and clover, the canyons, the forests—she roamed the whole continent and had finally seen and lived all that she had yearned for in her primordial bones.

But then one day, the vixen caught a glimpse of a man on horseback galloping in the distance, beyond the fields of heather. It was the season after a drought left fissures on the land, the creeks all dried out. She gasped: Was he a phantom? He looked dashing, with his scarlet waistcoat catching the evening sun's prisms. The sheen on his horse, silky like almond milk, so healthy, contrasting with her own coarse, knotted fur. Surrounded by brown-eyed dogs with tongues out, tails wagging.

The fox desired, for the first time in a long while, her previous life. A surge of nostalgia, like a death trap hewing the edges of her den, curled her tail, softened her fur. She suddenly recalled desires from her human self, never fulfilled—narratives she'd once imagined that never came true: stumbling like other pretty girls upon fairy castles in the wilderness, upon romance . . . a gallant man on horseback, reaching his arms out as if to rescue her . . . she began daydreaming, letting desire steep her in amnesia, of what life really had been, as a human.

The horseman disappeared after she saw him once, but she could not stop thinking about him. The fantasy began to beset her day and night, the prince and his steed running across the field, bringing snow, bringing ice, bringing water, bringing warmth.

The steel of his sword formidable in the sun, battling dragons and ogres just to pull her out of her solitude.

George Washington owned a pack of handsome, lean foxhounds. One of his passions was foxhound breeding and fox hunts, the gentleman's sport. He would conduct the fox hunts at his manor in Mount Vernon, Virginia. In spring, the hounds bayed, the horses leapt and raced over the open fields, and beyond, the Potomac River roared.

Before daybreak, George would eat an early breakfast, then mount his horse in a blue coat, a scarlet waistcoat, buckskin breeches, boots, a velvet cap. He carried a whip. He brought friends, many gentlemen who wanted to participate in a gentleman's sport. Their main quarry was the red foxes—bushy, spry creatures that teemed in the hills of Virginia.

George loved his horse, a slate-gray steed he named Blueskin. He loved his hounds, whom he bred himself—he gave them names like Truelove, Sweetlips, Countess, Vulcan, Singer, Duchess, Juno, Doxey, Madame Moose. In his diaries, he described his chase one morning after breakfast: "found a Fox just back of Muddy hole Plantation and after a Chase of an hour and a quarter with my Dogs . . . we put him into a hollow tree, in which we fastened him, and in the Pincushion put up another Fox which, in an hour and 13 minutes was killed—he was a conquered Fox we took the Dogs off, and came home to Dinner."

The early hours had fallen, the wind dry and frigid, and the fox spent the whole night collecting food—a vole here, a dormouse there. As a fox she had the ability to use the earth's magnetic fields to calculate the distance and direction of her prey. The rings of shadow on her retinas darkened as she gazed toward magnetic north, and when the shadow aligned with the sounds of her prey, she could find their exact location. Once she detected a shape crawling in the tall grass, she leapt into the air northward, around twenty degrees from magnetic north, landing on the rodent's throat, and that's how she caught her biggest trophy, the rat.

Now dawn was fast approaching, and she heard galloping in the distance, the sound as strange as alien landings across ancient craters. She saw the prince had a whip. His dogs were searching for her—their tails were no longer wagging—they snarled, their teeth sought blood. She understood finally, on a primeval level, the danger she was in—that her blood was scented like pungent soil, like pollen or poisonous berries.

She turned her magnetic abilities to her predators. She raced and raced through the grasses, the fields, the fences. She raced and raced and ran out of breath and collapsed in shame. With her hind legs buckled beneath her, she wondered whether she should surrender and give them her life. Vixens like her only knew shame because of their past lives as humans. Her every limb flooded with it—at having been fooled by hope, by romance, at always being the despised, hunted thing.

In the forest, she managed to find a tree with a hollow. It would be her hideout for the day, when she was weary. She climbed inside, tried to rub her fur off with the lichens and jagged bark, tried not to release her scent, but her body was secreting it everywhere: the rocks, the flowers, the dried-out gullies all smelled like her. She had nowhere to escape, so she hid—climbing farther and farther into the tree, until at last she found the deepest pit inside the hollow where blight had chewed through most of the heft. With her breath harried and heaving, she curled into a ball and collapsed. Ants crawled across her languorous body, making their mass migrations.

Soon the lowest branches began rustling with the sound of sniffing dogs, and by nightfall she was running again. She ran through the forest, thickets and twigs snapping beneath her paws, now blistered with sores. Above the clouds, thunder tore through the sky like the moan one makes when mauled by a bear. She was alert to the rain about to pour, hoping it would disorient the hunter and his dogs. She heard the dogs ransack her den, she heard them snarl, maddened by lust. They were getting impatient in their pursuit— they could smell her—they knew she was somewhere close.

She ran through cities, hid in small towns, camouflaged by her ability to shape-shift—the pearl in her throat responded to her distress, cast a light from her body so she could become one with the reeds or the marsh or the pavement. She tried not to excrete too much and fed on insects, flying bugs. Small towns were the most dangerous: fox hunts are considered a rural art born in the endless expanses of countryside, where there were open spaces and perfect views of stars. Nowhere to hide for a fox with a red, bushy tail.

One day she ran into a thick coppice, thinking she had evaded her captors. She had just gathered enough wild gooseberries for a bright jeweled dinner when she turned around to an awesome sight: a foxhound appearing through the underbrush. He was a handsome hound, spotted with a crown of cedar fur. He was bigger than her. He could overpower her easily. His eyes a scarlet pus that ate away at his pupils; his nose wet, infernal; his fur reeking of a terrible domesticity; his breath smelling like he'd been fed and fattened with raw game. All the wildness had been leached from his being, and now he was a captive. At the sight of her he almost buckled with excitement.

"Oh boy," he said, circling her. "Oh boy, oh boy, I've caught you, my wild one, now my master will reward me and I'll be the bravest and the best dog in all the land."

At first she tried to bargain with him. "I'll give you a better reward than the master ever could," she declared. She imagined gnawing on the dog's mangy head, his meat for brains.

"You're just trying to trick me, vixen."

"Human life. I've been a human before, and you can be, too. Trust me. I'm magic. Aren't you tired of following them all the time? They are the only species on earth who could control other species like you and me."

"You're stalling. My master told me never to trust a fox. I don't have time for talk. I need your body now." He sputtered this, drool dripping from his jaw, and lunged at her. She arced backward and instinct made her jump vertically in the air, like when she hunted for prey buried under snow. His teeth missed her by a wide margin, and that miss was his fatality—he left himself open, his pale throat in front of her, and she bit him.

Red trickled on her already red fur. The hound squealed, yelped, whined, and the shriek satisfied her. She clamped down, she did not let go as the dog thrashed and thrashed. Now she knew what she was, what they'd always suspected, what they'd always been afraid of. One hit in, she delivered the coup de grâce. She was a victrix, and a demon.

After so much starvation and running, it was only natural that she would begin biting the skin off her quarry. He was hers now.

A sudden flash reminded her of a time when she was still a teenager in Allentown, Pennsylvania. Since she'd transformed, she had not harbored many memories of her human life, but the image of her school returned to her, fluttering. She was reading at the library a book about the circulatory system, the pages open to a diagram of the heart. For the next week's science exam, she was memorizing the parts of the heart: right aorta, right ventricle, left aorta, left ventricle, coronary arteries.

A boy from the same class sat down next to her. She forgot what his name was, Matt or Stan or Mick—he had been held back one or two years, and he had a sprinkle of freckles across his nose. His face was hard to read—they had never spoken before, but she knew he wasn't doing well in the class, always mumbling, always at a loss for an answer whenever Ms. Archer called on him.

He sat down next to her, took out his notebook. He stared at her for an uncomfortably long time until, without warning, he reached over her and tore the page out of her textbook. "I need this," he said. "I lost my textbook."

"It's mine," she said, reaching toward it.

"I heard you got all As. I'll give it back if you let me copy you."

"No. And I don't get all As."

"But look at you." The sneer in his voice was suggestive, almost flirtatious. His voice had croaked recently into an ugly rasp. "No one wants you here. You have nothing better to do than study."

She ignored him then, shut her book, and slipped it into her backpack.

"Don't you and your family eat dogs?" he snickered, holding the sheet over her. "Even the history teacher says so. You people eat dogs."

"My parents are white," she said, as if her adoption status absolved her of his accusations.

He guffawed, and at this she shuddered involuntarily, because he was right, in a way. The history teacher did mention in class one day, in passing, that in the summer he had visited some provincial town in Asia where the local delicacy was dog meat. Sometimes this teacher, Mr. Brady, brought his own dog, a beautiful German shepherd named Lass, to school, and her classmates would take turns petting it. Shaking his head, he said, "What a shame that a man would butcher and eat his own best friend."

For the final project that semester, Mr. Brady assigned a research paper about any period in history, as long as it occurred in the nineteenth century. She chose one of the most brutal assassinations in history, the deposing of Empress Myeongseong in Joseon-period Korea.

She spat out his blood—soon, when she'd had enough of the chewy, awful meat, she had to retch it out as well. She collapsed against the bloody loam. She was groggy, bone-tired. The meat of the dog enervated her. But she could not just stop. Now that the corpse lay before her, she was afraid. One of the master's own prized foxhounds was missing. They could smell the hound's blood—it was out in the open. They would have no mercy now if they caught her. She remembered the prince had a gun. A rifle that could fire multiple rounds.

One of the most chilling things about composure and civility, she realized, was the murderousness hidden beneath manners. One can be dignified while tearing something into obliteration.

And then she had an idea. She would shape-shift even better with a costume. She tore at the hound's fur until she carved a new skin. Inch by inch, claw by claw, she entered the hound, made a coat out of her hunter. This new skin—this new identity—would be her hideout, for now.

· · · · ·

The assassination plot against the last Queen of Korea, Empress Myeongseong, was called Operation Fox Hunt. History calls the execution of this plot the Eulmi Incident. The forty-three-year-old Empress opposed the Japanese occupation. At the end of the Joseon Dynasty, she collaborated with Russia and other foreign governments to retain Korean national identity.

Operation Fox Hunt was orchestrated by the Japanese viscount Miura Gorō, along with up to fifty other men. On October 8, 1895, a team of male assassins stormed the Gyeongbokgung Palace in Seoul, infiltrating the courtyard where the Queen's wing was, north of the Hyangwonjeong Pavilion. They were dressed in strange gowns and armed with sabers. None of these men could recognize her or knew who she was. They forced the Empress's consorts out, stripping them and raping them, demanding information about the Queen. They killed at least three women whom they mistook for the Empress. According to historical accounts, the assassins found her, carried her through the hallways past her gardens, raped her, beat her, sliced her open, dismembered her, threw her onto firewood, doused her in kerosene, and set her on fire. They cremated her in front of a live audience. This was the price of disobedience.

Ever since she socked Matt or Stan or Mick across the face with her textbook, knocking him to the ground and bestowing a yellow-green bruise on his temple, she had been suspended and shunned by her classmates. Even before the "incident" she didn't have many friends, but now even the other outcasts avoided her during lunch or after classes. Even her own foster mother, who had adopted her when she was two years old, became distant.

"You can't get angry like that," her adoptive mother said. "I know that boy was out of line, but, darling, you have to take the high road sometimes."

Many years later, her mother would offer this same advice to her when her boss at a chain restaurant put his hand on her ass as she was counting the cash in the register at the end of a long night and played dumb when she shouted at him, spilling all the bills on the floor at his feet, running and raging all the way home.

She stalked the streets in the skin of the hound. This kind of camouflage was consuming: she became the dog, the hunter. The sensation disturbed her—his body didn't just envelop hers, it was supplanting, usurping hers. She was adapting his senses into her perception as well. The keen potency of smell, the pricks on her nose opening a floodgate, overpowering all her other senses. It disoriented her walk, made her vision foggy, turned the world black-and-white. Smells of white pines, mud, the beating organs of other animals in the forest, even the fearful sweat of skulking men. Their hunt forestalled, waylaid by the missing hound. She heard them call for SweetTooth. They had named their dog SweetTooth.

What call would she answer to? Where could she go from there? When she was hunted, she felt alive with the constant threat of defilement. When she was no longer hunted, who was she, even? Invisible, at peace. In her human life, she had weathered chaos of a different order. She wondered whether she should gargle it up, the fox pearl, spit it out, give it back.

Recently, a history professor, Jeong Sang-su, discovered a classified German diplomatic document stating that the Empress survived her assassination plot and was alive four months after the

Eulmi Incident. It was a decrypted text that the German ambassador to Russia had sent to the chancellor, which stated that the Russia consul to Seoul had received a top-secret request asking if the Queen could flee to Russia.

Another document, from Britain, discovered at the National Archives in the United Kingdom, stated that the Empress had escaped during the incident. The evidence was compelling that Empress Myeongseong had fled Korea in disguise. She had done this before in the midst of other assassination attempts: covered her body and passed as a child, fleeing their thirsty swords.

Imagine this was real, and the Empress slipped out of the pandemonium of that bloody and cloudless day incognito, escaping into the Russian legation, where she lived out the rest of her days as an exiled widow of her nation. Eternally indoors, she raised houseplants and wrote anonymous poems. A stranger, exiled not just from her palace, from her beloved and besieged country, but from the realm of the living. A living ghost.

If British and German intelligence were reporting the facts, then Empress Myeongseong had outfoxed the hunters. The brilliant Queen Min survived Operation Fox Hunt. Who wouldn't want to believe this story, that the woman who attempted to guard her country's sovereignty would live through her own brutal assassination—who wouldn't want it to be true?

Mr. Brady circled this section of her history paper and marked in red, *Questionable source and statement. The assignment is a research paper based on real history and fact, not conspiracy theories.* He gave it a C+.

Despite the ugly episode with Mick or Stan or Matt, she loved libraries. During her suspension, she had endless time to herself.

She read poetry, she read about animals, especially foxes. She learned foxes were contradictory figures, both solitary and communal, primordial and contemporary. That foxes harnessed the magnetic poles to locate prey. That foxes could live in every eco-system, from the lushest to the most barren—the city, the jungle, the arctic tundra. For thousands of years, they made homes out of every continent on earth except Antarctica. That when foxes screamed, it sounded terrifyingly human: at night, in neighbor-hoods at the edges of brambles, their shrieks sounded like women screaming bloody murder. That foxes screamed to communicate, to stake territory, to attract mates. Female foxes screamed while they were mating.

She wrote, too. Poem fragments at first, then entire paragraphs and stories. It was known that for epochs, fox spirits retreated into the mountains to write and read, just as she did, and they wrote long lyrical epics. It was known that once her great-grandmother had done the same, before she came down the mountain and married a human.

The first sentence she ever typed on a computer was, *The quick brown fox jumps over the lazy dog.* That one sentence contained every letter of the alphabet. In typing the sentence over and over again, she recognized writing as a sort of utopia where the beasts of the chase may evade the hunters. The quarry prevailing. Moved, she typed and typed and practiced until all the words were meaningless.

William Faulkner wrote a short story, "Fox Hunt," published in *Harper's* in September 1931. In the story, the rich protagonist, Harrison Blair, buys back his childhood family estate in South Carolina to go on fox hunts. For three years he tries to catch a fox, to no avail. One day, with his wife and three servants as his witnesses, Blair runs ahead of his hunting party, and eventually his hounds, and discovers the fox in a briar patch.

He gets off his steed and wrestles with the fox, trampling it to death with his boots. The violent death of the fox occurs simultaneously with his wife leaving him for another man. In his descriptions, Faulkner conflates the wife with the fox as Blair's quarry, uncontrollable and wild, but Blair himself is not a sympathetic character, always looking for a new game to play.

After seventy-two hours as a hound, she began to recognize she would rather tear herself up, rip herself out of this protection, than remain hiding in this skin. The brooks had lost their color. She'd drunk from the dirty river, spat out foul water. She could no longer hunt like she used to hunt. Her celerity, her nimble senses, gone. She'd even lost her magnetic compass, which had been her only comfort besides the beautiful den she'd lost. What was this life for, other than solitary suffering? Other than a fruitless fight to survive? She began to molt. Shed the senses, the fur and teeth and blood. The handsome, shiny short-hair coat. The wet, vital nose that smelled everything near and far.

When she was twenty-two, she became a dancer to pay off her tuition at Columbia, where she was studying literature and poetry. By night, she performed at clubs, dinners, dance halls, receptions. She cited the careers of prominent dancers like Jadin Wong, who danced at clubs like the Forbidden City in San Francisco, as her inspiration. By day, she wrote poems. She read novels by Kathy Acker and Clarice Lispector, poetry by Lucille Clifton and

Mary Ruefle. Her verses were getting better. She was getting accepted to small magazines and readings.

Four months into her dancing, she noticed a face in the crowd, that of her childhood bully, whose name she found out was neither Mick nor Stan nor Matt—it was actually Terry. He had become an investment banker at Merrill Lynch. The venue was a newly opened club called Den of Shadows, styled like an old Shanghai opium den, on Mott Street. It smelled like smoke, flowers, and brandy. The clientele was the kind she most detested: a certain type of young professional man, interchangeable, who wore button-downs and heavy jackets in Manhattan's mossy summer heat. Terry was in a group of such men. They hooted at her, whistled, made gestures, licked their lips. Although he made no such noises himself, she sensed something invasive in the way he looked at her. When their eyes met, the vacant, calculating lust she saw on his face was devoid of recognition.

She let him buy her a drink, to confirm this. "Do you remember me?" she asked. As he handed her drink to her, he slid his hand on her waist.

"Trust me, if we'd met before, I would have remembered. Your performance was incredible. I memorized every detail." His fingers circled her back. She stiffened.

"I'm sorry, it's not like that." She pulled his arm off.

"Hey, hey. Not implying anything." His voice grew softer. "Come out with us after this. I'll make sure you have a good time."

"Even if I was interested, I couldn't. I have another act in forty minutes." She leaned in close as if to kiss him, and he closed his eyes. "Maybe you blocked it out of your memory. I don't blame you. I socked you in the face at our high school library in Allentown, remember?" she whispered, and she felt his neck stiffen, the hairs on his face standing up.

"And now you want to fuck me. What a world we live in!" She gave him a conciliatory pat on the shoulder, then walked away with her whiskey Coke.

When the Master of the Hunt discovered her hideaway, every hair on her body stood and she scrambled into the brambles. A seismic panic button. A quake. The words she heard: *Tally ho.* He took out his whip. The sky fast dusking, turning dark, ink spreading across a bolt of cotton.

The master's face glowed white as phosphorus. There was nothing gentle or genteel about this gentleman and his rifle. From a distance, one could view the scene as fateful, even sexy—at the edge of the forest, the fox and her hunter. Living on her last lifeline, she finally confronted him, the subject of her fear. The perfect conquest. He would relish punishing her. There would be a scuffle, branches rustling, the sound of gunfire. And finally she'd emerge as the prize, the trophy.

When the master leaned downward for his kill, he was startled by a movement—the fox, in her last stance, had departed the earth—she was jumping up, toward the magnetic north, shooting toward the sun to catch the prey that remained unseen, burrowed underground, and she screamed her fox scream, the shrieking of a woman, the trilling of the dead—

In Finnish mythology, it was the fox that was responsible for the northern lights. The name for aurora borealis is "revontulet," literally translated as "fox fires." According to the beast fable, a magical fox swept its tail across the snow, spraying snowflakes to the sky. Thus, the green fire blazed in the star-studded night. You could say that the moment that *Whoop!* was delivered, the fox ascended into that heavenly fire.

In the story where Empress Myeongseong was caught, the one in all the history books, she was laid to rest in a tomb in Namyangju, Gyeonggi, in 1897, two years after her death. Her husband, King Gojong, arranged a mourning procession with scrolls, giant wooden horses, and four thousand lanterns honoring her memory and legacy. Korea had fallen under Japanese colonial rule, which remained in place until 1945.

In the story where Empress Myeongseong got away, the one we want to believe, she lost everything that meant something to her: her country, her husband, her identity. At first her displacement and subterfuge would disorient her and unbury far-distant memories of childhood—transport her back to when she was eight and orphaned, and the outside world smelled rotten with garbage, and that was all she thought was possible. Little did she know how sweet it could be: lilies opening in the winter gardens in February, the smell of braised octopus and winter radishes. In the world she left behind, the people mourned her, they mourned their sovereign country. In the frozen waters of her exile, the secret might bring her a little pleasure—neither her assassins nor her subjects knew: that just beyond the floe, her heart was still beating.

The Haunting of Angel Island

PARTS 2–3

2

When Axiu arrived in San Francisco on the SS *Chiyo Maru*, she was twenty-one years old, five months pregnant, and without her husband. He had left Canton for America three months before, to be admitted as a paper son to a family in Salinas.

At that time, neither of them had known that she was pregnant. But now that she had finally arrived, she felt like a dust mote dragged by her belly, its sordid swelling. On the ship over, she was beset with fevers, and nausea that left her expelling all her meals. She barely remembered the three weeks at sea, except the rise and fall of her body, its seismic panic—the farther the ship traveled, the less she could recognize herself, her own skin, her own hands. On board she had developed a mysterious rash, and it inched down her arms like little tides.

After they admitted the first-class passengers into San Francisco, Axiu, along with the other passengers, boarded the ferry to Angel Island. When it docked, a long wooden path awaited them, and uniformed immigration officials welcomed them by taking away their luggage. Axiu's one trousseau was dragged, along with many of the other immigrants' luggage, into a shed at the end of the wharf. It was the first time Axiu saw the white devils in the flesh: one of them was quite young, perhaps only a few years older than her, in an ill-fitting uniform. Earlier he had climbed on board the ship and checked all their papers. Axiu noticed his light-colored eyebrows, his light-colored eyelashes, which reminded her of corn silk, they were so translucent.

It was this officer who separated the new arrivals: he ushered the women and children to one side, the men to another, and then they walked in these formations to the administration building, which rose like a strange white palace. Axiu was not accustomed to such architecture—to her, it appeared both majestic and austere, with white-painted wooden walls and a colonnaded porch, surrounded by forested hills, facing the sea. Date palms rose from plots of earth, lush with brown-tipped leaves. In their new formations, Axiu began noticing the other women in line: Most of them looked Chinese, but some were from other countries—a Russian mother with child, Sikh wives, and groups of young Japanese women. When they finally entered the main examination room in the administration building, she was further separated into a group of Chinese women. After they were culled according to their identities, each group was led to separate "waiting rooms" inside the building, which were really just isolated spaces cordoned by high steel fences.

The room was already fraught with the nerves of all the new arrivals, but now that they were contained between these fences, the fright was palpable. One woman had her head down, rocking a sleeping child on her lap as if on the edge of a nervous breakdown, and another woman openly wept. Axiu noticed the stark wooden paneling on the walls, the chicken-wire clerestory windows, netting the view of the sea. Not a carving or aesthetically pleasing shape in sight. Even on the walk up to the administration building, the barbed-wire fences had dampened the stunning views of the eucalyptus grove that surrounded them, the palm trees and their low-hanging fronds.

Eventually they were called to meet the inspector in the main room. He was a man in his fifties or sixties, gray-bearded, broad-shouldered. Beside him was an interpreter, a diminutive bespectacled Chinese woman. They did not introduce themselves. Axiu was immediately curious about this interpreter, childlike and moon-faced, who spoke fluent English. What's more was that Axiu was certain that she'd seen this woman on the ferry, packed along with the rest of them, obscuring her face with a long silk scarf.

"How long have you been pregnant?" the interpreter asked her in somewhat accented Cantonese.

"I do not know. It must be around four or five months."

"Are you planning to give birth here?"

It seemed like a trick question. "Why, I don't know. . . ."

"It says here in your file that you are joining your brother, who arrived here in the States a few months earlier. Who is the father of your baby? Where is he?"

She found herself flushing, lightheaded. Her husband had told her to lie and say she was his sister, because wives were not allowed to enter the country, but blood relatives were.

"My husband, sir. He was back in China. He died recently, before I left." She made the lie up on the spot, and the inspector remained unconvinced.

"How old was he?"

"He was thirty-six. He died in a boat accident."

"How often were you intimate with your husband before he died?" The woman who was translating now seemed apologetic, as if embarrassed for Axiu. Her eyes strained as they avoided Axiu, who stood horrified at this question, unable to muster something to say. The hard expression of the official, the intensity of his gaze, seemed to cleave into her, and she felt dizzy imagining what he might be imagining at that moment. She wanted to exit, rescind this decision, reject this journey, head home immediately, but it was too late. She was trapped here, trapped in this pregnancy, already a liability in this country.

"I do not recall, sir." She flushed. To her horror, the inspector guffawed at her uncertainty and took a note on his pad. Then he ripped off a ticket and began to issue an identification number. Axiu readied herself for the next step, so eager she was to leave this man behind. But in her relief she craned her neck and then the man stopped altogether when he noticed the redness there. The man barked at the interpreter, who then asked Axiu, "What is that rash on your skin?" The woman's voice, compared to his, was perfectly calm and nonthreatening, and Axiu almost marveled at how mismatched a pair they were, as if the act of translation ended with mere language.

Encouraged by this woman's steadying demeanor, Axiu tried

to shake it off—probably just some insect bites or a burn, she guessed. When the interpreter failed to relay her answer to the inspector, Axiu pleaded: "Tell him it's not serious. Tell him it's just a sunburn. It will heal in a day."

This time, the interpreter gave her a pitiless glance and said, "I can't tell him that. He has eyes, you know."

"We're going to have to send you immediately to the hospital to be treated," he said. "You're not to be assigned a dorm in the main building until this has been taken care of."

At these words, Axiu was, for the first time, legitimately terrified. A guard came and escorted her out by the arm—the way he gripped her with his meaty hands, she felt like a criminal. Axiu felt hot against the stares of everyone in line, whose worry she felt not directed at her but themselves. She shot another glance at the interpreter before exiting. The woman had already moved on to the next detainee, without a glance in her direction.

The guard led her past the administration building, up several sets of wooden staircases to a white building on a wooded bluff. This was the hospital. The door opened to a room full of nervous detainees, and she was sent to the waiting room for Chinese and Japanese women. Finally, when it was their turn, she went into the doctor's office along with several other women.

A man she assumed was the health inspector told them all to strip down naked. A couple of nurses, one Chinese and one white, flanked him. This time there was no official interpreter, except for the Chinese nurse, who spoke in simple phrases and half gestures. Because Axiu, along with all these women, had been flagged as possible agents, they were to be given a full nude inspection. Axiu felt despair. Never had she undressed fully in front of anyone, even in front of her husband—there was always a bolt of silk, a sleeve, or darkness, something, to hide herself. The nurses took measurements of her body and checked them against her papers. At first they measured her height, but then they also measured her waist, her hips, her belly, her spine. Through all of this, Axiu tried to reassure herself that it was standard protocol.

Then the doctor asked them for a stool sample, and the nurses began issuing shallow wooden pails. A test for hookworm, a common disease that Americans believed immigrants from Asia carried—so every Asian arrival must provide the sample. Each woman was directed toward a cordoned-off section of the room, and asked to do their business there, with everyone still in the room.

Incredulous but lightheaded, Axiu squatted over the pail with her pregnant belly, attempting to control her bowels and failing. The whole time, she grew dizzy trying to hold her breath. The thought of everyone collectively taking a shit made her feel nauseous again, as if she were back on the steamship. When she finally handed the pail to the nurses, they immediately sent it downstairs, to the laboratory, for "testing."

"Female of the Chinese race. Height, five feet three inches," the doctor muttered, when she emerged. She did not understand anything he was saying, though she understood he was talking about her. "Five months pregnant. Moon-shaped birthmark on her lower back."

In his examination, the doctor traced his finger along her rash down to her birthmark. His cold nails against her back, she shivered. She had not been touched in a while, and the strange foreign doctor's finger probed into her spine. He then administered a white cream onto her rash, kneading into her skin with unnecessary force.

"What's this medicine?" she asked, but he did not answer. Neither did the Chinese nurse, who fidgeted with her braid.

. . . . .

After another hour in the medical facility, she was finally discharged, but she felt as if all her muscles had been flayed. Her rash was painful: the longer the cream penetrated her skin, the more she felt her skin inflamed. The guard then assigned her to a bunk bed on the second floor of the administration building.

It was a cramped, airless room with wire-netting bunk beds, half of which were covered in drying laundry. The smells burned her nostrils. There must have been about fifty, sixty beds, all stacked together one on top of the other. The women used every last available space to stake their belongings—the chandeliers were draped with wet stockings and blouses, so that even the source of light emitted gloom.

To her relief, Axiu was assigned to one of the lower bunk beds. By then it was dinner hour and the women had already shuffled off to the dining hall, but Axiu had no appetite. Exhausted, she curled into a sleeping position and cherished this rare moment of peace. The blanket she was given felt coarse, like fox hide, tangled with the smells of other women's bodies.

3

Opposite Axiu's bunk was Mrs. Yee. Back in China, Mrs. Yee had a different name, Mother Bai. Mother Bai was primarily a midwife, and she was known to deliver the babies of almost every family in her southern village, but she wore many hats: in addition to her "official" job as a midwife, she was also a healer, a diviner, and a fox spirit medium.

Mother Bai came from a family from Shandong so poor that they ate bark off of trees and boiled grass for suppers. In the north, it was common practice to worship fox spirits. When a local woman was rumored to have been possessed by a fox, the Bai family, along with all the other poor villagers, thronged to her home to ask questions and seek cures. The possessed woman, she was told, became a medium in front of all their eyes. She jerked in all directions, she muttered, she spewed noises in a language no one could decipher, she approximated the sounds of an animal in heat—and finally, after what seemed like hours, she fell on the ground in a trance, and woke up a medium. The medium told the Bai family that in order for their son to revive, they needed to marry their daughter off to a man from the south.

And so off she went, the teenage bride-to-be, in a caravan of sorts, journeying the long, craggy miles from Shandong to the village in the Pearl River Delta to wed her husband, who was twenty years her senior. She could not remember much of him; only that he was quiet, studious, provided her with a modest shelter. Three years after their daughter was born, he died. She was twenty-two and already widowed, living in their empty house with just her toddler. Soon there was an infestation of foxes: she found her clothes torn and eaten, her menstrual rags stolen, her stores of food raided and spilled. Chicken bones and tufts of fox hair and fur appeared in her husband's former study.

One night, the fox spirit finally visited her and told her that it could bring her financial independence for the near future, if only she surrendered the area of the study to them as well as surrendered her daughter to be wed into the fox family. Mrs. Bai considered her options: She could agree to the fox taking residence, but she refused to give up her daughter like her own mother had forsaken her. She didn't want to hire an exorcist to eradicate the foxes, either, for she knew it would result in karmic consequences. So she decided to offer herself as an imperfect substitute for her daughter; in exchange for peace, she would serve as a medium for the foxes and worship them for the rest of her days.

Many fox mediums were forged this way: through a mutual arrangement with a fox, which bestowed the medium with favors and supernatural gifts. She developed a loyal customer base as midwife, healer, fox medium, and shaman. People came to her with just about any affliction—physical, emotional, or spiritual. She administered medicine for the ill, divinations for the wayward, exorcisms for the bewitched, and rituals to commune with the spirit realm for those beset with grief. She was respected well enough that many families sent her gifts during the Spring Festival, affectionately calling her Mother Bai. She raised her daughter as a single woman, and this was unheard-of in a village like that. This went on for about thirty years.

And then just like that, it all disappeared. One day, a Taoist priest visited the village and requested her services. After asking her a series of difficult questions she easily evaded, he frowned and began chanting a hateful sutra to exorcise the fox, who had begun flailing inside her body until she vomited a poisonous red sap. The fox, wet and squirming, slid out into the puddle and the priest wrung its neck with a string of mala beads.

Then he professed to the village that she was a fraudulent fox medium, and thrust the fox's emptied husk of a body forward as proof: *Go on*, he said, *ask her anything*. And so in the span of one miserable season, business dried up, famine struck her village, floods drowned the crops, bandits moved in to wreak havoc and loot the homes of her neighbors. Still, the bandits skipped her home: true medium or not, bandits remained afraid of her.

Her only daughter, Anqing, weak from starvation, died giving birth. Her daughter's husband, Ho Mock, grief-stricken, took the baby and moved to Canton, abandoning his life in the village. Eventually Mrs. Bai heard that he sold his house for a meager sum and bought the papers of an American-born Chinese on credit, making the crossing to California.

A few years after her son-in-law vanished, a group of angry townsfolk rapped at her door, accusing her of defrauding them. Many were irate former customers—they had consulted her, and she predicted good fortune; what they faced instead was disease and devastation. They emptied her cupboards of rations, they spilled her rice. They sacked her medicine drawers, her herbs and roots and flowers, the ones she'd spent her whole life collecting—the ginseng reserves, the dried Osmanthus flowers, the teas. They plundered her makeshift altar to fox spirits and to Mother Taishan, the goddess she consulted in her divination practice, the one she summoned to communicate with fox spirits. They smashed the goddess's statue against her altar, and at her feet landed the broken head, which she snatched up and ran away with as they set her house on fire.

Some of the people who had done this, she had delivered from their mother's womb. She had cradled them when their faces were still wrapped in a film of caul, cut their umbilical cords, ran their first baths under clear springwater steeped in herbs. She had been the first one to welcome them to their lives, but of course none of them remembered. All they saw then was a pathetic old woman who had no relation to them—the lowest of the low—a widow, a fraud, and a crone.

"Repent, old witch! Repent for your lies!" they cried as flames tore the roof of her house, the smoke incinerating all other senses.

A sympathetic neighbor let her hide in her house for a few months. In the first week, Mrs. Bai could not eat or sleep—she did not even dare to dream. Instead, she ruminated. So she sold lies—so what? She was not special: judging by her customers, everyone was always lying to each other all the time. Husbands lied to wives, wives to husbands, to children, to in-laws—if anyone asked her, lies were the standard procedure of belonging to a family. In fact, in many cases, lies were actually the glue that held families together. It wasn't that Mrs. Bai was lying to her clientele, it was her clientele who lied to each other and themselves. In most of her cases, the lies had already been circulating long before it occurred to anyone to consult her. They only sought her out not because they were clueless, but because they wanted confirmation for their suspicions. And she was paid handsomely for substantiating the lies they told—most of the lies, in fact, were not hers. For example, when one woman made an appointment with her to ask if her husband had gone and impregnated a village girl, the husband came to her first before his wife's appointment, slipping her a bag of coins to have her tell his wife he hadn't. And then they lived happily ever after. Until now.

At first it felt like America was finally her way out, to another start. When her son-in-law requested her to take care of his son while he worked long hours at the mining camps, she was grateful. She hadn't seen the man in years—since he left with the child, he never bothered to even write. Then on a Saturday, his brother, Kee Mock, showed up at her neighbor's inquiring about her. It was her first visitor in over a month. Kee Mock informed Mrs. Bai that he was also making the journey as a paper son. He asked her to come with him as his "mother," that his brother in America had requested this. It turned out their real father had died and left his sons a sum of money. The papers were bought, the tickets procured—Kee Mock had gone to see a hawker for Gold Mountain and secured everything they needed to make the trip. He even gave her a coaching handbook, full of questions to study and memorize about this invented life: the life of one Mrs. Tet Sam Yee.

Before she died, Anqing had been eager to become a "Gold Mountain wife," having seen the finely dressed women at the ports, their arms heavy with gifts and luggage. And now, in her daughter's place, Mrs. Bai felt it was her duty to go.

Upon her arrival at Angel Island, the newly minted Mrs. Yee right away sensed the presence of fox spirits. The old impulse she'd long suppressed revived itself overnight. Pungent fox scent dampened all her clothes, and whiskers chafed her neck at odd hours, especially at dusk. Mrs. Yee had not felt this since she was twenty-two, at her fox medium initiation ceremony. That ritual possession took place over the course of one evening, in which she experienced every sensory extreme: cold as if she had sprouted a glacier inside her lungs, heat as if molten rock had replaced her innards. She screamed and danced and ran around the neighborhood naked, setting off a ruckus in town. Outside her residence, she planted a fox shrine in the mossy peat. She slept outside the first few nights, the rain casting a glow. She gave it offerings: tofu skins, radishes, the rest of her rice. She had never felt more alive.

She didn't dare repeat that behavior here, in the presence of so many other women. The first night, she felt a sensation like wind slashing everyone's turbulent sleep, though all the windows were closed. Beset by the ghostly motions, Mrs. Yee could not sleep. Perhaps she'd grown so used to the vertiginous rocking of the ship that she could no longer find rest without the whole world moving beneath her. The walls seemed to breathe on their own.

The buildings of this detention center were new, but the wooden walls were ripe for hauntings. Mrs. Yee saw poetry on the walls, carved with penknives or forged in ink. Some of the poems, she suspected, were written not by women, but by fox spirits. How else to explain the tattoo-like quality of the ink on the wall, the sharpness and depth of the strokes? Surely the poems were not carved using regular knives—the penmanship of the calligraphy seemed near-perfect, almost supernatural. Foxes were attracted to liminal residences, lodging houses, and this detention center was a veritable playground.

Every day, the breakfast bell rang, and the guards showed up to escort her and the other women to the dining hall, where they all ate together in collective disgust and dolor. To Mrs. Yee, this routine eventually became a rare source of comfort, even though the meals were so bad: stewed vegetables that melted into mush, rice gruel that reminded her of pig feed, all the different iterations of bone and cartilage without a trace of salt.

Eventually the women all came to adore her, since she gave them advice and herbs, sometimes a divination, and occasionally an ointment for sores or aches or homesickness. She even had a cure for hookworm, which was desperately in demand. They sought her out for tips on backaches from too much time spent on the bad mattresses. Several women discovered her reputation as a fox medium and begged her to light an altar for their journeys, to pray to the fox spirits that they'd be protected and eventually landed. And so she did: she fashioned a small makeshift one, very simple, but it would have to do. The head of Mother Taishan, set sideways, her broken neck carefully hidden with a piece of cloth. A few stray incense sticks stacked atop a small porcelain ewer from home, the matches procured from the Chinese cooks. After years of not practicing, Mrs. Yee found herself hypnotized once more by the burning. Against the charred joss sticks, the faces of the women flushed with the distinct beauty of hopeless hope. They offered both her and the fox spirits fresh persimmons and pomelos, all sent from their families in San Francisco's Chinatown. One woman even offered a whole roast duck, dehydrated and brined, wrapped in red wax paper.

To read a flame, to read the color and shapes of ashes—to enter the state of trance—Mrs. Yee had to motion to welcome the fox spirits. Her hand like an eagle, swinging over the smoke to capture its tendrils. This was her at her most vulnerable, her arms open, ready to receive. Then when the spirit slid into the flame, she could hear herself assuming its rasp, the small throb in her throat like a drum, answering the women's prayers.

On her tenth day on Angel Island, Mrs. Yee was summoned for interrogation. In the interrogation room, light poured from the barred windows. There was a chair for her to sit in, and she faced the immigration official—a frowning man with a blond beard. An interpreter sat to his right, and a stenographer, whose hands rapped against a typewriter with metallic clangs, distracting her from listening to the questions. There were about two hundred questions in all. How many stairs led to the temple in the village? What was the distance between her house and the dry goods store? Who was her son's teacher? Was there a red bridal chair for the bride at her son's wedding? What were the birth dates of her grandchildren, and where were they born, at what address? What was her son's American address? What dialects did her merchant husband speak? In what year did he open his business?

She regretted not studying the coaching book more closely. What arrogance, to assume her own clairvoyance would be an asset! In that room, in the face of the officials and their dubious gazes, her extra senses abandoned her. She'd been stripped of her power, her authority. The humiliation of drawing a blank on these questions she should have known was something she foolishly did not anticipate. Many of the questions she answered truthfully, so therefore they were incorrect. Her village was next to a river, yes, but not the village of her paper husband's. She said there was a palanquin at her son's wedding banquet, but did not remember the date, the number of guests, or the dishes served. "I don't know" was the most legitimate answer she could muster.

The interpreter spoke swiftly, barely looking at her through his spectacles, wearing his Western clothing. All were strangers, all were men, and Mrs. Yee understood that other than the Chinese interpreter, all had a say in her fate. Later that afternoon they would go into the city to interrogate her paper "husband," and she knew that if enough answers did not match, they would reject her and put her on a ship back to Canton. She hoped that they would chalk up her errors to her seniority rather than her identity.

"Forgive me," she said to the interpreter as kindly as she could. "Have pity on an old woman, why don't you? My memory has never been sharp, but especially not now." He peered at her in pity but did not relay her message to the official.

By the time Axiu arrived, Mrs. Yee had already been in the detention camp for a month awaiting the results of her interrogation. When she woke up next to a girl who was the spitting image of her daughter, Anqing, Mrs. Yee saw it as a portent, a lucky sign. Even though Anqing had already been dead for five years, it was a bitter loss that Mrs. Yee had never stopped mourning. The fox spirits must have sent her, this pregnant girl, whose gait, profile, and widow's peak were so familiar it was enough to confuse Mrs. Yee from time to time, make her question where she was. Axiu even had the same mole underneath her right eye as Anqing. At times Mrs. Yee wondered if the month she had spent aboard that terrible ship actually pulled her back in time, to the past where her daughter was still alive.

One evening, Mrs. Yee surveyed Axiu's belongings, starting with the tiny jars of medicine and herbs she carried in her satchel. A few of the ingredients alarmed Mrs. Yee.

"Who prescribed you these?" she asked Axiu. "You should never eat wild ginseng while pregnant!"

"It's okay. I had no appetite on board, and still don't. I'm starting to wonder when I'll ever want to eat again."

"You must eat!" Mrs. Yee offered Axiu a pinch of herbs and dried fruits from her own paltry reserve, the ones she recommended specifically for pregnant women. Angelica root, dehydrated loquats, sweet hawthorn.

But Axiu refused, saying, "I don't want these. I really have no appetite, Mrs. Yee."

Exasperated, Mrs. Yee said, "This isn't about *you*, Axiu. It's about the baby, who might be hungry."

"I don't want that."

Mrs. Yee asked Axiu what she meant.

"I never decided to get pregnant."

"What woman *decides* to get pregnant?" Mrs. Yee exclaimed, incredulous.

"What if my daughter turns out to be a miserable person, and blames me for bringing her into this life?"

"How do you know you will give birth to a daughter?"

"I have this strong feeling she is. Why else would I have so many dreams about having a daughter? And daughters, you just know the kind of life a daughter is going to have. It's no life at all!"

"You've suffered no losses, girl. You have never lost a child." Mrs. Yee found herself rubbing her eyes, thinking of the evening her daughter went into labor. It was true that she had tried, tried to deliver the baby safely, but it was also true that she was partial to her daughter, not the baby, when the eleventh hour arrived and it came down to the agonizing decision of who to save, and that perhaps heaven had wanted to punish her, because even when she made her choice, fortune was reversed and her daughter was not spared in the end.

Axiu was quiet, waiting for Mrs. Yee to continue.

"You know. You're right," said Mrs. Yee finally. "You're right about daughters. It isn't a life at all."

They sat there, staring at each other from across their bunks, Axiu plaiting her long hair. Mrs. Yee did not remind her of her mother, who was always too vain to care about what was in her mind. To be chided, then reassured, by Mrs. Yee—Axiu was oddly stirred.

"Do you have any daughters?" Axiu asked suddenly.

"I did. One," Mrs. Yee said. "I wish I could have done more for her."

"Why?"

"She died young. She was only a few years older than you."

"I'm so sorry."

"She died giving birth. My grandson is alive here in America, but . . ." She trailed off.

"But you would trade him for your daughter to come back?" Axiu asked.

"Nonsense. What has happened has happened." Mrs. Yee sighed. She suddenly felt very tired. "You know, I can't help you myself if you want to . . . do *that*, but I do know a way," she said to Axiu slowly.

"How?" Axiu grabbed Mrs. Yee's hand then, genuine gratitude in her eyes.

"It's that interpreter, Tye. You might have recognized her as the only Chinese woman who's working here. She can help you get one, but you have to pass the test to get out of here first. And you have to pay her. It's long, it's bitter, but it's possible."

"But I barely have any money."

"There's always a way. I've talked to Tye before, she seems to trust me because I'm just some old lady. You know, she may seem callous, but she's not a bad woman. She has networks, connections. She will help you get rid of your problem."

Later that day, Mrs. Yee wondered if it was really the right thing to do, tell that girl where to get the procedure done. At dinner, she saw Axiu talking to Tye, whose eyes then flashed right to her. Then Tye began walking in her direction.

At first Mrs. Yee thought she would be reprimanded for giving Axiu that advice. But then she recognized: *Ah*. It was just the news that she hadn't passed her interrogation. Mrs. Yee knew this because Tye was giving her permission to speak to visitors. Mrs.

Yee was finally going to see her son-in-law—maybe even her grandson—and that only meant that she was going to be deported. Only those who did not pass their interrogations could speak to their family members while on the island, because those who passed were landed in San Francisco, and could speak to their loved ones whenever they wanted. When Mrs. Yee heard Tye announce it, she felt lightheaded—it was as if the news wasn't real, as long as it was told in near-unintelligible syllables.

The next day, a Saturday, she met with her son-in-law. The visitation room was very small, and mostly consisted of weeping women talking to their lawyers or their relatives. Mrs. Yee waited for around ten minutes and then a tall, lanky man in a bowler hat and a threadbare shirt entered the room. He had aged remarkably since she last saw him. New hollows had sprouted under his eyes, and the man barely spoke. He had brought with him his son, who was around five years old, his hair shaved and his eyes black and beady, suspicious. At the sight of the child, Mrs. Yee choked back sobs.

"I can file an appeal on yours and Kee Mock's behalf," said her son-in-law. "We'll hire a lawyer, and he will send the appeal directly to Washington, D.C. We just have to wait a few more weeks."

"Some of the women have been waiting for a year for this appeal."

"We don't have much of a choice at this point. Would you rather go home?"

"I'm an old woman, I will not last here for much longer."

The next Monday, when Tye delivered the news to Mrs. Yee, a noticeable hush fell across the mess hall. In the end, her intuition had been correct. She, along with two other women, were to be sent out on a boat to *The Mongolia* in Meiggs' Wharf, sailing back to China in the next week.

Mrs. Yee struggled to finish her bowl. The bench under her, the long table set with that day's meal—cloudy, mushy pork with chives—all fell into a void. All around her, the other women began to react. It was these other women who wailed and wept for her—she could not muster a reaction herself. And then she noticed Axiu, who had managed to push past those other women to kneel in front of Tye, her head lowered with her arms outstretched.

"Please," Axiu beseeched. "Spare Mrs. Yee, at least. She's sixty-four. She never broke any laws; she has never done wrong. Isn't there anything you can do to help?"

"There's nothing," said Tye quietly. "I know you're new around here, but I'm just an interpreter, I have no vote on what the outcomes are."

"But you're close with the immigration officer—I've seen you!" Axiu cried. "Surely you can talk some sense into him?"

Mrs. Yee lifted Axiu to her feet, whispering to her, "That stance won't be good for the baby. The baby doesn't want to feel her mother begging."

"I don't want you to go." Axiu clutched on to her.

"Nothing will happen to you," said Mrs. Yee. "I know this. I consulted the fox spirits last night, and they ensured me that you and your baby will be safe."

"But what about you?"

Mrs. Yee led Axiu back to her bunk, where she was prepared to pack everything. Mrs. Yee unwrapped the head of Mother Tai-shan and handed it to Axiu. "You know, I sensed something about you. You should communicate with the spirits now. I'm too old to keep practicing."

Her hands ceased shaking as they let go of the goddess. As much as the news devastated her, Mrs. Yee felt release. The shock of her discovery had long worn off—that her dreams, which had led her here, were wild projections. Now that she had tasted the Beautiful Country's beauty, she wasn't sure if she wanted to stay. She thought of her lost daughter, the burned house, the village. She thought of the faces of the ones who burned down her house and felt, to her astonishment, a warmth bordering on gratitude. She preferred that to the lachrymose strangers who projected their own anxieties onto her, a woman they barely knew.

Once again it was she who remained the most composed at the news. Once again it was she who took the responsibility of comforting everyone else. The pregnant girl in her arms was now inconsolable, weeping and shuddering, clasping the head of Mother Taishan like it was a flotation device and they were all wreckage floating on a sea. It reminded her of nights like this with her feverish and pregnant Anqing, whispering into her hair: *It's okay. It will be fine. I'm home now. You won't be alone in this world. Soon, you won't be alone.*

Turtle Head Epidemic

In late fall of 1967, an epidemic named Koro after the Malay word for "turtle head" swept through residential block 80 in Singapore's Tiong Bahru district.

It began with a pig. A buxom hog by the name of Papillon fell ill and passed away on a pig farm outside the Kranji-Pandan Reservoir in Punggol. Rumors circulated about the mythic swine, including one report that its sex organs had retracted into its body days before its death. A panic spread through Singapore like a porcine flu—boys and grown men alike suffered nightmares that the pork they had eaten for supper had infected them with the same genital-retracting illness that had killed the pig. Between October and December, hundreds of young men claiming to suffer from this peculiar disease were admitted to the hospitals.

Eighteen-year-old student Meng Li was one victim. A young man with long hair like a stallion's tail and a pale, gaunt face, Meng loved taking walks in his neighborhood in the evenings at dusk, when he could see wild animals creeping from the nature preserve across the bridge. Meng's parents emigrated from Hainan the year before he was born, in 1949, right as the civil war was coming to a close. They had never quite adjusted to their life in Singapore—his mother, for example, kept her superstitions. Early on during the epidemic, his mother refused to buy any pork, even going so far as to cook only vegetarian food.

"Don't eat at the cafeteria. Eat what I pack for you," she implored one morning before Meng headed to school.

"Let the boy eat what he wants," his father said. "You don't believe this nonsense, do you?"

"So four hundred men and boys in the hospital is nonsense to you? This is reality, Wang!"

"It's a psychological illness, dear. A mass hysteria. No one's penis is actually disappearing in real life."

His mother turned to Meng. "Listen to me, son. Promise me you won't eat pork. And promise me you won't speak to any girls. Stay away from them, especially the loose ones, do you hear me?"

This was easy for Meng to agree to. He was skeptical in general, ate only pickled vegetables and roti for lunch, and didn't talk much, anyway—besides his one friend, Bing, Meng rarely ever interacted with anyone, let alone girls.

That day, during the a.m. break, Meng found his friend, Bing Tang, in a crowd of boys making a commotion around a student sitting on a bench. They leered and shouted at her, but Meng noticed that she barely reacted—all she did was stare down at her knees, bangs covering her glassy eyes. The boys chanted, "Witch! Witch! Witch! Witch! We don't want you here! Go back to Canada! We don't want you here! Go back to Canada!"

When Meng pulled Bing aside asking for an explanation, Bing

replied, "That's Suzanne Hu. She's the source of Koro. She's the one bewitching all of us."

"How do you know?" asked Meng.

"Open your eyes, Meng, it's so obvious! Everyone she has been friendly with has gone to the hospital. And now she got Kamil!"

Kamil was in Meng's class, and the day before had gone to the emergency room. Everybody assumed Kamil's absence had to do with Koro, but everybody also knew Kamil was a devout Muslim who didn't eat pork. The origins of Koro had become a new point of contention that week, as *The Sunday Times* reported hundreds more men and boys claiming to suffer from it, some of whom were Malay Muslim. The Patient Zero swine had been dead for one month by then. According to the articles, many locals explained Koro in terms of an imbalance in the life forces of yin and yang: Men and boys carried yang in their vitality and semen. Malevolent fox spirits, who took the shape of young women, seduced and extracted life essence from men, often possessing them or infesting them with yin-illness. Naturally, blame began shifting from the pigs to the women in the community, especially the beautiful young women.

As everyone shouted and jeered, Bing's classmate, a popular and handsome boy named Hakeem, walked up to Suzanne, crouching forward so that their faces were level. With a flirtatious flourish, he said, "Why don't you talk to us? We just want to start a conversation, you know, get some facts straight about you."

Suzanne lifted her chin toward Hakeem and smiled slightly, then went blank-faced. Meng sensed the fury simmering beneath her expressionless composure, and as he watched, the anger mutated into a spite that frightened Meng. She cleared her throat and spat on Hakeem's face, prompting him to stumble backward in disgust. The boys began screaming even more loudly, and one of them took out a small carton of milk and dumped it on her. The white liquid dripped over her hair, her neck, the collar of her school uniform, and she closed her eyes, making no sound, not a snarl or a whimper. She began to resist as the rest of them pulled a fishnet over her head, twisting her hair into knots, but it was pointless; there were too many. Bing screamed with them, grabbing Meng by his shirtsleeve. One boy had locked Suzanne's left arm in a vise grip, and Bing held on to her right arm as she struggled. With his other hand, Bing handed Meng a carton of chocolate milk. "Spill it!" he screamed. "It's what she deserves! Spill it!"

Meng was dizzy. Around him, the boys chanted, "Spill it! Spill it! Spill it!"

In the middle of the circle of boys, prompted by the trance-like force of their yelling, he opened the carton and poured it over her. If it was true that she was bewitching all of her classmates, then she needed that lesson, Meng reasoned. Brown liquid dripped down her already-wet clothes and everyone cheered. Briefly, she opened her eyes, focusing on Meng with her glassy gaze. The spite was gone. He saw that despite the fishnet over her face, despite the milk and the scowl and the cowering, she was still preternaturally pretty. At this, Meng couldn't help but marvel.

Suzanne was one year older, one of those rare helicopter children who came from the West to Asia instead of the other way around. She lived in a mansion in Bukit Timah owned by her grandparents, who had recently passed, leaving the house empty aside from the caretakers who were still employed by the estate.

When the teachers learned of the incident with the milk, they dismissed her from the rest of her classes that day, but not a single adult disciplined the boys who had cornered her. The day after the milk incident, the principal requested Suzanne to be transferred into Meng's class, 3B, placing her two seats in front of Meng. She was not even introduced at the beginning of class. Meng peered at her, though he tried not to. She appeared unbruised, without even a single mark on her arms, which had looked so swollen the day before.

As Professor Shen lectured about Japan's occupation of Singapore, Suzanne took an orange out of her bag and rolled it beneath her palm on the wooden school desk until the rind broke and nectar leaked out onto the unfinished pine. She tried to wipe it off but splintered her hand. "Ow!"

The professor looked at her and asked, "You have a problem, Ms. Hu?" All eyes fell to her, but she wasn't fazed.

"Actually, yes."

"Care to explain to the class?"

"I'm being hunted."

Snickers all around the classroom.

"What are you talking about?"

She ripped open the rind and bit into the orange, and juice rolled down to her chin. Then she got up and left the room before anyone could stop her.

A silence as thick as the Indonesian haze. Professor Shen excused himself to go look for her, appointing Meng as the interim classroom leader, but as soon as the teacher shut the door, the class erupted into uproarious gossip. The rumors about Suzanne were mutating before his ears: one said that she was a Wiccan who had practiced black magic in Ontario; another, that she had a sexual relationship with her half brother, who was full Canadian. Yet another said she seduced other students by inviting them to the back of the baseball field after dark where the lilac bushes grew wild and pungent, and as soon the unlucky boy got excited, she would snatch his penis away and vanish behind the Angsana trees. The U.S. ambassador's son, a blue-eyed bully named Brian, had been bewitched by her and went absent for two weeks. With Kamil, too, Suzanne had been friendly, often lending him her notes, letting her fingers brush against his as he returned them to her.

No one noticed Meng slipping away from the ruckus of class 3B. No one advised him to venture to the roof of the building, but he had a hunch that Suzanne was there. He had sincerely felt guilty for what he had done the day before, but he did not want to admit that in front of the others.

Climbing to the top floor, Meng inhaled deeply, smelling none of the dust and particulates of the week before. He opened the door and saw her standing there on the roof, her skirt and school bag blowing in the breeze. She didn't look human then, more like an apsara, a divinity. Her eyes were eerily greenish. She was already maneuvering her legs over the railing before the spell broke and he realized what she was doing, before he uttered, *No*, before he recognized her for what she was, neither goddess nor witch—a damaged girl, contorting herself against the railing, cradled by the air in a wager with gravity. In his alarm, he ran toward her, grabbing her arms before she lost her balance. She spat: "Don't! Don't!"

He yanked her down toward him, and Suzanne collapsed backward. Together they toppled over, away from the ledge, onto the rooftop surface, the sun eating their faces. He felt himself gripping her arms as she yelped, "Let go, let go, you piece of shit! Let me go!"

Vertigo overtook him, and when he opened his eyes, she had disappeared. Her body's weight was also gone, and he couldn't feel the heft of his own: his arms, his legs, every joint and muscle seemed like a random arrangement of cold and limp appendages belonging to some other body. Even his head felt superfluous, barely attached to his neck. Had she jumped? Had he stopped her? The sky stopped aligning with the rooftops.

Meng managed to regain some of his balance as he walked home, but something in his body felt off. It was as if his parts had rear-ranged themselves, his body like piles of bricks that had once been a house.

He couldn't taste the dinner his mother made for him, a clear bone-and-turnip soup with rice. No matter what was in his mouth, there was always a strange, sour aftertaste. That night, the nightmares were the most vivid he'd ever had. In one, he was about to make love to Suzanne, but he couldn't feel her at all. All sensation had left not just his nether regions, but the rest of him as well. His fingertips glided down the nape of her neck, but he had to imagine what it felt like as he saw it. The pleasure only came to him visually, when he combed her hair with his fingers and gathered it in his hands, or aurally, as she sighed. Waking up, Meng was damp with sweat and, inexplicably, soil. His hands and fingers had cuts on them and little pieces of leaves, as if he had been somnambulating all night outside, in some wilderness. He wanted to masturbate, but he was too terrified—he felt sore and numb.

That's when he noticed his penis was retracting into his lower abdomen. When he pulled back his pants, he didn't see anything strange, but he felt a shrinkage, a withdrawal down there—strange prickly sensations that were not unpleasant but peculiar enough to raise alarm. Warm tremors took hold of him, soldering his groin to his belly. A spark, then a fizzle—and then the heat was gone, and in its wake he felt stabs and palpitations in his abdomen, a stony, frigid chill, as if his insides had morphed into a slab of cold igneous rock.

It was early morning. He was sweating so much he needed to go outside. He no longer felt like going to school; he got on the bus going the opposite direction and waddled toward Holland Village, toward the Botanic Gardens. Instead of doing what other boys had done, like pull their penises out and hold them in place with clothespins or green yam stems, Meng went about his day wandering the streets with the newfound alienness in his body. He didn't rush to the hospital in a panic. He didn't confide in his family.

This wasn't to say he didn't suffer. He suffered and kept it to himself, pacing wildly. He'd always carried a blade in his pocket, and so he used it to slash at plants—mostly dead branches, lianas. Then the thought fruited: Whatever was happening to his body was a test, perhaps even punishment for his cowardice, his complicity. For the moment when Bing had handed him the carton of milk, when he had made the choice to be weak and small-minded.

The morning rush had passed. He walked into the Botanic Gardens, where old women were gathering to practice their calisthenics. Overnight the haze had returned, dousing the horizon he couldn't see back into a baleful shade of gray. He picked a newspaper out of the trash. The headline read: "More Young Men Fall Victim to Koro Epidemic."

In the story, the reporter interviewed all sorts of "experts" to explain the phenomenon. A physician in Singapore called Koro an "acute hysterical panic reaction to a dynamic morphological sudden symptom formation." All of this was a fancy way to say that Koro was a psychological illness that caused anxiety, panic, and a cosmic fear of death. For treatment, he recommended shock therapy, serotonin reuptake inhibitors, and moxibustion.

A spiritualist from Malaysia called Koro "a procession of parasitic fox spirits bent on possessing humans," and advised men to carry peach branches to protect themselves. He recommended pepper jam, ginger tea, or turtle soup for replenishing this masculine energy, if afflicted. On the next page, there were six recipes for turtle soup.

An anthropologist from England called Koro a "culture-driven mass psychosis," caused by Chinese superstition and folk beliefs in fox spirits. This anthropologist cited a previous Koro epidemic that occurred in Sichuan, China, in 1908, where locals immediately blamed women for the penis-retraction illness. Soon, across the city, brothels began shutting down, vandalized and raided by mobs of angry people. Locals patrolled the streets with swords and knives, setting off fireworks to ward off the evil female fox demons. One girl was beaten to death with peach branches; another had been drowned in a lake. Meng thought immediately of Suzanne, and chills came over his body.

Folding the paper in half, Meng developed his own theory. If the rumors were true and she had been the cause of a Koro infestation at his high school, then surely she would know how to reverse it? Surely she would know how to lift the spell, the curse? Everyone at school either harassed Suzanne or shunned her. The one thing nobody tried to do was to befriend her. On the park bench where he settled himself down, Meng contemplated this experiment, watching the old women's stances, their nimble arms. He was sure his plan would work—he just had a few errands to run.

Meng found his turtle at the bird and fish market where his mother always bought eels, mackerel, quahog, and occasionally a king-sized jackfruit. They were all sold out except for one. This last turtle was listless at the bottom of a grimy plastic bucket. The seller told Meng it had been rejected because it was so unmoving, and this made the other buyers uneasy. But rest assured, he said, it was alive and well.

Though lethargic, the turtle was quite handsome, hiding in its iridescent honeycomb-patterned carapace. Meng had read some-where, probably in his Eastern Religions class, that ancient schol-ars valued the turtle as an essential creature of longevity and vital forces, a symbol of the yang positive principle, signifying life, light, heat, and maleness. According to these pre–Ming Dynasty scholars, turtles concealed a powerful layer of yang in their shells, enough to revitalize a young boy's life after a fall, enough to in-vigorate the eunuchs who served the princes in the Sui Dynasty and allow them to become high-ranking civil servants in the pa-latial courts. It was said that these eunuchs, who ate turtle soup every day, remained spry and lissome all their lives. If pork or foxes were the origin of the Koro, then the turtle was surely its antidote.

When Meng brought home the turtle that night, his mother raised one hand to hit him, but used the other hand to wipe the dirt off his cheeks.

"Your teachers told me you were not present. I was going to call the police." His mother looked haggard, her perm unkempt, her glasses fogged. She was horrified at his slovenliness, but Meng could tell she was moved by his gesture to nourish the family. Meng found himself, for the first time in a long time, seeing her eye to eye. Last year, they had buried his uncle, her brother, and she had refused to let any boys or men in the room as she and her sisters dressed the corpse, out of respect for the masculine principle. Women, she argued, had a special relationship with that gateway, that liminal space between life and death, as they carried in their bodies the feminine yin, which was associated with the passage to the realm of the ancestors. According to her, Meng could not expose himself to the corpse—it would pollute his living force and impede his growth into a young man.

But one day, Meng opened the casket when she was not around, and stared directly at his uncle's body. In life, the man had been hot-tempered, given to murderous rages even in the presence of his children. He had died young, in his forties, a victim of alcoholism, and the lines on his face were still shallow, smooth. For a long time, Meng stared at his uncle's face in repose, fascinated by its complete composure, how blood no longer rushed to his cheeks, how the vein in his temple was now invisible and no longer twitched like a trip wire as it had during his life. In death, his face did not match his face in life.

Mother and son now sat together at the kitchen table, between them the turtle wrapped in a plastic bag, crawling weakly toward the table's edge. On a normal day she would have demanded his whereabouts and reprimanded him, but that day, she was just relieved he was safe. She buttoned up his shirt collar, muttering, "Meng, I'm not going to ask where you went, but I really can't keep waiting for you all day." Then she picked up the turtle to wash it. The water ran over the turtle's shell, painting it black. Meng stared into its cold yellow eyes.

"I want to cut him before you cook," Meng said to his mother. In a gesture of reassurance, he said quietly, "I'm sorry I was gone today. I just . . . I just had to go to the market and get this. It's for a friend."

The knife was trembling in her hands, so Meng took it from her. She began gathering lotus root, wood ear, dried dates, and herbs. He beckoned the turtle to come out from its shell.

"Who is this 'friend'? I told you to avoid girls. Have you listened to me?"

"I never ate any pork," he said. "But there is one girl who has been . . ."

"You have it, don't you? Koro? That's why you brought the turtle home?"

"I'm not sure," he lied. "I'm just taking precautions. Cut me a break, Ma. I didn't want to go to school, and I didn't want to go back home, either. . . ."

Ceremonially, he cut the turtle's neck, and a stream of thick blood leaked out. He asked his mother to make a soup from its head and blood just for him; the rest of its body would feed the family the next day. As she cut the rest of the turtle, she lamented, "Home should have been your first resort, not your last."

"I want to bring someone home for dinner tomorrow," he said. His mother froze. "Is it the girl?"

"Ma, promise me you'll treat her kindly. She's had a rough few weeks. And she doesn't have anyone."

"You're asking me to make a promise when you've broken yours?"

"Ma, hear me out, it's my experiment. She's been bullied at school, badly. She doesn't have family in Singapore. I want to help her, and maybe it'll make me feel better."

"There's probably a reason for all that bullying. I mean, she could be one of those fox spirits!"

At this point, his father came out of the bedroom, having overheard the conversation.

"Let me remind you that fox spirits are *fictional*. I don't see why you're not happy about this, dear. Meng has never brought home a friend before. And a girl! Why not welcome her?"

"On one condition," said his mother.

"What's that?"

"You will carry this branch wherever you go with this girl." And she shoved a peach branch, with the petals falling, inside Meng's backpack.

That evening, after he ate the turtle blood soup, he tried to masturbate in his room. It was as if all sensation had abandoned him, from his epidermis to his bones. His penis hung in its foreskin, and he couldn't feel it in his fingers. Panic started rising in his belly until he felt nauseous and lightheaded. He went into the bathroom, trying to vomit. He couldn't. Only phlegm came out of his throat and mouth.

The phone rang then, and Meng answered, still nauseated. It was Bing. "Hey, Meng, where have you been? I was worried that you, too, went to the hospital."

"I'm okay. Feeling sick, but not *that* kind of sick," Meng lied.

"If *you* had gotten it, I swear to God, I would go exorcise her myself."

"That's unnecessary, Bing."

"Are you crazy? She's wreaking havoc on everyone in our high school! Did you know that two more boys went to the hospital, including Hakeem? Our very own track star, no less!"

"Oh, wow. I hope Hakeem is okay!"

"Seriously, though, she's a slut. She came up to him while feigning an apology, and then took him home, and the next thing you know, he's in the hospital, crying about his penis. I swear to god, she strikes the moment you let your guard down."

"I get that, but do you have any verifiable proof? Like, have you seen her?"

"I haven't yet, but listen. My uncle is a Taoist priest, and he can exorcise fox spirits. He has a temple he goes to every once in a while, and he can get me some talismans. Then we can vanquish her once and for all. Help me get her, man. It's for the sake of all of us!"

After Meng hung up, he felt genuinely conflicted. He had never heard such fear in the voice of Bing—it was as if Bing had become consumed with the need for revenge. What had that girl done to Bing that he was so worked up? As far as Meng could tell, Bing barely interacted with her, aside from taunting.

The next morning, Meng went to school. He knew where to find her. Entering the grounds through the back gates, past the lilac bushes where she had reportedly seduced Hakeem, Meng ran up the fire escapes toward the roof. This time she was not at the railing. She was sitting under the window out of sight, smoking a cigarette. She turned toward him, and to his surprise waved for him to join her.

"The view for dying is better here," she said. This side of the rooftop overlooked an array of buildings, some high-rises, mostly just apartment complexes under construction. Painted cranes lifted men into the sky.

"Hey, I'm really sorry about the milk thing. I'm so sorry, okay?"

"Don't mention it. Seemed like you didn't have a choice."

A long pause ensued. He tried to not look at her.

"I'm surprised you're here. I mean," he stammered, "if I were you, I would cut school altogether. Why do you even come if you just stay on the roof and smoke?"

"Because anywhere is better than that . . . house. It smells like death there, literally."

"What do you mean? I would kill to live there! Don't you live in a mansion?"

"I hate tropical places, it feels disgusting. I can't leave home without my clothes feeling like plastic wrap when I get to my next destination."

"But school is dangerous for you. You know, Hakeem's returning tomorrow, and plotting something possibly. My friend Bing wants you gone, and he's not the only one! Why not just go to the mall or the park?"

"What the hell would I do at the mall?" She spat out her cigarette and crushed it under her shiny black loafer. "Why do you care so much where I go, anyway?"

Chagrined, he deflected her question. He did not look at her. After a moment, he let the question that was simmering on his tongue go. "So you're not doing it on purpose, then?"

"Not doing what?"

"You know. What they say you've been doing." Meng tried not to sound accusatory, but he could see her defenses flaring.

"I haven't been doing *anything*."

"They think you're the one who's stealing their sex organs."

"I have nothing to do with their mental problems."

"I'm not sure if it's a mental problem. It's real. People are sick."

She glared at him but didn't say anything.

He added with some trepidation, "It's okay to come to me if you need someone to talk to, you know. I won't say a word to anyone. You can trust me."

"Trust. Ha!" She started laughing bitterly and shoved him, hard. He noticed it was the first time she had touched him voluntarily. "Anyways, I have nothing to hide. You can tell your little friends that, or you can tell them to fuck off."

They stayed there for a moment wordlessly, taking in the view of the forlorn town blocks, the cranes moving over the chlorine swimming pools, the lone hawker center, the palmetto trees swaying in the gray blank of the haze.

Finally, Meng blurted out, "Have dinner with my family tonight. My mom's making a soup. I'm sure you haven't had home-cooked food in a while, right?"

The question caught her off guard. He hoped she would say yes. He hoped she would say no. "Well . . . why not?" she finally said, holding up a pen and her left hand as paper. "Write your address down here."

She smiled at him wanly as he took her hand. To his surprise, his skin started prickling again, and sensation began to return to him. His muscles finally relaxed. So this was joy—the gross feeling of his insides moving, guts throbbing, his organs coming back to life in a full-blooded orchestra. A spell untangled. He held her pink wrist steady as he wrote down his address and said, "See you then."

She laughed and lit another cigarette. "Now leave me alone, you loser."

He left her in high spirits, opening the door into the building and practically skipping down the stairwell, humming "Suzhou

Nocturne," a song his mother used to sing to him. It was during this skipping, two flights down, that he witnessed, outside the narrow window of the fourth floor, Suzanne in the air, her body falling down, down, down, not fast but slowly, billowing like a flower or a feather in the late autumn breeze. He blinked once. She was falling. He blinked again. She was not.

He ran down the stairs, panting and sweating, screaming at himself, tumbling over the steps, howling when his knees hit the ground-level floor. He threw the door open, slamming it against the wall on rusted hinges, bracing himself for what he would find, and discovering nothing but an empty courtyard: begonias and tiger lilies and daisies unmoving beside the windows that looked into Classroom 3B, full of students taking their History of War final, all except two empty desks. None of his classmates looked up from their examinations, and even Professor Shen sat at his desk, focused on his notes. It seemed virtually impossible for them not to have noticed a girl falling. Meng imagined her body hitting the cement, ruining the manicured daisies, staining the soil.

He raced around frantically, not sure what he was looking to find. He followed the length of that building searching for her, then ran back up to the rooftop, looking down from the approximate location where she would have jumped. There was no body. There was no Suzanne. Did he imagine the whole scene?

It was ten minutes past the agreed-upon time of half-past seven. They'd made a place for her at the table, right across from him. His mother was fidgeting with her spoon; his father, absently reading the news. They had even worn their best clothes, because they hadn't received a guest in ages. Still, he did not want to begin. He breathed raggedly. What he had seen was real, but at the same time, it was completely unreal—so unreal that he had not bothered to tell his mother that Suzanne would not be coming, that there was no way she could. Somewhere in the back of his mind, he thought she would maybe still make it.

The hour was descending, the clock struck eight. Meng could tell his mother was tense, by the way her shoulders were stiffer than usual, her posture high and strained. His father, too, seemed to be fading—he had set the paper aside and was now staring vacantly at the door.

Another half hour passed, and Meng could no longer stand it. "Hey, why don't we at least try the soup?" Meng suggested.

"Are you sure?" his mother asked. "Should we wait?"

"No. Let's eat." Meng was crestfallen. He took the ladle and started serving his parents the soup. Then, at last, he served himself a bowl of soup from the other pot.

The blood was curdled into the soup, but he couldn't taste any of the tannins; the broth was hot, cloudy, the turtle meat delicate, melting in his mouth. Star anise and Sichuan peppercorns crackled under his teeth. He couldn't taste any of it. He could only think of the crime scene that hadn't materialized that day.

Mrs. Li only had one small bowl of soup before she cleared her own dishes. His father picked the turtle clean, ate most of the rice, eel, and bitter melon.

"So, this girl," his father said. "She told you she'd come to dinner?"

"She did, but I guess she changed her mind," Meng muttered, unable to tell the truth, for which he had no proof. At this Mrs. Li relaxed a bit.

"It's probably for the best," she said. "We'll save a bowl of soup for her." It was a small gesture of kindness, and for that he thanked her.

"Son, you best make sure she's okay," said his father.

After his parents had retired and all the bowls were washed and dried, Meng turned off the lights and went upstairs. Tiong Bahru darker than the night sky, the stars all clouded. Maybe what he had seen was real, after all. Maybe they had discovered her, bloodied and still, at a site he hadn't checked, and were covering her body with a cloth.

It was only much later, after he'd dozed off a bit, that someone began knocking on his window. It was ten past midnight. His family's small condo was on the fourth floor, and outside the window there was only a balcony, no stairs attached.

Rattled, Meng slipped the peach branch out of his backpack and moved toward the window. There, beyond the curtains, was Suzanne, standing on the balcony, slightly leaning. She was in the same uniform she had been wearing earlier that afternoon.

An inexplicable fury formed inside Meng as he opened the window. "How are you doing this? What are you doing here?" he hissed.

"I have to confess something," she said. In the moonlight, with her black hair framing her face like crow feathers, she looked funereal, despondent but at peace. "I die a lot. And I can't really die. See, I've already attempted it many times, and it's pointless. I don't know how I can explain it to you."

Futilely, he held up the peach branch, its wilted petals engraved against his palm. "What the hell do you mean?" he cried, bewildered but exhausted. "I saw you. I watched you fall."

"You don't understand, Meng. I didn't mean for you to see me." She reached out and grabbed his hand. "Since I've turned eighteen, I can die as many times as I want and be reborn again each time with no consequences. It's this habit I have that's meaningless. This afternoon, I died twice—I died a second time after the fall. You don't know this, you'd left, but I died the day we first met, too. After they got the fishnet over my face. They beat me so badly after dousing me with milk that I had to die to recover from my wounds. Can you imagine? Three deaths in three days!"

The warmth of her hand gripping his, mixed with the fragrance of the crushed peach blossoms in his palms, disarmed him. Slowly she climbed in through the window, looking around his room. In the presence of her body, so vulnerable and close, his fearful anger transformed into something else. Her face was pale, and he could see it clearly despite the darkness.

"So today, your friend Bing brought these Taoist talismans in his backpack, and in the evening after school he came up to me and just threw them at me. Those slips of paper immediately paralyzed my body. There I was, again on the ground, and this time the death felt true. Anyway, he stayed there until I transformed back into a fox, and luckily, he did not have enough talismans to vanquish me completely, so in my fox form, I escaped." She showed Meng the scrapes and bruises on her elbows and knees. "I'm so sorry I missed dinner."

"I'm sorry," said Meng, suddenly ashamed. "Bing . . . Bing doesn't know what he's doing. He's my friend but also a complete idiot."

She drew herself close to him, and he began to recognize the feeling that had made him shrink up next to her. He could finally admit it was desire. Her scent of evening primrose, the sudden peach-fuzz flush on her cheeks, the sound her breath made when her voice softened—all of it intoxicated him. He wanted her. But what made his desire any different from that of all the other boys? Could he take that risk? He knew what might come next, and he was afraid.

She leaned forward, and it took all his willpower not to sink in or shrink away. In the end, he didn't resist as she put her lips on his. They kissed for a while in the dark, and it was the opposite of what had happened in his dream. He did not have to imagine what it felt like to caress her as he did it—her flesh felt warm and smooth, hairless, and each of her ribs felt human. He moved his hand upward toward her chest, and she held it in place, then pushed him forward. Astonished, he felt himself down there, he felt himself grow rigid.

"I'll prove it to you," Suzanne said. "That it's still there." She pulled him onto the bed. She unbuckled his pants, and he tried to stop her, feeling ashamed.

"Are you sure?" he asked.

She laughed. "Let's just check."

She pulled his briefs down and pressed her leg against him. Her fingers started stroking.

"Look at it. Do you feel this?" He felt it. He sighed, his head leaning backward like his neck was about to snap. "Are you afraid?" she asked.

"Maybe," he said. He wanted her so badly he could die. But something was preventing him from going there. Something felt wrong—like somehow he wasn't entirely there, like this moment was a scene he was viewing from another vantage point, another room where he had different knowledge and sight.

"It's all right." She withdrew her hand. "I think I get it. I won't, then. I mean, look at you—you're totally fine. This disease is bullshit."

Meng joked, "How can you promise that it'll still be there tomorrow, and the next day, and the next?"

She sneered at him. "Somehow, I trust it'll always be there." She walked toward the window and lit a cigarette. "Don't mind me," she said. "I need to smoke."

He climbed out of the window with her. She took a long drag. "Have you ever been to Canada?" she asked.

"No, never."

"Well, in Ontario, there's snow. And it's the strangest stuff ever. It falls, you hold it for a moment, you feel the miracle of it, then it vanishes when you go inside, turns into sweat in your palm. I could relate to snow. It's everywhere and nowhere at once. I miss it so much—I mean, snow makes me cold, and cold is the only thing that makes me feel at home."

It filled him with sadness, the realization that their homes could never be the same place. "I've never seen snow before," Meng admitted. "And . . . I mean, I don't know if it's possible that I will get to. It will never snow here."

Suzanne dropped the cigarette and squeezed his hand. Her hands were covered in ashes. He felt something brushing his backside, stroking it—a soft, pleasant sensation. She stood up, and three white tails emerged behind her, plumed and ghostly in the moonlight.

"Do you know the story of Azi the Purple?" she asked. "It's a folktale my mother used to tell me. About a hated fox spirit who haunted the mountains in ancient times. She fell in love with a man and accidentally stole his life force away, bewitching him. That's the danger of lecherous women, the story goes. It's not that she was a fox spirit, it's that she consummated what was in her heart. When villagers raided her den, they killed her, carved up her body, and feasted on her heart. This, the organ that led to her death."

He had thought he'd been looking for the human in her all this time, but as he watched her tails fan out from underneath her school uniform, Meng saw how wrong he was. It wasn't her humanity, but her marvel—her alienness—that drew him to her. He didn't want her to leave, though he knew it was inevitable.

"Well, that's only one story," he replied, after a brief silence. "I grew up hearing another. A young man named Xu was walking with his grandfather across a bridge and saw a beauty, who later appeared at his residence claiming that they were predestined lovers."

Suzanne laughed. "She was lying to him, obviously, to get his attention."

"Well, the lie worked, and she earned the approval of his grandfather to marry into the family. But it was not a happily ever after, even for a predestined couple. After his other family members harassed her and belittled her for 'being a monster,' she decided to leave, refusing to take their verbal abuse. According to her, their treatment of her did not reflect the romantic fervor and pure intentions she harbored for Xu. So she departed, and she escaped unscathed. To me, it was always the aftermath of her departure that was the most unforgettable."

"And why was that? What happened after?" Suzanne was staring at Meng like a child without defenses.

"Well, she went to another world. She went on a pilgrimage to the palaces of the moon, studied for divine examinations, and truly became a celestial. Every now and then Xu would hear from her, but always through a disembodied voice reciting spectral poems to him at night. She became a divine transcendent, only after—because—she left her marriage. Her name was Shuzhen."

"That name . . ." Suzanne said slowly. "That's so funny. Before we moved to Canada, my parents renamed me Suzanne, so I could fit in. I'd almost forgotten my other name, my Chinese name, until you told me this story."

Meng glanced at her, and she was smiling. Behind her, the tails had disappeared. In their place was the low-hanging moon, its yellow plumpness like a peach too heavy for its branch.

After a few months, the Koro epidemic eventually subsided, and the boys all returned to their lives. Hakeem continued to be a track star, beating the national record for hurdling. Bing went back to hating Hakeem, but for the rest of high school, Meng and Bing grew apart. Suzanne no longer attended the high school and, curiously, no one ever spoke of her again. Meng did not inform anyone of what had happened between them. Sometimes he wondered if he'd imagined their encounter, and if he told anyone, would they even believe him? Slowly, he, too, began to forget. Instead, Meng put his focus on perfecting the turtle soup recipe with the help of his mother.

Years later Meng and his mother opened a Bukit Timah restaurant called the Turtle, specializing in turtle soups. With his wife, Lili, he welcomed two sons, Ang and Ming.

After his father passed away, his mother let him join her in dressing the corpse. He dipped his hands in a bowl of cold water, as if he were about to knead bread. Instead, he smoothed the lapels on the suit his mother chose and laid his father down carefully.

"Won't all this yin upset my life force?" he asked as his mother took her husband's possessions out from a leather suitcase: a pen-knife, a gold watch, a notebook scrawled with short poems and notes about his patients.

"You've survived an encounter with a fox spirit," she said. "So it's okay for you to see your father before we let him go." Over the years her full figure had begun hunching forward determinedly. Her recent sorrow was forgiving to her features, which were still fine, as delicate and childlike as in her youth. "I want you to go somewhere for me. In the fall, please return to Hainan, where your father and I met, for the field festival. You may see off your father in our ancestral home."

And so in late September of 1984, Meng, his wife, and his two children traveled to Hainan for the Double Ninth Festival—the first time Meng returned to China since his parents left so many years ago. That year's Double Ninth Festival, attendees awaited the gods and ancestors' arrival on the fields. On the golden autumn streets of Haikou, Coconut City, the firecrackers didn't scare the ghosts, the ancestors returning on this blessed day.

Vendors sold chrysanthemum wine, acrobats and lithe young dancers gathered in red uniforms on the street, and fortune-tellers made predictions on folding tables under the swaying palm trees. Local pet shops had little booths where children could look at animals. Meng's sons and Lili were delighted to watch the rainbow-spotted goldfish swimming with the turtles in the tanks. Haikou had an island charm distinctive from Singapore; Haikou felt like a real island. Loosely dressed, sipping his chrysanthemum wine, Meng felt relaxed, content.

But soon one fortune-teller in particular caught Meng's attention. A circle of young men surrounded the seer, listening in a rapt haze. She appeared to speak first in dialect, then switched languages every so often, warning these young men of a beautiful fox spirit that would come to hunt them down in the days after the Double Ninth Festival.

"Just because the ocean looks blue, doesn't mean it is," she said as the men looked at her, bewildered.

A horn blew, and a parade started, scattering the smaller vendors. The fortune-teller collected her cards and walked into an alley, disappearing from sight. The clouds parted, revealing a watery orange sun, and a light sun shower began, prickling Meng's ears. Then he remembered this meteorological phenomenon: a fox rain, they called it. Evening settled over the horizon, and beyond the street, Meng could see the ocean.

Dazed, Meng turned toward the parade, which was actually a wedding party. Four strong, tan handlers held up an old-fashioned palanquin. The curtains stitched over the palanquin were bedazzled with sequins. Something about the ostentation was alluring and vulgar at the same time.

"Look, Dad!" his son Ming cried. "The bride!"

There, under the transparent veils, was the bride, sitting with a cloth over her head. Meng felt a strange urge to follow the wedding party until she revealed herself. Lili, annoyed, tugged at him, but he motioned toward the procession, and she followed.

Down the street they walked, closer and closer to the sea, until the bride stepped out of her nest. She was wearing a golden dress, atypical of Chinese brides. Gorgeous she was, a fairy-tale vision, so resplendent even the unimpressed Lili let out a sigh.

"Who is she?" she asked a neighbor.

"I don't know who she is, but the husband is a millionaire from

Shanghai," a spectator whispered. "No one knows why they chose to have their lavish ceremony here."

When the cloth came off, he recognized her. In late fall of 1984, an epidemic named after the Malay word for "turtle head" swept through the isle city of Haikou, spreading fast through Hainan like a cloud.

The Fig Queen

A woman wanted to become small. So she shrank, smaller and smaller still, until she was small enough to fit into the calyxes of the foxgloves she'd planted last winter. Her garden was now a jungle, a hemisphere, and the bees had transformed into helicopters overnight. They welcomed her as her neighbors; they offered her honey. The neighbor's fig tree grew wild over her fence, and soon figs were falling from the branches, their purpled flesh an endless feast.

The woman was finally living a life of abundance—everything that once felt small and cosmically insignificant was now huge. Her tiny apartment, once so cramped, with the couch in the kitchen and the desk on the dresser and the bed in a loft over the desk (she never could sit up straight while answering her emails) suddenly became palatial.

Taking it all in, she realized that she missed nothing from her old life. She did not miss the drudgery, the neuroses, the loneliness, the back pain. Now look at her! She could eat and drink all she wanted from this garden and never go hungry. She could feed on nectar that tasted like marzipan apples, relaxing from the perch of her favorite foxglove all day. She could revel in the view of the garden that was now her kingdom—all that she'd planted, all that blossomed from the tiny seeds she'd once held in her hands.

Eventually she realized that someone else was now living her life. Someone else was making appointments, going to work, going on dates, going to therapy, picking up groceries, cooking, making calls for her. Someone else was watering the plants and flowers in her garden, someone with her exact physical appearance. A doppelgänger—or a replacement? At first she felt indignant, pacing around in her calyx. She was anxious that this impostor would ruin the life that was hers, the life she'd grown from the ground up. She paced and paced and waited every night for this alien version of her to come home, at first afraid that this replacement's unknown personality would render her unrecognizable to her friends, her coworkers, and her family. Lurking beneath this fear, she was also worried that none of them would recognize her transformation at all, and her disappearance would go unnoticed.

Months went by, and she realized that this impostor was not ruining her life. In fact, this impostor was living her life much better than she had. This impostor was getting a promotion and negotiating for a salary she never would have thought to ask for. This impostor was booking a trip to Lisbon, where she'd wanted to go ever since she read Pessoa's *The Book of Disquiet* in college. This impostor was making new friends and reconnecting with old ones and hosting dinner parties where she successfully mixed these two groups together on the couch in the kitchen over the coffee table that doubled somehow as a dining table. This impostor was always the brightest person in the room, commanding everyone's attention and cracking jokes that made everyone laugh. This impostor was always laughing off the "nihaos" and "konnichiwas" from men on the street because she didn't take things so *seriously*. This impostor was going out until four a.m. on weekends, plopping down on the couch wearing short skirts and six-thousand-dollar leather jackets from designer brands she couldn't afford, that she'd believed she could never pull off. This impostor had a skin-care regimen that made her glow all the time; in fact, the dark spots on her face finally vanished, her blackheads gone. This impostor found a lover who took her on ski trips and family functions on weekends. The impostor would be gone for days at a time, busy with her fulfilled life.

She'd never hosted dinner parties. She'd never taken trips. She'd never had a boyfriend. Suddenly she was getting anxious again, anxious that she had not adequately lived her life, and now she had given it up to a doppelgänger who was going to enjoy all the things she hadn't, that she'd always wanted but had been too afraid to pursue. One day, the impostor brought home the lover, and she watched them from the perch of her petal—herself, on the bed, making love to a stranger. Hold on, though—she looked closer, and realized it wasn't a stranger at all, but the man who, just the year before, had broken her heart. Left her by the curbside in front of a bodega, left her crying into her iced coffee, the ashes of her cigarette dusting her bare knees. The man had said he wasn't looking for a relationship, that he didn't like her like that, even though they'd slept together a few times already; he wanted her for sex and only sex, no, never mind, he wanted just friendship; sorry, he was sorry. This man had never taken her outside of his apartment, let alone to Thanksgiving with his family upstate. She had not met a single one of his friends.

And now there he was, with this impostor, whispering sweet words, like how he wanted to show her off to his friends, go to Europe with her, the words she had fantasized about before, uncannily—eerily—coming to life. She watched them for the rest of the night. For the first time since her transformation, she wanted to be noticed. She shouted at them, waved at them, but they could not see or hear her. She was a voyeur spying on her own existence. She began to understand that this was her worst fear coming true. That perhaps, just perhaps, something essential inside her was rotten—something primordially hers, fixed and unsalvageable. It caused people like this lover, and all her former lovers, to abandon her. But when someone else occupied her body, this didn't happen. And just like that, she heard herself climax. A hot hiss of breath escaping from a throat that looked just like hers.

Last year when she was still seeing that man on and off, they had been careless and drunk one night, and the next morning she was so hungover that she forgot to buy Plan B. Soon after, he ghosted her. It was incremental: At first he would not respond to her texts until two or three in the morning. Then he stopped responding at all. This should have been the first sign that she was better off without him, but in those weeks of silence she felt as if her body were decomposing. It must have been the oxytocin, she rationalized—it was just chemicals tying her to this man, nothing more.

When she missed her period that month, she was still in a haze, barely eating or sleeping, and so didn't notice at first. But after several more weeks passed, she decided to go to her gynecologist, who administered a pregnancy test. *Positive*. Before she imagined an actual child, she imagined the child's potential trauma: Who would want to be born into a world where even the love between one's parents could not exist? She thought back to her own parents, who'd barely spoken to each other for most of their marriage outside of the most essential topics, namely her; she couldn't tell if the silence stemmed from habit or bottled-up resentment. She felt as if her own body were mocking her with its fertility. If this love was going to be barren, then why didn't her uterus get the memo?

She went home and watered her foxgloves, her dahlias, her camellias. Then she sat on her plastic chair and wept. She suddenly craved bruised fruit. The tree from the neighbor's yard dangled its branches over the fence, swarming with black stony figs, fat and ripe.

For the first time, she noticed the swarm of insects by the fig tree. They were tiny fig wasps, though she didn't know it at the time—she thought they looked like gnats or mosquitoes. Concerned, she consulted her book on gardening and insects and came across the entry on fig wasps. A fig, it turns out, is not a fruit but an inflorescence, a cluster of tiny flowers that needed special wasp pollination. The pregnant female wasp finds the tiny ostiole, or hole, at the bottom of the fig and crawls inside with the intention of laying eggs. As she lays her eggs, she also pollinates the florets.

Several facts about fig wasps stunned her. The first was that, in the process of trying to squeeze through that impossibly narrow portal of the male fig, the pregnant female wasp loses her antennae and her wings. The second was that, once she crawls inside, she lays her eggs and dies. The fig's enzymes slowly consume her, digesting her body until she becomes a part of its seeds and flesh.

The third was that if the wasp climbs inside a female fig, she still attempts to pollinate it, but, unable to lay her eggs, she just dies alone.

The woman had eaten so many of these figs, and it had never occurred to her that tiny wasps could be living and dying inside them. In the summer, she would sometimes go for days without eating anything else. They reminded her also of her lover, who loved figs.

Later that night, she called him, wanting to inform him about the test. She had never called him before. When he answered, they had a casual but flirtatious conversation that gave her hope, and she could not bring herself to tell him and ruin the mood. "How have you been?" he asked, finally. "Sorry I lost touch—I've been so busy, you know."

After hanging up, she made an appointment at the clinic for the following Tuesday. She thought about asking him to go with her, but she didn't want to put pressure on him or inconvenience him. He didn't want anything serious, he had told her; pregnancy was definitely a serious matter.

Nevertheless, when he started texting again, her body felt light, the lightest it'd been in weeks, and she felt herself sucked back into this airtight ostiole of romantic desire. They started talking more regularly and met up a few more times over the course of a few months before the incident at the curb by the bodega. By then she had already gone to the clinic, where her doctor informed her that she was seven weeks along and gave her a box containing two pills.

After taking the first pill, she bled profusely, her body cramping and clamming. She spent hours on the toilet every day, passively bleeding, and wondered if this was just all life was, all she was meant to do: Bleed, bleed, bleed. Blood would flow out of her until she ran out. No pads, tampons, or menstrual cups stanched the flow. A gloom, like a decomposing wasp, crawled inside of her, and the rot felt familiar, the rot felt true. She imagined herself suspended in a fig's red flesh, bleeding all over its flowers.

The next evening, the waves of nausea passed, and she felt enough strength to host him again. He came over, and as usual she fed him the figs from her neighbor's tree. His favorite thing about figs, he told her, was that they had no pits. How easy it was to just swallow them whole.

They sat together in silence, watching the sunset from her street-level window. When he reached for her, a small noise escaped her throat, a yelp. She turned her body away from him, suddenly protective of it. The nausea and lightheadedness returned, and she made up an excuse to go to the bathroom and vomit.

He didn't ask her what was wrong. Instead, he turned on the television and flipped through the channels, snacking on her chips, pretending nothing was happening. She actually felt relieved at his lack of curiosity, because she wouldn't know how to explain without telling him the truth. Finding nothing of interest on TV, he left shortly after.

Emerging from the bathroom, she threw out the empty bag of chips and the fig stems he left in the bowl, opened the door to the garden, and pulled up a chair outside. The sun had not fully set yet—the summer sky was delirious with pink streaks, like little scratches on skin. "Wow," she marveled, at nothing in particular. She wiped her mouth, which had gone sour, feeling small, so very small. *If only I were actually small*, she thought. *Perhaps it would make my problems go away.*

A movement in the fig tree startled her. A few roof tiles scuttled down from the eaves, and she looked up, but there was nothing. Figs fell, too, as the branches of the tree trembled. Then in front of her, to her amazement, appeared a tawny fox with flaxseed-yellow eyes. It was crouching in the long stalks of the foxgloves. She looked around for holes or burrows but could not find a portal through which this fox had entered. In the dusk, which seemed yellow now, too, the creature peered at her, regarding her with a mixture of trepidation and interest. She'd heard of foxes as omens before, usually auspicious. She beckoned it with a fig in her palm, but its wet nose did not stir. Soon the last ray of light shivered away, and the eyes of the fox lingered and winked. And then, before she was ready, it scuttled off into the night like one of her lovers.

Spring soon molted into summer, and she grew bored of her smallness. Around this time, the impostor was on her vacation to Europe. Imagining the terra-cotta rooftops of that city she'd never seen, Lisbon, and the deep blue of the Tagus River, she felt an intense longing.

The woman didn't want to be small anymore. She'd grown bored of the smell of flowers and the taste of nectar and honey and figs. The view from the foxglove began to madden her, fill her with despair. She watched a man next door pan-frying a branzino, and the smell of butter sizzling on skin made her desperately crave human pleasures again. She watched the fig tree and the female wasps kept digging and dying, digging and dying. She witnessed one female after another attempt to wrangle its body through the tiny hole at the bottoms of the figs. Sawed off, like cellophane or parachutes, pieces of wings fell from the figs.

Then she noticed that there were new tenants living in the figs.

Newborn female wasps were leaving—the daughters of the wasps that had decomposed had hatched inside the figs, orphaned from birth. Now they were nymphs, already gnawing their way out, embarking on the journey of finding another fig tree. The skin of the figs on the branches gave way to flesh and pulp, and the newly minted female nymphs were liberated.

That's when the woman considered: Perhaps she, too, could leave? Perhaps she could also journey to an unknown fig tree, escape this life once and for all. By this point, she had forged an uneasy communion with the bees and other insects that frequented this garden. She could ask them to relay her message to the fig queen, who had just emerged from the plumpest fig on the farthest limb of the branch.

Word got back that the queen had agreed. The woman found herself swooning: *Oh!* Emerging from her fig womb, the queen was unrivaled in her majesty, wearing a gown of pollen that resembled intricate lace. The queen's brown body was decked in a sleek armor resembling patent leather, and her silky wings fanned out, a holographic vision catching every errant ray.

Soon the queen descended on her foxglove, and the woman climbed on, gripping her thorax. The queen's body was sticky with nectar, and the pollen felt fluffy, like hairy flesh—the woman grew drowsy, but she didn't want to sleep. They were flying up in the air, and she saw her garden grow smaller and smaller, and yet it was entirely unlike being on a plane—no glass or metal separated her from the wind, which could not hurt her. From her vantage point, she saw the corner store. She saw her neighbors sitting on the stoop eating their figs. She saw the park where she used to lie out on the grassy knoll alone. She saw the botanical garden where the peonies and wisteria still budded, their petals all sprayed with rat repellent. She saw the statue of the weeping girl near the algae-green pond. She saw the fish market, with its display of striped sea bass, golden pompano, red snapper. She saw the bodega where she got dumped, and it looked marvelous with its display of bountiful melons. She even saw, for a tiny millisecond, a fox flashing in the graveyard where she sometimes walked her bike.

She was amazed. The journey to another fig tree felt like the farthest she'd ever traveled in her life, even though it had to be no more than a few hundred yards. When they eventually reached their destination, she almost threw up, her wonder mutating into dread. As she was dropped onto the branch of a new tree, she pleaded to the queen not to let her go. She didn't want Her Majesty to die so young. When she saw that the ostiole on one of the new figs was already open, she screamed at the queen not to rip off her wings. Instead of waiting on the branch, witnessing, she found herself running, climbing over onto the queen's antenna, launching herself into the red fragrant flesh of the fig. She would use her own body as a shield to save the queen. She would pollinate the fig herself.

As if the fig had heard her, the hole closed up once she climbed inside. Whole gardens of florets, pale and vulnerable, waited for her. In this red fig womb, suddenly she was more exhausted than she had been all her life. Too tired to remember anything about herself, too tired to save herself from being digested. Deeper and deeper she crawled into the fig, following its perfumed trail. It turned out that the fig, ever the hospitable host, had been expecting her, had already made a bed for her. On all fours, she crept as far as she could, the pollen falling off her, and curled into a ball on the soft pink bed.

In the red fig womb, she became an amorphous thing, a zygote, a fetus; she was breaking down. She was in a fugue state, where life and death had no language, the ending was a beginning was an ending, and she felt her own nonexistence like a warm airless room, a sauna. Her naked flesh in that air of fever vapor. Her lovely bloodless flesh in a sauna and then a clinic room, bent against the metal speculum. Her bathroom where she took that pill. The blood on the toilet seat, on the bathroom floor, all congealing. In her bleeding, she had spared someone from existence. She thought of her mother, who mentioned once offhandedly that she had gone through three abortions before finally choosing to have her. The one-child policy in China made her mother anxious about her body, its fickle patterns of creation. In the end, she finally had her daughter, and the trouble with daughters was that they, too, would eventually bleed. Without bleeding, who was she? Who was her mother?

In the kingdom of fig wasps, there were no singular monarchies. Every female wasp who made the journey of breaking her body was a queen—their coronation was death and decomposition. They were all mothers, and just like her, they were no mothers. The impostor living her life could have been any number of things: a demon, a fox spirit, a ghost. But perhaps it was just another version of herself, a self that was not broken, a self that did not believe she was broken—perhaps this woman had been sleeping inside her, underneath her pain, all this time. But instead of recognizing her, she'd called her an impostor. A doppelgänger, instead of something that she herself had dreamed, manifested, wished to life. In her fig womb, the city of Lisbon materialized. A balmy breeze blew through the open door leading to the balcony of the inn. The suitcases were packed. A note taped on top. *Good-bye. We'll meet again soon.*

Even if it meant death, the woman couldn't think of a better way to go—the juices and fragrance of inflorescence lulled her, and somehow she heard music. When she was ready to die, she fell asleep.

She opened her eyes, and she was back in her bed, covered in sweat. The alarm rang next to her. With wonder and relief, she felt a foreign yet familiar heaviness in each limb—how much effort was required just to arch the spine, to reach her arm out and hit snooze! The unsung effort the neck expended just to hold her head up! Every part of her, from her soles to her scalp, felt sore with muscle and bone. Even so, she had a newfound respect for this body, its dance with gravity. An hour went by before she could will herself to get up.

She cautiously stepped onto her kitchen tile, afraid she would crack it with the weight of her foot. Then she walked carefully outside onto her patio, then her garden. She watered her fox-gloves, her oxalis, her camellias. She picked up some figs that had fallen onto the ground.

Then she opened her laptop and checked her inbox and noticed it was full of emails from people she didn't know. Strangers, new friends, some whose names she recognized from the dinner parties. And many, many emails from that ex. His latest email was sent at 11:12 a.m. "Where are you??" was the subject line. The message was blank. She rolled her eyes. Oh, so *now* he was looking for her? She clicked through the rest of the increasingly frantic emails he had sent, and gathered that she—no, her impostor—had been in Lisbon with him and disappeared from their room that morning while he was out for a run. She checked the inbox history: according to the receipts from Tripadvisor, they had booked a terraced hotel room with a balcony overlooking the river. It dawned on her that now that she was back in her full-sized body, the impostor might have vanished. She wondered if she should reply, if she should book a flight. She could arrive at their hotel by the next bright morning, and he would be so relieved to see her that he wouldn't even notice she was different.

It had been her dream—to travel with this man. It had been her dream that he'd come back to her. For so many nights in the past year, the moment she closed her eyes she relived the way he touched her, where he put his hands, what he whispered as she drifted toward sleep—surprisingly tender things that had confused her; she relived the nightmare of iced coffee and cigarettes and the bodega. Sometimes she imagined an alternate reality where she chose not to take the pill. What then? Perhaps they would have been a family. She knew full well the impossibility of this fantasy, and yet there was safety in that certainty, in knowing it would never happen.

But that moment had passed, and now she found herself feeling something she didn't expect: amusement, even satisfaction, that she was not going to Lisbon, not for this man, no. She was amused that he was so confused by her whereabouts, that he probably at the moment felt abandoned, disoriented in a foreign country and suddenly alone. But she owed him no explanations about where or who she was. Today, tomorrow, she would go to the botanical garden, a ten-minute walk, smell the rat-repellent fragrance of wisteria and peonies, record their names. She would revisit the places she saw from the air on her journey—the neighbor's stoop, the corner store, the pond, the weeping girl, the fish market, the graveyard, and maybe even the bodega. If she saw the fox, she would hand it a fig.

Before she left her apartment, she gathered and washed some in a bowl. Then she drew a bath and soaked for a while, eating the figs one by one, swallowing even the hard stems. The steam and water loosened her tense muscles, and her aches started to vanish. She scrubbed herself until the dead skin sloughed off, and underneath, she was new.

The Haunting of
Angel Island

PARTS 4–5

4

Rumors flanked the beautiful Daji, who had arrived on Angel Island on the *Spirited*. Even in the close quarters of the women's dormitory, she had never been seen without red lips or a natural blush, what one might see painted on the cheeks of a Peking opera singer. Her hair was close-cropped, curled in a modern short wavy style, and she often wore embroidered silk gloves. Daji had a solitaire diamond ring from a previous husband she wore on her pointer finger like a North Star. Envious, the other women loved to mutter all sorts of lies in her wake.

But Daji loved gossip, even and especially when it was about her. The most common rumor was that Daji was a nine-tailed fox

spirit who would bring misfortune upon all of them. A hulijing—
fox woman, an informal term for loose woman, any loose woman,
but in this case it was literal. If she had to be honest with herself,
this rumor actually flattered her. Everyone knew that nine-tailed
foxes were legendary for their cunning wit and maddening beauty.
In some villages in northern China, there were still shrines de-
voted to these fox demons, and thousands of worshippers. After
all, the name itself, Daji, was notorious—according to the famous
sixteenth century novel *The Investiture of the Gods* by Xu Zhonglin, Daji was the name of the man-eating vixen disguised as a
concubine who bewitched King Zhou of the Shang Dynasty with
her supernatural beauty.

Of course, Daji's parents would never have thought to give her
this name—it was the new name she chose for herself when she
was negotiating the terms of her new identity, for which her now-
ex-husband paid a price. In her official documentation papers,
complete with the U.S. ambassador's seal, her new name was
Daji—it rolled off the tongue harshly. Daji, not the concubine of
a king, but the "wife of the wealthy merchant Wing Fu Ong." Ap-
parently this merchant had quite the reputation in San Francisco
as a handsome and formidable patriarch. Daji was sure she would
never have to meet him.

Daji neither confirmed nor dispelled the rumors about her, as
they entertained her—she loved to play into these women's projections, sow their fears. At first a few of the women tried to befriend her during breakfast, asking about her life in Shanghai, her
husband, her children, but she always replied with a smile. It was
a winning smile, half smirk, and it unsettled anyone who tried
with her. They always assumed that perhaps she was mute. Their
children would wake up in the middle of the night and discover

that Daji's bed was empty, then clumsily walk about looking for her. Daji would be awake in the moonlight, smoking a cigarette one of the smitten cooks had smuggled in for her, staring out the window, and these somnambulating children would appear in front of her, half-dazed, gawking. They were mesmerized by her spectral beauty, but they were also supremely afraid. Late at night, they whispered it to their mothers when they crawled back into the cots, rattling the bunks, tossing other women from sleep.

The one kid at Angel Island who wasn't afraid of Daji was Yingning, Mrs. Rong's daughter, who occupied the bunk bed above Daji's. They began talking after Yingning confessed that she had a superhuman hearing ability—she could overhear almost every private or hushed conversation in that vast, swarming room. Pretty and puerile, Yingning was a young girl, sixteen or seventeen, whose shy smile masked a layer of vindictive glee. She reminded Daji all too well of herself at that age, drunk with hormones and unresolved fantasies. It was Yingning who told Daji all the rumors—some about Daji, but mostly about other women. Together they would share a trove of stories: The woman who tried to jump from the rooftop after her infant son died. The interpreter who was having an illicit affair with an immigration inspector. The granny who was involved in a smuggling ring.

"Did you hear about the pregnant girl from, oh, maybe three months ago?" Yingning asked her one day during recreation time in the sitting room. Just minutes before, Daji had received the news from the Chinese interpreter that she was going to be interrogated the next day. Yingning's gossip was a welcome distraction.

"Do tell!" Daji said.

"This girl was not much older than me, but came here married and pregnant already, but her husband had arrived months before. Anyway, so she admitted that she didn't want that baby!"

"What's wrong with that? I can relate," said Daji. The day was clear and blue for once, and overhead, gulls flew in swift circles above the eucalyptus trees.

"Well, you know she tried to secure an *abortion*—she tried to ask the midwife at first, but then the midwife got deported, and . . ."

"And?"

"So this girl heard that an *employee* knew where these services could be provided. But then her plan completely backfired, because the employee ended up leaking her planned abortion to, you guessed it, the pregnant girl's *husband*!"

"So what happened to her?"

"Well, her husband all but disowned her. She had to be rescued and taken in by a missionary home. All that trouble to get to this country, only to be dumped in the end. Sad, isn't it?"

"But did she get the abortion?"

"That part, I never found out. Great question, though."

"I feel for her. I've been through something similar myself." Daji put her hand on the railing, and a dragonfly buzzed past them, darting in and out of view.

"Yes, I heard!" exclaimed Yingning.

Daji laughed. "What *have* you heard, I wonder?"

"Well . . ." Yingning hesitated for a moment. "According to some women here, your husband was a very successful merchant who met you in a Shanghai tearoom and whisked you away to Canton, where he bought you a three-carat diamond ring and promptly abandoned you for the sea, and then for another woman."

Daji smoothed her gloves. "Do go on. What else do they say?"

"Well, then they said you went mad, and got possessed by a

nine-tailed fox demon. That you were so weak and vulnerable and desperate, you traded your life to be possessed."

Daji's expression must have changed abruptly, because Yingning then immediately added, "But who believes that superstitious bullshit? I, for one, do not buy it for a second. Those women are the ones who are pathetic fools!"

But Daji knew there was some veracity to these myths. It was true, for example, that fox spirits possessed women in their weakest moments. That desperate women were indeed easy to exploit, that they willingly gave up their identities, traded them for a chance to transform into something else. What? It didn't matter. What better way to transform than through a fox spirit—a master shape-shifter, master border-crosser, who moved so easily between worlds?

One thing the rumors got wrong was that her diamond ring was, in fact, five carats, not three—sharp enough to bruise a man's eye. She could cut the wooden wall with it—and she did. The first poems that Daji composed on the walls at night when the moon was huge and she couldn't sleep, she carved with a small penknife, and she had refined the edges of the characters with the diamond.

Then one day in the afternoon Daji dozed off as she was memorizing some notes on her bunk bed, and upon waking saw that her ring was missing—someone had taken it right off her finger. She made no assumptions, though everyone thought it was Yingning. At first Daji snooped around, speaking for the first time to the women who had spread all the nasty stories about her. She didn't want to accuse Yingning directly, for fear, she admitted, of losing her only friend there. Daji wondered if she was actually relieved to rid herself of the ring, or any hope that she would meet her ex-husband again. When she was only a teenager Yingning's age, full of foolish, lavish hopes, she let him sweep her away with florid tales of Western palaces. The way her ex-husband would regale her with stories of the West—as if Shanghai was not already a microcosm of all that noise, waste, and exhaust. The West was not more enchanting than her home, she knew.

And yet here she was, responding to this call, memorizing the details of this stranger's life, the merchant Wing Fu Ong—the intimate details: when this stranger slept at night, how this stranger liked his pancakes cooked, how far this stranger's village was from the sea. This was not freedom, was it? To pose as yet another merchant's wife? It had been her ex-husband's parting gift for her: a chance to grow another new life, a ticket across the world—far, far away from him.

The next day, at her interview, Daji wore her best, most respectable outfit: a pale pink silk blouse, a creamy white hat and jacket and skirt, all pure lambswool. She decided to wear her silk gloves, since she was without her ring. The inspector was a broad-headed, flame-haired man in his twenties, who ordered her to the pulpit. Standing next to him was another officer, and beside them was the interpreter and a stenographer. The room itself was sparse, with only one window. Daji was distracted because she recognized the interpreter and the inspector as the very subjects of Yingning's gossip—the ones who were having an affair. She detected from their gestures that they were actively avoiding each other. She imagined Wing Fu Ong, her "husband," in that same room, answering all of their questions the day before, and tried to summon her courage.

It didn't surprise her when the young man asked her if she had been a virtuous woman before and after her marriage to this merchant.

"Would you define what you mean by virtue?" she asked.

"You know what I mean. Any respectable woman would."

"I just wanted to make sure that our communication is sound."

The inspector turned to the interpreter with a raised eyebrow, and she gave Daji a withering look. Clearing her throat, she said impatiently, "Have you ever had sexual intercourse before you met your current husband?"

"Yes," said Daji. "With my first husband."

"What were the grounds for your divorce?"

"He was always away, didn't have time to spend with family."

"Did you have sexual intercourse before you married your first husband?"

"No," said Daji emphatically.

"How many sexual partners have you had?"

"Two."

"Are you positive?"

"Positive, sir."

"Do you know the implications in this country, of lying under oath?"

Daji stared into the eyes of the officer. He really did think she was a prostitute. Here this man was, questioning her virtue, when she was certain that he himself was carrying on an illicit affair. It was clear that this man already had a verdict when it came to her. To him, the way she looked proved her moral turpitude, and no amount of speaking under oath would prove her innocence, her worth.

The night after her interrogation, Daji looked out the window from her ledge. She could never sleep at night, especially when the moon was so crisp and visible, a crystal goblet hanging low in the sky, about to pour down its light. Outside the window, she noticed the silhouette of a fox on the dock. A silvery one, walking alone, sharp-eyed and staring right at her. The fox then turned around, revealing a flurry of tails—one, two, three, four, five, six, seven, eight, nine—all snow-white and glinting carelessly like knives.

5

Normally, Mrs. Rong had a saffron-flowered complexion, pudgy and sweet. But these days, in the detention center, her blood pressure had taken a toll. When that woman quietly asked her, to her face, if her daughter had taken her ring, Mrs. Rong's affable demeanor switched to a pink-nosed rage. When she was angry, her face blossomed like a tea rose.

"I'm sorry—I have no idea what you're talking about."

"Never mind, then. I just thought I would ask." The woman smiled at her with her perfect white teeth. In the crowded barracks, where every normal woman was filthy and stank of sweat and depression, the sight of her perfect white teeth infuriated Mrs. Rong even further, so that even after Daji left it alone, Mrs. Rong seethed for days. The nerve of such an accusation! Yingning had her own trinkets. A gold necklace, passed down to her by Mrs. Rong's mother. A white jade pendant carved in the shape of a rabbit, which Mrs. Rong gave to Yingning for her twelfth birthday. The girl had no need for someone else's ring—her whole life, Yingning had wanted for nothing.

Mrs. Rong never thought to ask her daughter if this was true, for Mrs. Rong believed her intuition was unassailable. That is, until her merchant husband blindsided her by deciding to leave for America, opening a fireworks shop in Chicago. This was two years ago, and now he had finally sent for her and their only daughter, Yingning.

Though Daji did not bother her any further after the conversation, Mrs. Rong thought that woman must have run her mouth, because now everyone was wary of Yingning. Locks were fished out of the farthest corners of jewelry boxes and secured quietly, without a word. Of course suspicions would fixate on Mrs. Rong, even though they had no proof, no evidence that Yingning had done anything. These silly women had the nerve to turn on her! The poor girl only tried to befriend what was the obvious pariah of the group, and now *she* was turned into the pariah, dragging her mother with her.

Only a week ago, Mrs. Rong could gossip with any of the other ladies, but now they actively avoided her. At every meal she sat with Yingning, who stared blankly into her tasteless boiled rice and the fungal-smelling tea as if all the words had been drained out of her.

"You have nothing left to say to your mother?" Mrs. Rong finally said.

Yingning smelled the tea.

"Why do you speak to that vixen and not the other girls and boys?"

Yingning ate one spoonful and finally looked up at her mother. "I'm just not interested. They're all much younger than me. I'm sixteen, what could I possibly say to a six- or eight-year-old?"

"Little Mu is twelve. That's close enough to your age."

"Little Mu eats her own snot, did you know?"

Mrs. Rong noticed her daughter's oval face, a swollen red dot just under her nose, her eyes all droopy and ironic, her hair loosely swept to the side.

"Yingning, be honest with your mother. Did you take it?"

Yingning said nothing. Irritated, Mrs. Rong continued: "Why on earth would you steal when you have what you have?"

This must have finally hit a nerve, because Yingning snapped, with an expression Mrs. Rong had never seen, "Mother, not everything is about *things*! All you care about are things, and appearances, and acting proper and holier-than-thou, good god, it's so transparent. The way you smile at everyone with perfect contempt! You think I don't notice? You think I'm stupid?"

Yingning dropped her spoon and left her bowl half-eaten, leaving Mrs. Rong speechless. The other women were now staring at her, and she found herself livid again, not at her daughter, but at them. How dare they pry, these low-class women who were suddenly acting so much better than her, with their withering, estranged expressions!

"Excuse me," she said to no one in particular, and headed to the lavatory. Mrs. Rong thought back to their respective interrogations, which occurred the week before, on Wednesday and Thursday. It was two arduous days of questions, and when Mrs. Rong asked Yingning what questions they asked her, the girl had given her another blank look. And then she worried: What if her daughter failed, and she passed? Then what—would they be separated? She had been confident in her answers—but many of them seemed too difficult for a teenager like Yingning. Like the address of the hospital in their village. Or what crops were harvested and imported to the merchants late spring the year before they emigrated. Or what cardinal direction the kitchen door faced.

In the middle of her interrogation, Mrs. Rong had stumbled on that question. The official stared at her, studying her silence, and her neck stiffened under his scrutiny. She remembered the kitchen door, its red paint chipping—how one afternoon she let the chickens she bought from the market wander around outside that door before eventually killing them for a feast. And she had fixated on that feast—if only that had been the interrogation question! *What did you feed your neighbors on the Mid-Autumn Festival?* If they had asked that question instead of the kitchen door question, then she would have answered, proudly: three chickens, a pot of rabbit stew with fresh green onions, a mountain of steamed jasmine rice. They had a good life. If only her husband didn't decide to go here, this hostile shore. Daydreaming, Mrs. Rong had almost missed her chance to answer.

In the lavatory stall, Mrs. Rong came across the half-carved poem on the wall. It must have been Daji's poem, the one Yingning mentioned once:

> If I was truly a fox-woman,
> then I could shape-shift back into an animal
> and leap out of this human cage!
> The barbed-wire fences would not prick,
> for my luxurious fur would be too thick.

Then she noticed underneath the stanza there was another stanza, scratched lightly in a different handwriting. She recognized it as her daughter's:

> Yet, if I really could leap past this fence,
> I don't know where I would go.

> Do I stay here in this land that despises me
> or go back to a home I do not truly know?

The line cleaved into her unexpectedly. It occurred to her that up until now she had no idea what her daughter was capable of, whether it was stealing or writing poetry. This filled her with inexplicable sadness.

The morning after, Mrs. Rong woke up to a disturbance. Mrs. Burke, the matron, had entered the sleeping quarters at about six-fifteen, her eyes grim and lined with russet. Tye Leung, her interpreter, was standing by her side with a pad of notes, her face similarly stricken.

A woman had gone missing, they announced. Anyone with information as to her whereabouts had to notify the matron or any of the officers immediately. If any detainee harbored a secret or withheld information, that was a chargeable offense, subject to immediate deportation.

Mrs. Rong already knew who it was without asking. The matron said that the woman had been last seen late in the night, already outside the premises of the building. There was only one eyewitness, a child who saw her through a window. No one knew how she had escaped, but she was wearing a white gown with long sleeves.

The little boy then identified himself—he had to be no older than eight or nine. A crowd of women, now risen from their bunks, surrounded him. He said her sleeves "floated in the night," flying like what he imagined in the martial arts illustrations in his storybooks. According to him, she glowed like a goddess, she rose up in the air, and the sea and the moonlight seemed to move

along with her. She had been leaping and leaping into the sky, and
he saw her transform, upon landing, into her true form: a white
fox, with multiple tails. And that was where the matron drew the
line. "Enough," she said. "We need a more reliable witness. This
child was clearly dreaming."

Mrs. Rong glanced quickly at her daughter, who was slumped
and leaning against Daji's empty metal bunk, expressionless. It
seemed that Daji had left most of her fancy possessions there, and
Yingning was already rifling through the woman's leather satchel
amid the ruckus.

This time, Mrs. Rong smiled. In the end, her daughter couldn't
hide everything from her. Perhaps Yingning agreed with her after
all, that this vain woman needed to be taken down a few notches.
That she deserved it.

"It's true!" the boy cried in protest. "I swear I saw it with my
own eyes!"

"You need rest," said Tye, in Chinese, stroking his head, but he
pushed her away, crying. Soon his weeping turned into screaming
wails, and his mother, apologetic, bowed in front of the matron
and then wrapped the boy in her arms, in an attempt to both
comfort and quiet him. But the boy was inconsolable, and the
worst part, Mrs. Rong thought, was the truth she couldn't tell
him—that actually she believed him. They all did.

A Huxian's Guide to
~~Seduction~~ ~~Revenge~~ Immortality

Once a year I give myself permission to indulge in real tenderness. I dip an overripe fig in honey and eat it with yogurt. Then I allow some man to worship me. I make him go down on two knees and pray.

"Pray for what?" he'd whisper.

"Pray for whatever you like, as long as you pray to me," I'd reply. "I am your goddess."

Then I'd fan my hair out on my bed, splay my legs, and he'd dip his head down, put his palms together, and purse his lips in concentration. Sometimes he wouldn't know what to pray for, because his prayers had been answered. Sometimes he'd recite a novena he remembered from childhood. Sometimes he would take too long, and I'd watch him bend against the bed, his brows furrowed in thought. Sometimes he would start weeping, though this was rare. Then when he finished praying he would put his lips to my thigh and I'd arch my hips forward, and time would begin again.

Summer is a series of aches heightened, sharpened into blades. I watch it spin itself to the ground—the simmering sounds and scents of the city: lamb skewers frying on halal truck griddles, girls in puff-sleeve dresses with their manicured toes crunching over subway grates, Chinatown dumpsters full of baby's breath and rotten rambutan and slimy cockles, the sheen of sunscreen and sweat on the foreheads of commuters heading to Jacob Riis or Brighton or Rockaway. I smell and hear and see it all. I am always aching for meat. Months and months of listlessness culminate into a raw, bloodletting hunger. My sport is almost too easy for me, so I fantasize about switching roles, becoming my own prey. You look at your body in the mirror and want to consume it yourself. The taste of your own sweat, your own saliva, more thrilling than the taste of any other. The feeling gives you the impulse to go out there and find opportunities to defile yourself. To be defiled. To defile another.

I'm what they call a nine-tailed fox. A hulijing, huxian, fox spirit, fox fairy, fox demon, fox seductress, exquisite fox, all the names I can and can't claim as my own. Enchantment is my sport, and this city of ten million people and twice as many rats is my arena. I'm not heartless—I feed on the wicked. I observe from the margins—this in-between, this unseen place between dawn and dusk, this cockroach-infested apartment, this fur, this skin. I love this perch from which one can survey the world, gather the infinite wisdom of the city. Every street, every café, every gym or club or hotel lobby—all fair game for bad men who come out to play. I've noticed in particular how straight men are not cautious. They don't care about the potential dangers of inviting strangers into their homes or walking out in public spaces. They don't think twice like most others do.

My home is a studio apartment on the edges of Ocean Hill, Brooklyn, close to Broadway Junction and the sounds of the aboveground J crisscrossing the A, C, and L. It was vacated half a year ago by its owner, this whole complex up for foreclosure, then gut renovation. Last month, as soon as the windows were boarded up and the last squatters departed following an infestation of centipedes, I moved in and made my den. Just one flea-bitten mattress on the floor is all I need. Until the developers begin their gentrification, I am free to live in this liminal place and work. By work, I mean writing down all I learn from observing humans' habitations, their conflicts with foxes, the politics of it. My current project is a guide to help other fox spirits like myself get what we want: Love. No, scratch that. Revenge. Eh, I mean immortality, transcendence. It's a self-help book, if you will, a work in progress. Foxes are notoriously too proud to seek help unless from an actual god, so I fib a little here and there, like the lie that I'm already an immortal, that I already have nine tails. But we all lie sometimes to survive, isn't that true?

The rest of the time, I spend hunting.

I locate my targets with precision and caution. Certain men believe they are systemically oppressed because women won't have sex with them. They write manifestos about how unfair it is that they can't find someone willing to fuck them, how humiliating, and they blame this on women. According to the logic of these poorly written manifestos, if a woman is sexually active, then she is a slut and deserves to die, but if a woman does not sleep with these manifesto-writers, she is a bitch.

And some men move through this world with an ease that tells you vaguely what kind of life they lead, what kind of car they might drive, what kind of sheets they sleep in. When they wake up in the morning and walk outside their condos, they treat the larger world just like that—like the sheets they make love to their wives on, these men so wholly at home in what they do. And some men quit their jobs to go backpacking in Thailand or teach English in China, to distract themselves from their self-loathing, drown themselves in debauchery and local women that they feel free to exploit because life in such countries is not real to them.

And still some other men post long eloquent screeds on Facebook citing the statistics attached to sexual assault, yet in private, talking to the woman they're sleeping with about her previous trauma, they ask her if she reported her rape to the police—if not, then why not? Is it really trauma if you haven't been diagnosed?

Sometimes they are ordinary men, too. Most of the time, that's all they are. Men.

A HUXIAN'S GUIDE TO SEDUCTION

Vixens and enchantresses, you've come here from all walks of human life to learn how to seduce mortal men, extract their energy, their power, and acquire the elixir of transcendence that allows you to become huxian (divine fox transcendent) so you can get the hell out of the festering foxhole called Earth and ascend to Heaven.

If a vixen lives to the age of a thousand and gathers enough human essence, she will reach divinity and transform from hulijing (fox spirit) to huxian (immortal nine-tailed fox). The word xian connotes a blissful being, a perfected and immortal creature. Huxian, blissful transcendents, are free agents, unattached to any one house or temple or grave, and they live forever in their divinity and beauty, gaining the coveted nine tails. The huxian enters the cloud forests of Mount K'unlun, and above, the seven stars of the Big Dipper that she has worshipped all her life, which joins Heaven and Earth. After you arrive at the goal of transcendence and immortality, you forsake all human relationships.

To reach xian-hood, there are several ways. The first is self-cultivation—to isolate oneself on a mountain, refine the self in perfect solace, and study the classics. It's a process of meditation and purification, and those foxes who master this for one thousand years achieve true huxian status.

The second is a combination of self-cultivation and spirit possession—these foxes might haunt human residences, abandoned boardinghouses, and other liminal spaces. Sometimes at night, a fox might use their magic to possess a human's body and extract a bit of their life force. Sometimes they shape-shift into doppelgängers and steal life force from those unfortunate people's families. This is usually not fatal, but it sure leads to conflict. If caught and exorcised, these fox spirits are expelled from their residences. But if feared or worshipped, then they might enter into an agreement with a spirit medium and deliver their wisdom that way. I myself don't like to half-ass things, so this is not my preferred way.

The fastest, easiest way to reach xian-hood is through praying to the Big Dipper and metamorphosizing into beautiful women, bewitching human men and absorbing their life essence and yang force through sex and enchantment. This third, infinitely more dangerous path is the boat we are on, the way we have chosen.

· · · · ·

There was a man who drove a truck. Every so often he picked up hitchhikers and took them to motels.

There was a man who ran a Fortune 500 company. Every so often he traveled and conducted his affairs discreetly.

There was a man who studied at the local law school. Every so often he drove to the park looking for girls.

· · · · ·

I do not ever visit the graveyard, the cemetery where I was born. From the place dead bodies are buried, I came out, sprang forward, fresh-faced, peaches in my cheeks, a young girl with shapely limbs and a leonine prowl, hands and feet crawling on the earth. My metamorphosis began with the scent of rain-torn Easter lilies, all those deathly white flowers, some of them plastic, polluting the sacred ground of the dead.

People waste so much time on grief. People waste so much energy trying to please the dead, revere the dead, remember the dead. All those tangerines wasted on ghosts without the stomachs to enjoy them. But I do. I eat them whole, oily rinds and all. The citrus segments, the acids cooling all the cinnabar heat in my body. It was my first human meal, the tangerines left on a young girl's headstone.

I dug her skull up from the earth. I placed it over me. The contours of her bone fit snugly over my head, but its heaviness surprised me. Then I gathered all the flowers, all the dead bouquets, all the plastic roses and lilies, and mixed them with the wet sycamore leaves. I laid them out over my body and then I slumped down beneath a cypress tree. The night was clear, every planet naked and feral in the sky. Under the Big Dipper, I counted the holes between each star and worshipped my constellation until the leaves and flowers whistled through my fur. I summoned the oily pearl in my throat, closed my eyes, and imagined a mountain, K'unlun, the mythical Palace of the Sun and Moon where the heavenly nine-tailed foxes lived in harmony among hot springs and verdant waterfalls, all of them huxian, all of them divine.

Instead, I dreamt of clothes being ripped apart—wonderful hand-sewn clothes, stitched with the best fibers and selvages, torn to pieces. Instead, I dreamt of a hand reaching inside a silk robe and grabbing. Instead, I dreamt of mad violence in a field of lavender.

The girl whose skull I wore was only nineteen when she died. I could not imagine departing the world at such an age. All night, I dreamed of violet fields stained with rope and silk burns. Then I woke up, and I was a woman.

The dead girl was the third-generation daughter of a shoe repairman. Her father fixed and smoothed any and all of the scratches, scuffs, and burns that this city could inflict; her mother was a tailor and a laundress. They had a tiny laundromat and shoe repair shop in Sunset Park between a dollar dumpling joint and a day spa where the dead girl used to get bad copper highlights for ten dollars. The dead girl loved the smell of leather. The dead girl knew how to fix a zipper caught in linen, how to untie the most impossible knots, how to flame someone on an Internet forum.

One day she was out at Brooklyn Bowl with her friends, and an older man of about thirty-five approached them. She recognized him—he was one of the old regulars at her father's shop, always bringing in his broken shoes or old leather jackets. He was friendly with her father, often sliding him an extra five-dollar bill here and there, but a few years ago he had moved out of Brooklyn. The last time she had seen him was probably three years ago, when she was sixteen.

"Fancy seeing you here!'" he said, as if they were actually friends. He reached out for a hug, and she half patted him on the back, thinking that would be the end of it as she went to take her turn.

As soon as her ball fell with a thud into the gutter, the man began to give her some "tips," some "pointers." He demonstrated, with his arms, how to throw the ball, even though she didn't ask him, and she certainly did not feel comfortable when he came up behind her and tried to maneuver her arm such that she was holding the ball a certain way. Her friends intervened, and finally batted the man off by escorting her to the bathroom, where she explained in hushed whispers who he was—a "family friend," she said uncertainly.

But that was not the end of it. The man showed up at their shoe repair store a week later with a pair of scuffed leather oxfords that needed fixing.

"Look at these laces, they sure need an upgrade," he said, loosening the laces from the shoes, their discolored tongues hanging out. She removed the laces and sifted through the shoelaces on sale, then handed him a new pair. "I ought to properly thank you sometime," he said.

She did not politely say, *Sorry, but I'm not interested*, because she'd seen what happens to girls who reject men aloud, what happens when men's feelings get hurt, and so she was friendly, even asked him a few questions about himself, which he of course interpreted as interest, as flirting. So then when he asked her to go to the cineplex with him on a date of sorts, she did not decline, and when he said he'd pick her up at the store when her shift was over, she did not protest. Perhaps she was flattered, because he wasn't such a bad-looking man, and she had no idea why he would take an interest in her, a gawky Chinese teenager who didn't even get asked to senior prom.

It was a Sunday, late summer. Later, this man pulled up in the parking lot across the street at seven o'clock sharp just as he'd said he would, and she thought, *Who cares, it is just a movie, I do not have to even talk to this person, I can just focus on the movie—if anything, this would be a funny story to tell, this creep whose shoes were always inexplicably broken.* Within hours her thoughts would turn to regret. But then it was still before, and this man was smiling, because he had her in his car.

This man is you. You are the man I'm looking for.

A HUXIAN'S GUIDE TO REVENGE

Inevitably, on your journey, you will meet bad seeds who will test your capacity for patience. You will meet men who have committed crimes for which they were never punished. You will meet men who have never learned accountability, and in fact become indignant at the very thought. When the urge to take vengeance boils, try your best to remain coolheaded. If revenge is your mission, the best advice is to treat the man in question like any other man. Then proceed. Study your desire for vengeance. Study your anger. Examine it from another point of view. Remove yourself from your body—imagine you are a spirit floating in space, imagine yourself unencumbered by any weight, human, fox, or otherwise. You are on the top of the mountain now, the mountains from the classics and the poems, all blanketed with snowcapped spruces and a layer of shimmering mist. Are you still angry? Does the anger reside in both your being and your bones? If you find that this is the case, then you may keep going.

When seducing them, act completely ignorant of who they are, but once you have them in an open and vulnerable position, such as beneath you and tied to the bedpost, make it clear. List their crimes so they know and are aware that you are punishing them for a reason. Use your shape-shifting powers to scare them. Burn their own transgressions into their brains. Deplete them of their vital essence until you are sated, until you have gained enough breath to fill you. If they display insolence, show them what your powers are. If their arrogance persists, remind them.

Do not question your right to take revenge, nor second-guess yourself. Karmic debts will always be paid with karmic retribution. Remember that you are only practicing for your inevitable ascendance from hulijing into huxian. The journey from ordinary fox spirit to divine transcendent is an arduous one, but it is worth taking in the name of justice. Since huxians live in Heaven, they can deal heavenly justice. Remember, you are only exacting your vision of what you are on the verge of becoming.

I locate you on a Sunday afternoon on a dating app. I am making my breakfast and drop the raw egg in the frying pan, where it sizzles and hisses. Your pictures say a lot about you. On the outside, you appear to be a pretty normal guy. Some would describe you as handsome-ish: a pronounced jawline, a trim figure, and a lustrous full head of hair. In the first picture, you are holding a weight at the gym. It is a very basic photo. In the next photo, you are posing with someone else's dog. It is a very fine dog—wet-nosed, with long silky hair, a husky with ice-blue eyes. *John, 29, Manhattan.* To no one's surprise, you lie about your age.

I look very young. I list my age as eighteen. You chat me up immediately after we match. We talk about the weather, we exchange numbers. In our text exchanges, you don't mince your words. You immediately start commenting on my body. Do you do any sports? No reason, baby, just your legs, they look so long.

And when I comment on the beauty of your dog, you reply, sweetly, not as beautiful as you, and immediately after, counter that with: would you like to take my dog's place?

How many men have you slept with?

When was the last time you had sex?

What positions do you like?

Because it is a dating app, you do not question whether it is appropriate to ask questions like that. With her, you were what you consider gentlemanly, but with the girls on this app, you don't need etiquette or artifice.

I'm just being honest, is your defense. Why beat around the bush, why not just get to the point?

After all, it's not sexual harassment if the app is for sex, right? After all, why am I on the app if I'm going to be such a frigid bitch, right?

So I relent. I eat my sunnyside-up egg, cut it in half with my fork and knife. The runny yolk oozes out like the sun, a sudden shot of clarity.

. . . . .

There was a man who wrote a guide to picking up women and fancied himself and his followers "pickup artists." He held seminars in hotel conference rooms where he charged his followers something to the tune of two grand to hear his cheap pickup strategies and whine to each other about "the game."

There was a man who taught English in China and liked to have sex with his students. He posted on message boards online about how easy it is to sleep with these women, how American women were fucked by feminism but women in China were submissive and feminine and do whatever you want them to do.

There was a man who pushed his wife out of a window. When he called the police, he claimed that she killed herself. Later, he was acquitted of all charges and continued his illustrious career as a sculptor.

. . . . .

You were on your date with the girl who is now dead. You suggested a theater, the Regal Cinema on Second Avenue and Thirty-Ninth Street. In the middle of the movie, you took the girl's hand in yours and rested it on her lap. She thought about how to get out of this without hurting your feelings. She considered whispering in your ear to let go, but that could be read as playing hard to get, so instead she politely pretended to drink her Diet Pepsi, slipped out of your grasp to grab her cup. The cup stayed in both her hands for the whole rest of the movie. You were inching toward her ear, wanting to whisper all the dirty things you wanted to do to her, but she was so fixated on the film that you stopped yourself. You figured you'd save it for later.

The movie you chose was an indie film, *Simon Killer*, about an American man who goes to Paris. There was a scene where the man was getting a lap dance from a stripper, and you glanced over at her to see her reaction. Your date was visibly cringing, biting her tongue.

On-screen, the man begged the stripper to take him in because he had nowhere to stay, and she relented out of pity. The man called his mother in the kitchen while his new host was at work and cried. Then the man met a younger, paler girl at a café, and soon he started arguing with his stripper girlfriend. Even though she was housing him, he suddenly felt disgusted by her, he suddenly felt a deep disdain for her that perhaps had been his feeling all along. At the end of the movie, he killed her.

Because you paid for the movie tickets, you insisted that she come back to your home for a drink to discuss the movie. "I have to get going," she said.

"Just one drink?" you pressed. "Look, my apartment is just over there." You had chosen this movie theater specifically for its proximity—only about fifty meters—to your place, and its distance from the D train—at least a fifteen-minute walk. You squeezed her hand. You did not intend to let go, so she sighed in exasperation.

"One drink. Then, really, I have to go."

You suggest our first meeting be at your home in Kips Bay. You do not think this is presumptuous, and this is your first mistake. In privacy, sealed away from the public, you assume you have the power in any situation. Plus, you're lazy. What's the point of traveling even three stops on the subway? When I express a reasonable human hesitation about meeting a stranger at his home for the first time, you ridicule me, attempt to coax me out of my own discomfort.

Come on. Don't you want to have some fun?

Then you send me an unsolicited dick pic. A disembodied thing, bathed in thick yellow light. It was taken in a hotel bathroom with pink marbled floors. In the background, I can see your toes, which need a pedicure.

I do not respond to you for a while. Then, just to fuck with you, I Photoshop a *National Geographic* image of a yawning red fox next to your dick and send it back to you. It looks like the fox is about to bite it off.

So you into furries now? you reply.

Oh, you have no idea.

No one wants to see your dick pic, loser, I reply.

I'm sure this makes you both horny and angry, so you send me a flurry of messages.

So you want to see it in person then. I got it.

You want to play with it? Come on, you know you do. Want me to open my fly so you can taste it?

Do you want me to come over and **** you? Huh, you little *****? You little ****?

As soon as she entered your apartment, you poured her a glass of gin. It was clear you didn't really want to talk about the movie, but she went on about it in a fury, complaining about how much she despised the protagonist and his ilk, how movies like this don't serve any purpose except to sensationalize violence against women. When you disagreed, asking her to consider the nuances of this character, his complexity and humanity, she flinched, but you didn't notice this. You continued—this protagonist wasn't all bad, like look how even though he killed the prostitute in the end, it was evident he missed his mother throughout the movie. He was meant to be sympathetic, look at how many times he cried! Didn't she see, you exclaimed, that he was clearly hurting, that he needed help, he was lost, searching for himself in another country? Couldn't she at least relate to that?

And then she put down her glass, and that's when you went in, you planted a kiss on her lips. She saw that coming. After a second, she pulled away. But it was too late, according to you, it was too late for her to leave now, too dangerous out on the streets, and so you put down your glass and poured her another.

"I'll be a gentleman, I promise."

She went quiet, knowing what your intentions were, staring out the window into the fire escape of another apartment building, where a couple of teenagers were drinking beer and smoking. You got up and pulled down the shades. She must have been thinking about the last time she saw you in her neighborhood, how you bantered with her father as you collected your shoes, how he called you Johnny even though you never said that was your nickname, how he treated you as his "VIP customer" and gave you silver-foiled holiday cards and free packs of cigarettes. How on some days when you picked up dry cleaning from her mother, you winked at her, then still in high school, and snuck her a candy bar or a pack of Twizzlers, how her mother smiled at you and covered her mouth as she talked, suddenly self-conscious about her accent. Perhaps something about your full adulthood, the tidy austerity of your apartment, how your pots and pans were hanging off hooks from your kitchen, turned a switch on her mind and made her acutely aware of her own youth, how far apart you were from her, how you suddenly seemed like another planet altogether, an escape from what she had always known, yet just familiar enough.

You put an aux cable on your phone and asked her, "What are the kids listening to these days?" And she laughed nervously, but when her song came on she danced, even taking a few swigs of the gin, and you laughed and danced with her, swaying her, putting your hand on her hip. And perhaps she was lulled, nodding along to your overtures—she let you kiss her some more, shove your tongue down her throat and pull her to your bed even before the song was over.

When your hand wandered somewhere under her shirt, she began to protest, again, and then you whispered, "Ugh, baby, you're so beautiful, you turn me on so much," and you coaxed and coaxed her until she began to sigh in exasperation and mumbled, "Fine." When she finally relented, letting you take off her clothes, didn't you take it as a small triumph—another conquest, another notch?

But then there were some things you did that she didn't give you permission for, weren't there? Like when you took your phone out to record, no, that part was pure impulse and you wanted to capture her in the heat of the moment, you couldn't help yourself, you needed to record it so that you could always remember what a slut she was, that part she didn't consent to, isn't that true? And then when she turned around and noticed, screaming at you to get off, were you surprised? Were you unnerved to find her writhing, grabbing fistfuls of your covers like she was drowning?

"What are you doing?" she asked. And for the first time, you had no answer.

"What are you *doing*?" she demanded, the sob in her voice like a pulse. It was too late to say anything. She forced you to delete it from your phone and then immediately called an Uber, gathering her dress and her bag and slamming the door—and how did that make you feel? Ashamed? Regretful? You didn't protest when she walked out of your apartment building in the cold, did you? Tell me, was the night too dangerous then?

· · · · ·

There was a man, a security guard who worked the night shift, who saw an attractive woman trying to exit the building, and so he decided to lock the door.

There was a man, a nurse, who was charged with impregnating a twenty-six-year-old woman in a coma.

There was a man, a famous film producer, who regularly invited young aspiring actresses to his hotel room to "discuss his new scripts" over cocktails.

· · · · ·

To the gentlemen scholars of yore, the ways of fox spirits were mysterious. These erudite men were perplexed, flummoxed by our loveliness, they mistook us for lustful demons when it is not lust but a need to ascend to heaven that drives most of our actions on earth. They were fascinated and terrified of our femininity, saw it both as an object of desire and as a pollutant to their male vitality, their essence or yang, the precious nectar of life, according to them. A fancy way to describe semen, if you ask me.

So these men wrote tales about us in their records of the

strange—they stripped us down into demure playthings or de-
monic wenches, described us as divine beauties and wanton
temptresses, and yet they never did speculate on our motives, our
feelings and thoughts, our whereabouts beyond the bedchamber
of their gentlemen-scholar protagonists. They never assumed we
had any interiority or fears or desires or friends or lives. We were
mysteries to them that they were unwilling to pick apart. Ji Yun,
a writer of fox tales, never attempted to enter our minds or har-
ness our thoughts, for even his most sympathetic fox women in
the end were still aliens.

When the gentleman scholars gave us sympathetic roles, our
virtue only depended on how much we pleased their male protagonists. Virtuous fox women selflessly gave up their chances at
immortality to take care of the men they met. Miss Ren, a beautiful fox woman portrayed by Tang scholar Shen Jiji, uses her divination abilities to help her lover make money in business and
pull him out of poverty. Miss Li, another beautiful fox woman
portrayed by Tang scholar Zhang Du, marries a scholar and becomes a perfect wife and mother. She fulfills her family duties for
twenty years, giving birth to seven sons and two daughters, and
finally dies in the end. Pu Songling, another famous chronicler of
strange tales, invented Lotus Fragrance, a fox woman who selflessly nurses her lover back to health even after she discovers he'd
been two-timing her with a ghost woman.

By virtue of their stores of male energy, the men's place in the
world is fixed—as protagonists, their belonging never wavers. But
fox women are and will always be aliens who prove themselves to
be worthy under patriarchy, and time and time again, they are
punished. Even the most overpraised and virtuous fox women
suffer bad fates. After Miss Li's death, all seven of her children

die, too. And the brilliant Miss Ren, in the end, dies after being mauled by a dog.

The day after she left your apartment, something started going viral that made you angry, didn't it? You didn't think she could be so savvy, did you, that as soon as she got home, she'd cried for a long time and poured herself a bowl of cereal, then found your LinkedIn, your Twitter, and your company website that listed your boss's contact information? You didn't know, did you, that she had an audience of her own, this quiet, shy girl—that she curated a persona, if you will, on a popular video app, and amassed quite a social media following—she could upload anything to a sea of strangers, all of whom were eager to validate her every thought and whim.

The girl had posted about her experience with you on her vlog. It was a fifteen-minute video of her at her most raw and vulnerable: Her voice cracked as she sobbed. "How many other girls and women experience this? It is not okay!" She'd included screenshots of your Tinder profile, your messages with her, all kinds of receipts. On the screen, she seemed like a different person. Not meek at all—in fact, she was angry, snarky—she mocked you openly even as she despaired. How violated she felt, how it was a disgrace that you should be employed after what you did to her. Then, under the video, she tagged your employer, your boss, your colleagues, even your ex-wife. (How did she even find her?) The comments rolled in, calling you a rapist and a predator, calling this girl *brave* and *strong*, a *survivor*.

But you're not like that at all, you wanted to protest, you are a nice professional man. You, dear John, did not feel ashamed or regretful for your actions—and now something else was on the line, wasn't it. You may have deleted the video from your phone, but you had a spycam set up in your room for backup. For more angles, sure. If she had the nerve to tag your employer, you were right to send the video to your friends on the group chat, the chat room, put it online in your own anonymous account for all the world to see, have a laugh, all in the name of good fun, your name cleared, where's the harm in that? Look at how willing she was! A sex tape surely discredited everything she said on her vlog. Clearly, she was asking—no, begging—for it.

And when the evidence traveled through cyberspace and infiltrated the rest of her life, were you watching from afar? You didn't even have to do that much work—the online mob loved to see an outspoken Asian woman shut up, and so they did it for you. The petite Chinese American girl from Sunset Park had to open her mouth, so now she was all splayed for the online trolls to see. And how they loved it: a shiny new piece of meat. Now the anonymous accounts were flurrying to her profiles, posting links to this video of her. Now the anonymous accounts all called her a faker, a liar, a hack. *Kill yourself*, the new comments read. *You do not deserve to live.*

Now the trolls doxxed her and found her dorm, her RA, they found her school pictures and posted an entry about her on a website. She was afraid to go to class now—she didn't know who among strangers or new classmates would have seen her. *Aw, man, come on, just one drink. Just one kiss.* Spy cams, video clips, screenshots, angles, wasn't all of that just a good time? Didn't your friends resoundingly approve, weren't they admiring and envious, didn't they call you such a "lucky man"?

The next week, she was dead. And the fact that you are still living your miserable life, going about your daily routine, eating bagel lox sandwiches and sweating at Equinox, commuting to the office to enter some data and in the evenings having beers in the East Village with the guys: well, John, I can't have it.

. . . . .

There was a man who got a thrill out of groping strangers on the street. He would strategically park his car somewhere close as he walked up and down the street looking for potential victims.

There was a man who thought that his predilection for teen girls was a basis for great art, great films, and he enjoyed a long and illustrious career making the same movie over and over again, year after year, even after such movies fell out of taste, even after it was revealed this man was an abuser.

There was a band of men who rose up in the ranks of the highest courts in the land. One of them sniveled and spat about his love of beer when confronted with allegations of sexual assault. One of them sexually harassed a woman and for decades after accepted private jet vacations and yacht trips from billionaire tycoons. One of them cited Sir Matthew Hale, a seventeenth century jurist who hunted witches, in his written opinion that ended the civil rights of child-bearing people across America, overturning *Roe v. Wade* and allowing states to determine whether any of us deserve the right to safely access reproductive health care and autonomy over our own bodies.

. . . . .

I take the J to Canal Street and transfer to the 6. On that narrow platform, I take out my compact mirror and apply my lipstick,

NARS in Vixen, a deep carmine matte shade. It is Friday, a balmy autumn night. Teenagers guzzle vodka in plastic bottles and pin each other against subway poles, their breath short.

I arrive at your apartment at eleven-fifteen p.m. I am wearing a cropped shirt and a skirt, silk hose that shows off my long legs, with an exposed seam running down the middle. In my leather satchel I've brought supplies: silk rope for light bondage, a tail-feather, a pair of handcuffs, a pair of shearing scissors, a cat-o'-nine-tails, and a foxtail anal plug.

When you open the door, you greet me with a smile, and then throw me on the bed. Immediately you paw at me, my clothes. Then you point at your belt buckle and nod. When I say nothing, you point again. Your next mistake is that you assume that your delight is my delight, your pleasure my pleasure. You shove my head down toward your buckle. I am angry, but I do not show it, not yet.

"Wait," I say, sweetly. "I want to play a game. I want to tease you a bit." I take out the feather and stroke your cheek with it, imagine you dead.

"Oh, you're a little freak, aren't you? A little Asian slut?"

"You don't know me."

"I know your type. You know, I once knew another little Asian slut like you. It's weird, but you remind me of her."

I try to control myself, because good foxes always do. But in that moment something snaps inside me like a twig under the weight of a too-heavy animal, and I clamp my hands against your windpipe, the sweat on your neck sliming down my knuckles. I relish this rage, this moment when your face pales with shock that I could have such marvelous power. I decide that I will prematurely enchant you—I wave my hand, letting go of your neck, and your body is paralyzed instantly. I take out my silk rope, handcuffs, and scissors, cuff your wrists, and then rope you to the bedposts with silk. Obedient now to the laws of physics, you are supine in your briefs, and I feel almost sorry for you.

"Son of a bitch," you wheeze as I cut your perfectly coiffed hair, the hair you take so much pride in. Somebody once said to never underestimate the illusive powers of a tall white man with a full head of hair. You definitely fit the bill. Nothing about you is handsome or good, your facial features are indistinct, foggy even, but you skate by with your arrogance because of that hair.

Brown tufts of it fall on the pillow. It is like weeding, my hands on your scalp, it is like planting a garden. You are trying to cringe, but in your paralyzed state you cannot. It takes massive effort for you to say anything, but I don't want to hear you, so I pull out the foxtail anal plug and put it in your mouth. The bushy synthetic fur of it gushes out of your maw like a wise man's beard.

"Do you even know the name of that Asian girl?" I ask. "Did you bother to remember her name before ruining her life?"

Even despite the spell, you are trembling now, shuddering like a leaf, and saliva drips down the anal plug in a pathetic trickle.

"She was Lee's daughter. You knew him, didn't you? Why don't you say her name?"

Of course, you can't say it, you can't say anything because I've shut your mouth, and your dank green eyeballs are barging out of your face as I recite your crimes. I dust the tailfeather against your stomach because I know you are ticklish, you want to laugh but can't, you want to cry and scream but can't.

I take out the cat-o'-nine-tails, with its knotted leather thongs, nine in total just like I've always coveted, like this whip is already a huxian. Your nostrils flare with a mixture of dread and—if I'm not hallucinating—anticipation, as if this is what you'd wanted all along.

So I flip you over and pull your pants down. Your ass looks like a desolate moon, round and silvery with sweat, perfect for a flogging. One lash leaves a beautiful scarlet welt on your skin; with each stroke, with each thrust of this delicious, knotted leather, I cite a choice you made, starting with a drink you drugged on a night long before the night at the bowling alley, leading all the way up to the night at the movies, and then the night she died. Three blows, four blows, do you like it? Did you know she jumped in front of a moving train shortly after her classmates and her whole school got ahold of the video? You must have known, did you not?

And then I say her name, again and again, until you finally choke on your own spit.

Not all fox women are virtuous like Miss Ren or Miss Li. There are some infamously dangerous fox women in our history and folklore. In his sixteenth century novel *Investiture of the Gods*, the writer Xu Zhonglin invented Daji. As a young girl Daji was possessed by a nine-tailed fox and rose up the ranks of the emperor's favor. Eventually she became his queen. Daji, acting as empress to the corrupt Emperor Zhou, the last of the Shang Dynasty, had the hearts of her enemies served to her on a platter. Daji was cruel and inhumane, but she was also controlling the emperor with her enchantment, and he, in turn, abused his power, leading to the fall of the Shang Dynasty.

Other fox spirits simply act like foxes. In Korean myths, the gumiho eats the livers of young men. The classic tale "Fox Sister" describes a young man going to his family's field and discovering their maimed cows. Night by night, one by one, the cows die with gashes across their bodies where their livers were torn out. Then his brothers start dying off, too, and he realizes it's their younger sister who is doing the tearing and the eating.

In so many of these myths, wicked fox women are almost always exorcised, dealt divine punishment from the gods or the men they have wronged. As a hulijing myself, when I read these tales of destruction and calamity I can't help but scoff at their misunderstanding, their nerve: Could these fox demons maybe have had important motives themselves, like living? Livers are very nutritious, and so are men, presumably. The difference between a xian (divine transcendent) and a yao (a demon) then feels illusory, arbitrary.

So, my dear foxes, don't count on men for recording your stories, demonizing you as if you were some beautiful, thoughtless monster drunk on blood. They do not understand you; they were always too fearful to, anyway.

·　·　·　·　·

There was a man, a public figure, who did not apologize for his actions involving violating multiple underage women's consent, and his publicist (God bless) issued a statement: *He is sorry that his actions made her feel this way.*

There was a man who blamed women for not having sex with him, so much that he loaded several pistols that he stored in his basement in case one day he should go ahead on a murdering rampage.

There was a man who blamed women for having sex with him, so much that he loaded a nine-millimeter firearm and drove to three massage parlors, murdering eight people, including six Asian women. He claimed that the parlors were a "temptation he wanted to eliminate." At the press conference, the police officer told the murderer's side of the story: "He was pretty much fed up and had been at the end of his rope. And yesterday was a really bad day for him, and this is what he did."

. . . . .

Finally, when you can't take it anymore, I remove the fox plug and bend down to suck the breath from your throat with a long, furious inhalation.

I steal your breath, and in stealing your breath, I steal your voice, I steal your ability to scream for help, I steal your ability to express your fear or contempt or disgust for me, for women in general. I steal your disdain, your spite, your propensity for speaking over women, your impulse to belittle and abuse. I steal your whining, I steal your begging, I steal your spit, I steal your tears, I steal your apologies, until I empty you and you are a husk of a man, not too different from what you were before. In the end, when I've taken all your breath, I put the foxtail plug back in your mouth.

When will these dog days of summer be through? I am tired of men like you, yet every night I hunt. Only once in an epoch of the moon do I take long, drawn-out breaths like this. Usually I am good at containing myself—usually I do not feast or indulge, because there are always consequences for women who feast, even in the spiritual realm.

But here I am, taking your breath away, breathing in your life with all the fury and glory of my gluttony. Dear John. I am moved by this transaction. I will ascend to heaven now. This is a love letter.

• • • • •

You ask me how it feels to take these men's lives. Honestly, this is how it feels: like the moment you kill a mosquito, flatten it with your free palm. When you smear it against the white sheet, it leaves a bloodstain. And then you realize the stain is your own blood.

The night after our rendezvous, I am in the mood for love. I watch a Wong Kar-wai film about star-crossed lovers who never consummate their affection for one another. I admire Maggie Cheung's poise in her qipao, the way she tilts her face away from the object of her desire, the way she bathes in muted pink light at the window. What's the point of all that yearning? I wonder.

I go searching for someone, because it's that time of the year, when revenge has filled me up to the brim and I seek out something true, something real. This time, I find a man—he might work a shift at a bar in the city center, he might sing in a choir somewhere. We are stranded on the street in front of a grocery store that also sells hydrangeas and orchids in pots and he might ask me before he kisses me on the mouth, to which I say yes, and cup his face in my hand. I might buy a bouquet for myself, which he'll pretend to give me, we might share an ice cream, honey-flavored, the candied honeycomb leaving an aftertaste like rain in our mouths. This time, I might take him home, to my den on the fifth floor, to my unmade bed that is the only piece of furniture in the whole apartment, with its cold sheets and the window spitting out cold squares of light, a breeze that reminds us that summer will end.

This time, I am touched so tenderly, he makes love to me like I am already immortal, and by morning he is gone, he kisses me on the temple and disappears back into the grime. As I rise, he's already leaning against a subway pole, reading the news on his phone, his bloodshot eyes soft in the morning light.

I've spared him. I've set him free.

A HUXIAN'S GUIDE TO IMMORTALITY

When a fox dies, she faces the direction of the place where she was born. No matter how many metamorphoses, no matter how many cycles of life, she cannot forget her origin.

Because you are an exquisite fox, and because you are an exquisite woman, you hover in the in-between—you are the golden mediatrix between the day and the night. You are the crepuscular phenomenon of the Heavens taking on an animal form. Betwixt and between, you can then either cycle back into the earth or become huxian, a Celestial fox. The Celestial fox has gained the nine tails that signal transcendence and moves into the Palace of the Sun and the Moon. She has mastered the rain and the wind, time and space. She is no prisoner, she is no prey.

Nine life cycles in, when you've exacted your revenge and are satisfied with the men's essence you've gathered and collected, make a pilgrimage to your original birthplace—likely a mountain covered in mist. There, you will self-cultivate and finally meditate, refraining from all sex and basking in perfect solitude. This could have been your whole life, but it is not the one you chose.

After a hundred days, you may come across a frozen river or lake. Put your head down next to the ice and listen to the sound of the water underneath. Below the ice is the region of the yin, the female element, and the dark world of death. Obtain effluvia from the sun, the moon, the stars, the Big Dipper, and mix these with your collected essence to brew an elixir, the essence of immortality that you will place inside your pearl.

You can now shed your physical body, and escape into immortality by shijie, a simulated corpse. A gateway to Death will open up. You were never afraid of such a gateway, but if a shiver fleshes itself through you, keep going. Remember how you transformed—a midnight ritual in the graveyard with a skull. You must enter Heaven through this threshold of Death.

For a moment, you might feel brief hesitation to let go of this world. After all this time, you've never felt at home. And yet, there have been so many moments when you've carved pleasure out of sorrow, beauty out of ugliness, that you overwhelm yourself with sudden feeling. Nostalgia might sicken you as you remember all the love you've made on this earth, and how in the end you really couldn't find that one Love so legendary. So you linger for a moment, shocked that after all your efforts, you still hesitate to let go of that desire that made you so weak.

Is that just the condition of being ~~a wanderer, an immigrant, a woman~~? The entrance is open. Go, go, go before the ship departs—

—because once you ascend to Heaven and step into the Palace of the Sun and Moon, you can observe how different the air is. How good it feels to live inside a place not designed by and for the folly of men. As a Celestial fox, you have let go of all human relationships, and instead you can roam in the open sky, transcending both the divine and human worlds. After living a confusing life as a transient human, how good it feels, to kick back!

To be free, and yet home, at last.

The Girl with Flies
Coming Out of
Her Eyes

Imagine you are a young woman. Imagine you want to cry, but you can't, because of a sickness where your eyes make flies instead of tears. You've had this illness since the day you first turned into an adult, but you don't remember that day because you don't remember a day in your life when it was okay for you to cry. Every time you cry, flies come out of your eyes, and they are loud and brash with the freshness of being alive and they destroy everything: subway rides, dinner parties, family outings, relationships, silence, you name it.

You learned this the hard way. When your boyfriend of one year cheated on you, he admitted it was because you told him about this inane Kafkaesque malady of yours and that ever since then, he'd wanted to test it to see if it was true. In order to do that, he had to prod you a bit, intentionally. In return, your flies ended up chasing him for the better part of a week until he showed up wild and unkempt at the foot of your brownstone stoop, groveling not just for forgiveness but more importantly for deliverance from flies. It was early morning, but he was unshaven, his shirtsleeves torn, he carried an offering: that coffee maker you had been eyeballing at Target. You took the coffee maker. He tried to hold your hand through the screen door. You didn't have the heart to give anything he requested—your forgiveness, your hand, your acknowledgment that he was still a good guy. You shut the door and locked it. Then you moved away from that city, all the way west, to another coast where he would never find you. You couldn't risk another fly infestation, and besides, you didn't even know how to control the flies once they were loose in the world. Your preferred solution was to open the windows and set them free.

Years later, perusing *The New York Times*, you came across the headline "Four Bees Living in Her Eye, Feeding on Her Tears." It was the story of a Taiwanese woman who went to the doctor for a sharp pain in her eye after Tomb-Sweeping Day. She'd spent the weekend traveling to her ancestral grave site, weeding around the gravestones of her family plot, offering incense and pears. A gust blew something into her eye and she thought it was soil or sand, so she rinsed her eye with clean water. But the water did nothing— her eye kept swelling painfully, so she went to the hospital. Under a microscope, her doctor plucked out four tiny bees from under her eyelids, bathing in her tear ducts. The sweat bees had been feeding on the salt and moisture of her tears, and all four of them were still alive. If any of them had died inside her tear duct, she could have gone blind.

After reading the story, you couldn't help thinking: If only *your* situation ended after four flies! From this story of the bee woman, you discovered that there were many more insect species that fed on tears, that this phenomenon had a name, lachryphagy—bees, butterflies, and, yes, even some flies coveted a delicious cocktail of tears. Butterflies in the Amazon drank the tears of river turtles, stingless bees slurped up crocodiles' tears, and all these insects would swarm and feast at the prospect of a woman's lachrymose despair. For some reason, this made you feel hopeful. Perhaps there actually was a scientific explanation for your condition, perhaps you weren't a freak.

You turned on the *Maury* talk show, watched the mothers cry at the results of paternity tests, neglected daughters cry at the appearance of their lifelong absent fathers or mothers. You marveled at the naturalness of their eyes watering, even on camera, how delicate, how apt and effusive their crying was in the face of the ugly things that happened to them. You convinced yourself that their situations truly warranted their tears and their problems were much, much worse than yours. During a lie detector episode, one woman confronted a man who ran a secret human trafficking ring she didn't know about, and he failed the lie detector test about both his STI status and whether he slept with the sex workers he employed. During a paternity test episode, one woman found out her long-term partner was not the father of her baby, but she swore she did not sleep with anyone else. She passed the lie detector test that they administered to her. It was an immaculate conception on television. The lady glowed with emotion, but the audience booed her. *Crocodile tears*, one audience member said in disgust. The fallacy was what test to trust: the paternity test or the lie detector test. Indeed, the audience members were split into two groups: those who believed in miracles, and those who didn't.

You envied people who could cry. You envied those women on television—how pretty and broken they looked with salty cheeks, inflamed and red. You envied the painterly smudges their mascara left on their faces. You envied the woman you saw crying on the long-distance bus to Philadelphia. You wondered what she was crying about: Did she take the wrong bus? Had she lost a family member? Was she going through a breakup? Either way, for a moment you were tempted to comfort her but feared that if she stopped crying, you would start. It was the best contagion and the worst contagion.

Have you ever tried to sleep in a room where a single fly was buzzing? It's impossible. Sometimes it would land on your cheek, softly. And so the only time you'd feel the relief of silence, you'd gain the anxiety of touch. The possibility of infection. Night was when you *had to* avoid crying, even though to most other people, night was crying's prime time. Other people had the luxury of crying all night, but not you. Like a sentry, you guarded your eyes, you guarded your sleep against weeping, sobbing, crying, sniveling, lamenting, ruminating, and even laughing, because more often than not for you, laughing led to flies.

But you could not always guard yourself. One day you were in line at the grocery store and the headlines of the magazines shouted about death: a pop idol you loved had just died by suicide. A single fly inched its way out of your eye and you took out the flyswatter you always brought everywhere and killed it in front of the cashier. One day you were at the women's health clinic and the pregnant young woman next to you told you that her partner left her when he found out. You bolted out of the waiting room to let the flies out. Another day you saw your mother trying to revive the tulips that had just died in the garden, without success, and you burst into flies.

You couldn't understand—you had always kept the flies under control—you'd developed a series of techniques, expert strategies for suppressing them. Exercise: crunching your facial muscles until you resembled a dried date when you were lonely. Exercise: beating your face with a throw pillow while singing a song about survival. But then another day arrived and the person you liked stopped appearing at your doorway, stopped calling, and you were listening to the pop star you loved who died the year before sing a song not about survival but sadness, which broke the rules, which triggered a plague. Flies buzzed everywhere, and suddenly you realized you weren't alone anymore. They buzzed like bad death metal, they buzzed like buzzards, they buzzed like the phone of someone more popular than you. They buzzed and buzzed and buzzed and buzzed until the plague touched the invisible walls around your heart you had erected after the last boyfriend gave you that coffee maker six years ago. The coffee maker had long since hissed and wheezed out its last cup of coffee, but you didn't bother throwing it away. You wondered if you were going to be alone forever as the flies flew out of your eyes, aiming straight for the pears you left in the sun too long without eating.

Then you remembered the woman whose tears nourished the bees living in her eyes—you were the same age as her, twenty-nine.

How windy that day must have been, when she tore out the weeds on the graves of her family members. Perhaps it was her grandmother who triggered the itch in her eyes—the memory of a beloved matriarch, getting more and more brittle with time. The oxalis, the wild oats, the red clover, all growing from the dirt where she lay. Maybe she had driven hundreds of miles that weekend, to see the light gleaming on the terrain above the road. Did she let herself cry out there on the mountain where her grandmother was buried? Did the wind whistle, stirring the hairy legs of the bees inside her eye? Did they scrape, scrape until she was on her knees—had she mistaken those sensations for the ghosts of her female ancestors entering her body as she swept, weeping? Did she feel hopeless—that no matter how much she swept, wept, or weeded, the tombs of her history would never be clean?

Your family once had a plot on the Mountain of the Marvelous Peak outside Beijing. The last time you visited, you were only sixteen and already at the edge of the world. Outside your grandparents' burial site, there was a stone shrine to a fox spirit who had become a huxian, or fox transcendent. You had placed an offering there.

The fox had been born with a curse—that unlike other foxes, she could not shape-shift, and every time she tried, she would be swarmed with flies and ticks and wasps and ants and every affliction imaginable. So she could not join the other foxes in their quests toward transcendence, building their stores of vital essence from humans to achieve the elixir of transcendence. She avoided humans—just as she avoided romance, seduction, and enchantment, unlike her peers, who pursued the love and affection of humans until the very end.

Instead, she retreated to the mountains to study and write, carving out a perfect solace out of solitude. In her self-cultivation, she hunted rabbits and gathered fresh herbs and wild vegetables. She worshipped the Big Dipper and the Queen Mother of the West, obtaining effluvia from nature—from sun, moon, and stars, from trees, moss, and mushrooms—to build her own elixir. She lived in an abandoned pavilion next to a stream that led to your ancestors' plot of land, drank from the same brook your ancestors drank from. She surrounded herself with literature: *Spring and Summer Annals, The Classic of the Mountains and the Seas, Water Margin, The Plum in the Golden Vase,* and *Dream of the Red Chamber.* She studied the classics, the cosmologies, the ancient and modern poetries, for a thousand years, until she reached the edge of the cosmic order. One nightfall, her wick winked out the last flame, and her inks and paints ran out. The Elixir of Immortality was complete—once she drank it, she was meant to transform, and then she would never be the same. She was so frightened that the swarm would eat her alive, but this time there were no bugs. Only a lambent column of light shattering her pavilion with its brilliance. She had finally become a huxian, a transcendent, a fox immortal with all nine tails. Of all her peers, she was the only one who became divine.

You like to think that perhaps the fox spirit had blessed you with this curse that day when you touched the shrine with your fingers, when you left what you had offered, a penny or an apple core. You like to think that you would someday learn something from it, grow, though you still had no idea what, or into whom.

You decide that you need to drive away—far, far away, into the remotest desert possible—for a crying pilgrimage. Like the fox from your ancestral village, you would read and write, practice self-cultivation in the form of expression, release. From your home in Los Angeles, you speed across San Bernardino, Mojave, Joshua Tree, Death Valley—in the skinless 114-degree heat, you feel safe. You rent a cabin by yourself, bring groceries, plan to cook a huge meal, finish it, gnaw the chicken down to the bone, then cry as much as your heart desires, let the flies rise up above the arid open air and buzz, swirl in beautiful, bountiful circles. At night you cry under the giant bulbous stars and the flies that emerge would cry with you, multiply your crying by thousands, millions.

Flies possess compound eyes: held to a microscope, these eyes look like geodesic domes, masterful architectural marvels, with photoreceptors that can detect light and color spectrums beyond human or animal imagination. Flies have the fastest visual responses of all species on earth. You learned this on one of your despair-filled nights, the nights in the real world where you were tempted to cry and instead Googled your way through volumes of forgotten biology. If your eyes could secrete hundreds of creatures with the capacity for the fastest sight in the world, then perhaps you, too, would someday adopt this sight, which would allow you to see everything, detect every slight movement or small susurration. The pulse points on a lover's body. The rate of their breath before leaning in for a kiss. Beneath the flies and the stars, you imagine beholding this world with such eyes: the howling wind would be visible, plainly, the sky would split into a thousand fractals, symmetrical as heaven. You laugh at the bigness of this all. The thought that there is a spectrum beyond a human spectrum comforts you. The buzz becomes a kind of tawdry music. You open a beer. You laugh and laugh and then there are flies.

The Haunting of
Angel Island

PARTS 6–8

6

It was common knowledge that no woman should go into the lavatory at night alone. The second-floor lavatory was said to be haunted by the ghost of a woman who had failed to answer the questions correctly during her interrogation and killed herself mere hours before her deportation.

In the beginning, several occupants reported hearing a young woman's voice through the drainage pipes as they washed their hands. A shrill, sad singing—sometimes, if they were brave, they'd press their ears against the cold pipes, so hungry they were for melody. They found the voice and the song to be beautiful, because they were tired of the noises of the sea, of the foghorns,

of the English language—they longed for a music familiar from
home: the sounds of woodwinds and bowed strings, dizi and pipa
and guqin.

Sometimes, as they washed, they would squint and see her
form in the water dripping from the black faucet, a wraith struggling to rescue herself from the drain—they could soon make out
her wraith eyes, her wraith mouth, the muscles of her shoulders
and her arms, always swimming—and they weren't afraid, because there was something familiar about her movements, how
she struggled and struggled against an impossible current, the
tangle of all the women's hair in the drain. Then her voice would
hush, a quiet before a squall of wind. She'd start whispering in
the water all the wrong answers she relayed to the immigration
official, every answer that dragged her down to the depth of
where she was. The women would keep listening, because they
wanted to know—they wanted to know what she got wrong, why
she failed as badly as she did. *Yes, my father's job is with a shipping
company. Yes, they sell sails sewn by laborers from the north.*

Then quickly the ghost's whispering would tear open into
screaming, as if someone had hacked into the hollow of a tree
where all the hornets lived and swarmed. Hearing such a scream,
the unfortunate women in the lavatory reported a spitting head-
ache, and the pain of the migraine was beyond anything they
could comprehend—listless, they crumpled onto the cold floor,
their hands holding their skulls to prevent them from splitting
open. In the midst of all this, they would see her—the ghost,
fully formed, a young beauty not a day over twenty, peering right
at them on the dirty tiles. She reminded them so much of their
cousins, sisters, childhood friends, surely this ghost would not
want to drag them to the death she chose for herself?

In fact, the young woman who lived this life was unmarried. Her real name she never revealed to anyone, but the name she adopted was Fanglu, the name of the daughter who didn't exist. The paper daughter. Back when she had just arrived, she understood the stakes of her interrogation. The pale men with hulking shoulders, their glasses fogged with heavy breath. One of them, in particular, had a bald head and his expression chilled her, stupefied her. She couldn't afford to be distracted by the liver spots on his face—if she failed, there wasn't a husband who could advocate for her from San Francisco and request to have the decision overturned. The witnesses they brought were strange men she had never met before, and their matter-of-fact, rehearsed explanation of their relationships to her unsettled her rather than comforted her.

Most women who came through the immigration station were married and connected by family, but she was of the small minority who were unattached, therefore she was suspicious to immigration officials and the other detainees alike. Sure enough, the bald man asked the question "Why are you unmarried?" and it disoriented her.

Her answer was simply, "I did not have a chance to." And then she saw the corners of this interrogation officer's mouth lift into a horrifying smile. The smile disturbed her more than his usual stern expression—it was as if his facial muscles were deflating, and every dark thought that he had kept to himself he would squeeze out, infecting her.

"Well, if you go home, I'm sure you will find one," he said.

She knew that was it. Later that evening, she got the results—as expected, she did not pass. She would have to return on the *Olympic*, setting sail in several days—and she did not know where she could hire a lawyer for her to appeal her case. In the evening, the moon hung heavy, and she saw the outlines of the trees. She went into the lavatory and thought maybe she could crack the window open.

One woman in the barracks, a newcomer, heard the ghost story in the dayroom and laughed. Curiously enough, her name was really close to the name of the ghost—Fenglu—and she was also an unmarried, unattached woman who had sailed from Canton to be a paper daughter of an American-born Chinese. Back in Canton when she acquired the paperwork, she was told that Chinese men could apply for admittance with their credentials as students, merchants, or citizens, but women could only apply through their social ties—as wives of merchants or daughters of citizens. Bristling at this, she still learned the details of her fake life diligently—for months she studied the coaching books before she chucked them overboard when the ship stopped in Yokohama. Back home, she had been a trained actress belonging to a theater troupe that had gone out of business. She had acted in small productions of ancient plays and operas such as *The Peony Pavilion* and *The Palace of Lasting Life*. Why should the role of paper daughter be any different from acting these parts?

But now that she arrived on this island, Fenglu wondered whether all that studying was worth this detention. After only a week of eating the unappetizing food, Fenglu felt her joints grow weak like milk bone. A loner, she couldn't stand to be in the washroom with so many other women, with their tangled hair and pungent odors, so she often went to the lavatory at night when no one else went. Nothing scared her, and besides, she would welcome the chance to hear a singing ghost. It would remind her of her theater troupe days, which seemed so long gone.

One night, Fenglu forgot to wash her face. She rubbed the corners of her eyes and cheekbones with soap until she found a lather. She rinsed herself off with too-cold water, and when she looked up, she saw a woman standing behind her, staring at her in the mirror. She was around Fenglu's age, wearing a loose green dress, and, like Fenglu, she wore her hair in a chignon wrapped with ribbons. In the mirror, the woman was breathing heavily, but Fenglu felt no one's breath behind her—the air was still. This woman was the wraith that everyone was afraid of.

Fenglu did not move. The phantom in the mirror shut her eyes, and began singing in a high, sonorous voice, like a child's. Her voice was clear like the sound of a brook running through a forest floor. Fenglu had heard this tune somewhere before. It reminded her of music she would hear in her hometown, a folk song, perhaps. Back before joining the theater troupe, when she was working in a silk factory, she would walk home on the main drag of road where on holidays street performers and acrobats would crowd the walk and full-throated girls sang in heavy makeup and headdresses, their songs perfumed with longing. It had been what inspired her to become a performer.

When the song was over, the singer began screaming. There was no whispering, no lull between song and scream—the girl just shrieked and shrieked, her hands clawing into her face. Fenglu, lightheaded, ran her wet hand against the gooseflesh on her forearm.

It occurred to Fenglu that the screaming did not disturb her. In fact, Fenglu felt like it was the sanest thing she's heard since arriving on this island—the only acceptable response to what was happening. That droves of them had to be subject to such humiliation, have their bodies strip-searched and measured against the edge of metal rulers, confined to these wooden quarters on these metal bunks so narrow that one nightmare could send a woman crashing to the floor. Fenglu didn't understand why these women projected their fears onto the ghost, as if a female wraith were more terrifying than arriving in this hostile country. The ghost woman's endless scream felt truly honest, unlike the behavior of most of the other women, who pretended that they were going to emerge from these barracks and barbed-wire fences the same women they were before, that they were going to make it in America and strike it rich like the Gold Mountain wives they'd always dreamed of becoming. Just a few more days of eating shit, and they'll earn their place in this society!

In the mirror, Fenglu touched the wraith's face. She had meant it as a gesture of encouragement—maybe even solidarity. As soon as her finger touched the cold surface, the screaming stopped. After a slow moment, the wraith began to smile at her. The cheeks of the girl all crumpled in glee. This was not a face designed for laughter. At first Fenglu felt a thrill, a triumph, that she had calmed the girl down, finally—that she had done what everyone else had failed to do. But the more she looked at the girl, the more she felt a bloodless pounding in her temples—a blister of nerves edging toward her mouth. The girl was not calm. She was not calm at all.

In the morning, the women were bewildered to find Fenglu asleep on the tile of the lavatory. A few of them had screamed, mistaking her for a corpse. This woke her up. Her shoulders and spine throbbed all the way to her tailbone. Fenglu rubbed her eyes, which were wet with tears. Had she cried in her sleep? That was funny—she had decided, as soon as she arrived in this country, that she would never cry, not until all of this was over and she was safe in the comfort of solitude. If she could ever enjoy such a luxury again. The sounds of living women—their gasps, their whispers—filled her with dread. It turned out that Fenglu could only fall asleep soundly to the sound of a ghost woman's screaming.

7

On weekday mornings, the women gathered in the dayroom to wait for the arrival of the deaconess, who always took the ferry to the immigration station. The Chinese women called her Guan Yin, the Goddess of Mercy. The Italian women called her the Angel of Angel Island. The Russian women called her the Smiling Woman, for she was always smiling. The Japanese women called her A.B.C. Mama, for she taught them English and American manners.

A tall and handsome woman with salty blond hair, Deaconess Katherine Maurer led daily English and Bible lessons in the dayroom. Then, late afternoon, she would move on to the detention center, where the men and older boys were held.

Of all the women in the administration building, Mrs. Luo was the most devout convert to the faith. The Bible, she felt, was full of the most exciting stories, some that reminded her of the stories she grew up listening to at home. Prophets, kingdoms, plagues, and, of course, palace intrigue. It was a welcome distraction from the reality of where she was. Besides that, she was fascinated by this religion's obsession with forgiveness. In her Bible studies classes, the deaconess kept emphasizing God's forgiveness, God's grace, God's patience, God's tolerance. All qualities Mrs. Luo wished her husband had. Every day she asked the deaconess to relay messages to him, check in, make sure he was eating. Mrs. Luo needed the deaconess to assure her that Mr. Luo was learning the same tenets of Christian faith.

Her husband had come with her on the ship, but they had immediately been separated upon landing. He was led to the detention center, while she and their son had stayed in the administration building. They'd been on this island for almost a month now, which was not long, but with the absence of Mr. Luo, their status as a family was slipping away from her. If she had to be honest about it, taking a break from her husband was a welcome respite. They had not been apart for this long in more than twelve years, and she did not miss the sound of his carping. He never missed an opportunity to hound her for the smallest things—his floor not swept, his soup not salted. She did not have to do those things here, and so time passed slowly. She felt like she'd been quarantined for a year, and naturally began to focus her energies onto something else.

Like this new faith, which was so bent on forgiveness. Mrs. Luo was struck by the idea that all of these white Christians spent their whole lives begging for forgiveness even though thousands of years ago someone had died so God would forgive them all. So what happened after they were forgiven? Did they live their lives at peace, free of all guilt or shame or want?

This life appealed greatly to Mrs. Luo. Her son, Lim Kun, was a ruddy-faced little brute who had endured beatings from Mr. Luo since he was only two. As a result, he became quite violent himself. From a young age, he had been bellicose with other kids, pushing and shoving younger boys. At Angel Island, there weren't many other boys, so he shoved the girls.

"Stop that!" Mrs. Luo would shout, but Lim Kun was at the age—ten—where he carved his whole identity out of rebellion. In response to her recent conversion to Christianity, her son was veering in the opposite direction: more and more, he was privy to superstitions about ghosts, foxes, and demons, which he must have heard from the other children.

One morning she was watching him in the yard, and above him she saw a formation of blackbirds over the concertina wire. Were they crows, blackbirds, or ravens? She couldn't tell the difference. They made glorious arcs in the sky—if they hovered close or swooped down, she could see their feathers gleaming purple in the sunlight. Some of them had red tufts on their wings.

The deaconess, who happened to be standing next to her, murmured, "A murder of crows."

Mrs. Luo misunderstood, thinking that the birds were about to be killed, so she scanned the premises for her son. To her horror, she saw Lim Kun in a group of children throwing stones at a row of blackbirds that had been resting on the fence. One of them he struck with such force, the bird flew into the barbed wire and fell onto the ground, alive but bloodied. The children then surrounded the blackbird and piled it with stones, screeching in delight. They repeated this several times with the birds.

Even as the deaconess and Mrs. Luo ran to break up the circle, it was too late to save the grackles. Their feathers jutted out of their flesh, their beaks open. Evidence of carnage was everywhere. Lim Kun, the ringleader, said, "Mother, we want to cook them for dinner. Do you know how to roast it?"

"Roast! Roast! Roast!" The children chanted.

"Why did you do that? What did these birds do to hurt you?" Mrs. Luo asked, swiping the stone from Lim Kun's dirty hand. At that, he looked at her with all the scorn that a ten-year-old could muster.

"They are demons!" cried Lim Kun. "If we don't kill these birds, the ghosts and demons will come out of this forest and eat us! We are not protected here!"

"This is nonsense, Lim Kun. If you could only learn Christianity and *faith*, then maybe . . ."

"Maybe what? Maybe we'd miraculously be fed something edible? Why should this stupid bird fly past the fences but not me? Not us?" Lim Kun retorted.

At this, Mrs. Luo did not know what to say. But the deaconess firmly put her hand on Lim Kun's shoulder and said, "That's enough, young man. That's enough."

He recoiled at the touch—for the first time in years, Lim Kun slipped behind his mother, holding on to her arm. Stunned, Mrs. Luo grabbed her son's hand and gripped it as if he were slipping away from her already. Turning to the deaconess, she said, "The kids want to cook the birds. They are hungry. They hate the meals they've been having here. You can't blame them."

The deaconess was uneasy, muttering something about certain birds being inedible, how Mrs. Luo ought to discipline her son, who was spiraling out of control.

It occurred to Mrs. Luo that she could explain the situation in terms of what she learned in Bible studies class. "Please, Deaconess, you have a reputation as the Goddess of Mercy. Would your Christian God forgive these young children for being hungry, and hunting for survival?"

The deaconess sighed and nodded. "I suppose you're right about that. May God forgive these children."

Mrs. Luo convinced the deaconess to procure some coal from the kitchen and a shovel from the gardener and bring it back so she and her son could dig a barbecue pit. Later that evening, the children and their mothers gathered around the fire they built. Mrs. Luo, along with the other mothers, defeathered the blackbirds that her son had helped kill. Altogether there were maybe four or five: a murder.

They roasted them in the fire on a spit, and the meat was so tough and stringy that it could not be chewed off the bones. Sliding a wing off the spit, Mrs. Luo glanced up at her son's bucktoothed smile. Lim Kun licked the crisped skin, the spots burned black. His molars had recently fallen out, the last of his child teeth; she knew for certain that he could not properly chew the meat.

In the firelight, he played with the bones other people left on the ground. "This is so good. So, so good," he said over and over. But at the end of the night, he was still hungry.

8

There was a story Mindy heard once about a woman living in the walls of the capital. The story was called "The Red Girl," about a chaste fox woman who befriended an old city guard. The guard was lonely in his tower, and so every night the beautiful fox girl would show up to his post bringing wine and food, and they would feast and drink together until dawn. His other guards wanted in, but they never saw her. Later, the fox girl admitted that when the guard was a young man, he had rescued a black fox, and she owed him this kindness, a karmic debt.

Mindy thought of this story when she first arrived on Angel Island. Disoriented from the twenty days at sea, the smell of pickled onions and cuttlefish, the salt air prying her pores open, Mindy looked to familiar comforts—the books she carried, of which there were too many: a King James Bible in English she acquired from her school in Canton, books of poetry, and two collections of classical tales: *Occasional Records of Conversations at Night* by He Bang'e, and Ji Yun's *Miscellaneous Records from West of the Locust Tree*. In the past decade, whenever she found herself about to have a panic attack, she disappeared into these stories. Even the long passage to America could not get her to part with them. By the time the ship reached Hawai'i, she had already re-read every volume, plus the coaching handbooks for her new life. By the time the ferry docked on Angel Island, she could recite any number of lines by heart.

At the end of the long walkway, Mindy noticed a plaque covered in cattails:

1775–PRESENT.
ISLA DE LOS ANGELES, ANGEL ISLAND.
WHEN THE SPANISH NAVAL OFFICER
JUAN MANUEL DE AYALA LANDED HERE IN 1775,
HE NAMED IT ISLA DE LOS ANGELES, AFTER ARRIVING
ON THE CATHOLIC FEAST DAY OF
OUR LADY OF THE ANGELS.

• • • • •

Mindy remembered learning about the Catholic feasts from her English missionary teacher back in Canton. It was Mrs. Downey who gave her the name Mindy, which she adopted to replace her Chinese name, and Mrs. Downey who taught her English, enough so that she did not need an interpreter. "Feast days are commemorations of the death of a saint, when people gather and celebrate," Mrs. Downey had explained. It didn't seem so different from the Red Girl's bringing her guard friend a feast to commemorate his heroic act. In the ten years since Mindy left the missionary school, she'd abandoned most of the religious rituals, but not her belief in God. To her, Gold Mountain was a metaphor for feast—the promise of America, the premise of her prayers.

The wooden house in front of Mindy, like the walls of the capital in the Red Girl story—a physical border not made for forever. Yet the fox girl lived and slept in the walls, and Mindy would live and sleep here, too, in this tinderbox palace on the border between the world and this unknown country, this unknown city. Towering against the verdant green hills, the palace rose like spring. All around, yellow wildflowers burnished the grasses like pyrite or gold. Mindy took a breath and ascended the stairs.

Settling in her narrow bunk, Mindy saw a ghost. No, it was someone she recognized from another life. Another girl who attended her missionary school—the radiant Hanna Tsai. Mindy had not seen Hanna in a decade.

Recognizing Mindy, Hanna practically shrieked. A sharp relief, Mindy felt, as the other woman ran up and embraced her. Hanna's softness a welcome burst of warmth. Mindy had not expected such a welcome. They hadn't spoken for so long.

"I missed you," Mindy admitted, and meant it. Hanna had not changed much by way of appearance—same willowy figure, same bangs, same long ropelike braid down her back. Her bones marbled against her skin, delicate and light like her subtle scent of rose hip oil. But something had shifted. There was a glow about Hanna, an easy confidence she must have honed since they'd last seen each other.

Hanna and Mindy attended the missionary school for ten years before the Boxer Rebellion erupted. While Mindy studied diligently and practiced the teachings of God, Hanna skipped classes, ran off with boys on the Pearl River piers. Hanna never learned English well enough to hold a conversation, but she was slippery and mutable in a way that Mindy always envied.

Ten years ago almost to the day, on March 18, 1900, a troop of bandits infiltrated the wrought-iron gates around their school. Young, hungry mercenaries climbed into the school as they shattered windows, targeting anyone who dared cross their path. Mrs. Downey, who suffered a gash across her arm, hurried away with an envoy of American teachers. According to later reports, seven people died that morning: three missionary schoolteachers, four students.

In the confusion, Hanna had dragged Mindy and two other girls outside through a broken window. "I know where we can hide," Hanna whispered as they climbed through. Following Hanna's lead, they ran from the schoolhouse, turning through dank alleys for how long? Half an hour? An hour? They ran down Old China Street, then Hog Lane, then crisscrossed toward the piers.

For such a slim girl, Hanna was remarkably athletic—her muscular legs darted across the streets packed with markets, hanging birdcages full of lorikeets, handicrafts and ivory, people and fruit carts, avoiding them all with the spry acrobatics of a ghost, wriggling between narrow spaces—spaces that Mindy missed, hitting her elbow here and there, pains shooting from unknown parts of her body, until finally they found the edge of the Pearl River. Rain began pouring. Whorls of icy water needled their faces. Mindy could never forget the sound of slate-gray river, her heart pounding wildly, her hand suctioning against Hanna's grip. Open cuts from where she chafed against glass prickled against the pearled moisture, as Hanna pointed toward a hiding place—a row of floating boathouses on the piers. The four girls climbed aboard, hiding in one of the boathouses, covering the ornate carved windows with red cloth. Inside, there was a sitting area.

"They'll never find us here," said Hanna. They sat in the boathouse until the evening. Mindy thought it was charming, the ornamental edges of the boat, the vase full of water lilies, the chandelier dangling from the roof. At the time, it never dawned on Mindy what kind of place that boathouse was. All she knew was that she owed Hanna her life.

After the school shut down, Mindy never finished her education. But it didn't matter—Mindy had learned what she needed to learn. She was fluent in English and Chinese, and moreover she had a God to pray to. Mrs. Downey taught her well. Both the English teacher and Hanna vanished. Mindy still thought of both these women almost every day. A few years ago, Mindy returned to the floating boathouse looking for Hanna. This time, Mindy knew what kind of place it was. A flower boat, where Hanna was the flower, the star. In Hanna's room, Mindy saw a photo of her, bedecked in Qing silk and hair floating with tortoiseshell and nacre hairpins. The pearl among river stones. Hanna was working, but no one directed Mindy where. In the end, Mindy gave up looking and slipped away.

So perhaps it was God's will that propelled both Hanna and Mindy to migrate across an ocean at almost the same time, God's will that they should reunite, this time behind the wooden walls of an immigration station. When Mrs. Downey was not preaching God's will, she would tell stories of America that always seemed too good to be true. Mindy noticed that though Hanna never paid any attention in class, she perked up whenever Mrs. Downey described the Beautiful Country, just as Mindy herself did. Its trams, cornices, buildings, hills, valleys, cities stacked sculpture-like next to the sea, tall and golden like groves of Osmanthus trees.

Mrs. Downey's words were enough to convince Mindy to make the crossing. At twenty-four, she secured the papers of an American missionary's Chinese-born daughter. Such papers these days were rare: most papers for women came in the form of marriages. But Mindy was methodical and prudent—she had to be, to survive. She bought henna dye from the markets and dyed her hair light brown. Her eyes were wide and heavy-lidded, and she put powder on them to accentuate their largeness. With her face, Mindy could easily pass for half-American.

It didn't matter at the end of the day. At the last minute, the inspector decided to shuttle her off to Angel Island, too, along with the rest of the people in the second-class cabins and steerage—including Chinese men and boys, families from Mexico and Guatemala. No one talked on the ferry over. It was as if everyone was holding their breath, their anxieties spilling quietly overboard, unsaid. Mindy closed her eyes. She had assumed she could skip going to Angel Island altogether, because of her sterling papers and her ability to pass as American. Mindy had not been careful enough; she had messed up, being so overconfident. The papers were suspicious. She should have studied harder, been more vigilant in case she had to endure interrogations. But too late now.

Within the first week, Hanna read all of Mindy's books. Mindy was pleased to discover that Hanna had changed somewhat in the past decade: Hanna once hated school, but now she was well versed in Chinese literature. In her seven years working at the flower boats, Hanna had discovered an affinity for quoting poems to her guests, and then eventually she began writing the poems herself. After she got married three years ago, Hanna quit the flower boats to move in with her in-laws, but she continued to write poetry. At Angel Island, Hanna received constant deliveries of delicacies from her husband, who was a merchant living in San Francisco— dehydrated blood oranges, smoked meats, peanuts, and melons, some of which contained hidden coaching notes. The notes arrived carefully folded into cuts of meat, or stuffed inside a melon pit, smeared with honeydew seeds. Sometimes when they could find a moment, Mindy and Hanna studied the notes together.

The scheduled dates of their interrogations were days apart. Mindy's interrogations were a two-day-long process, and in total she was asked about two hundred questions. What shocked her was how easily she breezed through the questions, as if her fake life had already been implanted into her, replacing her old one.

"Where did you learn to speak English so well?" the inspector had asked.

"I've been speaking it all my life," Mindy replied. "Believe it or not, I am the daughter of an American."

Hanna did not fare as well.

"I think I messed up," she said. It was the afternoon after their interrogations, and Hanna was sharing her persimmons with Mindy in the bathroom. The two of them often wrote poems together, copying the style of Du Fu and Li Bai, recording them in little notebooks that Mindy procured from the deaconess. At every chance, they transcribed their poems onto the bathroom walls with a fountain pen that Hanna collected, another gift from the deaconess.

"I'm pretty sure I did, too," said Mindy, though it was a lie.

"I heard that if you write a poem here, the walls will listen. The walls deliver a message to the fox spirits," Hanna said. "They've made haunts, dens, and the women here have been communicating with them. The ones who write poems are liberated soon afterwards."

Mindy peered at Hanna's efforts. The lines holding her ideographs were crooked, clunky, but her individual strokes were elegant. "If that were true, then no one would be doing anything else in this house. Everyone would be scrambling to these walls to write. And besides, when did you become so superstitious? I can't subscribe to beliefs like that. I believe in God."

"Oh, please don't tell me you still believe in *their* God," said Hanna, laughing. The laugh, while harmless, cut into Mindy. There was so much about Hanna that remained remote to her, no matter how close they became again.

"I do. Why not? Besides, aren't the kindest people always the women of faith? Like Miss Maurer, or Tye Leung."

"I hate that woman, Tye," said Hanna. Hanna complained that during her interrogation, Tye had made some offhanded comment about Hanna's profession that she would not repeat. It derailed Hanna for the rest of the interview.

"Mmmm. Yeah, I mean sometimes I find her to be disingenuous when she tells us she's here to help and that this all is *good* for us," said Mindy, although it wasn't really true. She actually liked Tye.

"She—*they*—think I'm a whore," said Hanna. "Seems like my husband has a reputation in Chinatown. But why punish *me* for it? They actually think I came all the way across the sea to be his whore. Why go through the trouble when there's a demand for that at home? I should know that more than anything."

"To be fair, they think every woman is a whore," said Mindy. "What they don't know is that whores can also be great poets."

Hanna smiled, and Mindy blushed. "So you don't judge me?"

"Never." Mindy examined the freshly painted wall facing the sinks. Whenever the matron ordered a repaint, within a few days new poems replaced the old. If Mindy ran her hand against the paint, she could feel the faint grooves that the putty filled, where knives cut wound-like words into the wood. There, she began her own poem.

The next day, news arrived: Mindy had passed her interrogation and would land that Friday. Hanna, however, had failed hers.

Across the dormitory, a distraught woman rushed toward Mindy. "But you are the only one of us who can stand up to them for us," she said. "Your English is good, and your Chinese is even better than Tye's!"

"Mindy is *leaving*," said Hanna firmly. "What are you suggesting there, lady? Why would she want to stay in this hell?"

"I would trade places with you," said Mindy, gripping Hanna's hand. "I *want* to trade places with you. Once I land, I will find a lawyer who will appeal your case. Please don't worry, you know that most appeals get approved."

"Congratulations, you're getting what you've always dreamt of," said Hanna, ignoring Mindy's proposal. "Don't think I didn't notice, when we were young. You always lit up whenever Mrs. Downey talked about America."

"I won't rest until you are out there with me," said Mindy. "And besides. I only lit up because *you* lit up."

Hanna was right: This *was* what Mindy wanted—to land in America, the Beautiful Country. It was true it was her dream, but this dream only began because she saw Hanna's face. At fourteen years old, the only hope Mindy ever wanted in on was Hanna's. The only hope that could convince Mindy. Hanna would shine in a city like that. Hanna would not just survive—she'd *live*. The grand hotels, the opera houses, the parks, the gardens, the trams, the churches, the lanterns of Chinatown—all of that beyond the foggy gray bay. The feasts. The angels. The sibilant names of the streets. The strangers. Hanna could remain on Angel Island indefinitely, or head back on a ship to Canton. Where would she go? Would she return to the flower boats? Would she be welcomed back?

"I want you to have this," Hanna said as she was helping Mindy pack. "It's protective. It will keep you safe out there." It was a ring, a pearl in its center, surrounded by tiny stones. A freshwater baroque pearl from Canton.

"I'm the one who owes you a debt," Mindy said, but she gripped it tight. It was too much, the beauty. The pearl gleamed like it was supernatural. "I should be the one giving you the gifts."

She gave her books of poetry to Hanna: the Du Fu, the Li Bai, all her most cherished tomes. "Someday, you will write your own."

"That's a pretty thought," Hanna said, smiling.

There was no telling what awaited Mindy. She understood that the border, the walls of the capital, was all she knew of this city. To travel to the center now, suddenly she was afraid of what she'd find there, how her illusions would leave her, just like she was leaving Hanna. What good was freedom, if freedom meant she would go back to being alone?

But the day that her departure was supposed to take place, the fog hung over San Francisco so thick that everything it touched became invisible. It was the kind of fog that a person could vanish into and never come back. Judging from the quiet solicitude of the detainees at Angel Island, it seemed like many were thinking about doing just that. A group of picture brides were standing at the dock, waiting for their husbands to arrive in the fog. There was no hope they'd come, but the women still waited.

Mindy decided to walk outside for a better view, but when she walked out onto the long wooden pathway, her own hands vanished in front of her. Beyond her hands, she suddenly began to make out the shape of a woman at the very end. It was Hanna, standing on the wharf looking at the sea, her lovelorn face in profile behind the fog. She looked so peaceful she could have been a ghost.

No! Mindy wanted to scream, but then the fog bell began to ring.

That day, no one was allowed to leave the island. The deaconess never arrived on the ferry. The ships that were supposed to dock never made it. Rumor had it the fog had interfered with the clockwork in the lighthouse at Point Knox, and the ships already out at sea were out of luck. The lighthouse keeper was a woman, and for twenty hours she struck the bronze fog bell. Against the sound of surf and wind, it rang all day into the night, a peal that felt as heavy as a heartbeat. It sounded forlorn, like the bells they struck to mourn the martyrs and revolutionaries back home. In other moments, it sounded hopeful—a carillon from a faraway country that had nothing to do with her.

As Mindy turned around to return to the administration building, she began to notice the presence of foxes. One by one, they appeared in the fog, yowling and moaning in unison with the bell. From the verdant green hills, they walked toward her. Must have been hundreds of them, immigrant foxes, their tails curled over their bodies—some had one tail, some had seven, some had four. In the human-made thunder of the bells, Mindy waited for hers to arrive.

Lotus Stench

after the Pu Songling tale "Lotus Fragrance"

illian announced her presence with the sound of her suitcase rolling down the hallway, the wheels squeaking as if being dragged over gravel. Hearing it, Liana rushed to open her door. It was the first day of spring, move-in day, and Liana couldn't be more thrilled. The two of them were friends who'd met in the most unusual of circumstances: their cheating lover, Sang. An underemployed novelist who hated making decisions and loved attention, Sang had two-timed them for several months until Liana and Lillian found each other.

"Your place is perfect," Lillian said. She set down her backpack and smiled. Liana's apartment was on a fourth-floor walk-up, sparsely furnished with a small thrifted couch and an IKEA dining table, a snake tongue next to the living room window, its leaves browning at the edges. The space was cramped, but it didn't matter; between the two of them, they had very few belongings. Lillian's room was the guest room, a windowless space with a small futon on the floor, but she preferred no windows. Temporary, all of it, necessarily—but loved.

"Welcome. I'm so glad you're here," said Liana. And she truly meant it. In many ways, it was remarkable that they got along at all, let alone this well. A fox spirit and a ghost, forming this union born of rivalry—who would have thought! Liana uncorked a champagne bottle and poured two flutes.

"This is a beginning. Let's toast."

Liana had first met Lillian on an unseasonably hot day in October.

She had come home to Sang's studio early after taking a trip upstate. Immediately something felt peculiar. Take-out boxes on the dining table. A half-eaten pound cake, its crumbs spilled all over. Boxed wine, two empty glasses, one with a lipstick stain. Then finally Liana saw the open window—and Sang, outside on the fire escape, kissing a waifish young woman.

At this point, Liana and Sang had been dating for about six months. That week, Liana had traveled by train to the Hudson Valley for her mother's funeral, Sang having decided not to accompany her; he said he was hard at work on a deadline for his novel, which remained unwritten.

Whenever fury overcame Liana, she shape-shifted back into her fox form. That day in the studio, she degenerated, molting her human husk: her flesh shrank and crinkled, prickling with white-hot fur. Tails and whiskers razored her smooth flesh, soft and barbed like cattails. Her coat wet from summer rains. She slipped into Sang's laundry basket, full of the clothes she'd so neatly laundered earlier that week, which he hadn't even touched. She'd throw them in the cesspool tonight, she thought, seething.

Climbing back in through the window, Sang tugged on the young woman's hand. An alien smell, fishy and coppery—something like a mix of rotten seaweed and musk—settled over the apartment, and Liana was certain it came from the strange woman. Safely hidden, Liana peered at Sang's lover. Her face seemed familiar, but Liana could not place it. Had Liana seen this girl at the hair salon where she got digital perms in Chinatown? No, this girl looked like she got her balayage done somewhere much fancier—not a hair on her head was out of place. Or perhaps Liana had seen her at school—that would make sense. Liana had attended NYU, where Sang was also employed as an adjunct instructor teaching fiction. Perhaps she was one of his students? Liana wouldn't put that kind of relationship above him. Sang had always toyed with the idea—when they first dated, Sang had made the requisite student-teacher jokes, even though Liana had never taken any of his classes and they'd met on a dating app. As Liana searched her memories for clues, Sang peeled off the young woman's plaid skirt, one she could have bought at a Hot Topic in New Jersey.

This girl was very pretty, Liana could not deny. Her figure was lissome and thin, skin jutting out because of knobby bone, fragile and greenish like celadon. Wispy bangs, a flat moon-shaped face. She had a translucent, dewy pallor that matched her general dolor, as if she'd been shut inside her whole life. Liana recognized this type—she'd seen them everywhere in this city, in her own mother—abject women steeped in yin, whose spectral beauty, sorrow, and loneliness were permanent as grease stains. The smell, too, felt permanent. This girl seemed smart, had to know better than she let on. Despite this, it was clear she craved male attention, if only from the way she looked at Sang: half simper, half stare. Liana understood: she was the type who infantilized herself near men, when it was convenient, and this no doubt inspired a pity in Sang, pity that aroused him. She watched as he kissed the other woman on the clavicle, as it elicited an instant response—a whimper.

Then something dawned on Liana, something that startled her so much she lost her grip on her transformation. Instantly her human form reemerged, snapping the plastic laundry basket apart. Covered in Sang's rags, she sprawled in front of the undressed couple.

"What the fuck?" the other woman yelped, gripping the comforter as Sang scrambled to find his glasses on the bed. Slapping them on his face, Sang stammered, "Liana? Where did you come from so suddenly?"

He mumbled a series of excuses Liana did not hear. She had finally placed where she recognized this girl from—a class Liana had taken the year before, that one lecture with at least seventy-five students, English 401, taught by a professor whose syllabus only contained dead white men. Her name was Lillian. The Lillian in front of her had black hair, but last year in class she'd always looked like she had just arrived from an anime convention, with her oversized sweatshirts and saucer-eye contacts, her hair changing color every week, silver or lavender or red. It was hard to know what she really looked like underneath the hairstyles and makeup. During lectures, Lillian sat in the back, nodding off and copying notes from her friend.

All the expected feelings of betrayal or anger that threatened to throttle Liana in that moment dissipated. Because now she remembered: the girl from her class was dead.

. . . . .

Early in the previous semester, Liana and Sang had been inundated with emails about the news that a fourth-year student from the History Department had vanished. The story went that Lillian had gone missing from her dormitory, and her roommate filed a report. Two days later, her body was discovered in an alley beside the Humanities and Social Sciences Building. The girl had fallen twelve stories from an open window in the east wing of the building, from the office of a professor in the History Department. It was a mystery whether she had been pushed or fallen of her own accord, but the university and the police investigated and found no evidence of foul play. They brought a few people in for questioning, but no one was named a person of interest.

So there in the kitchen of Sang's studio apartment, Liana realized that the woman in front of her was a female ghost. It explained the pungent smell, and it also explained her preternatural beauty—a beauty she most certainly had not worn in life. Liana had met a few such ghosts in her lifetime—always gorgeous and pathetic, smelling of melancholy and death.

So Sang had a type: the supernatural woman.

"A ghost, Sang? Really?"

"I can explain!" He put his hands in front of his face.

"You could get violently sick from fucking around with ghosts. They swarm with death and disease!"

"I thought foxes and ghosts are more or less the same."

"Are you stupid?" Liana cried. "Foxes are flesh and substance!" She didn't think that Sang was silly enough to make such a false equivalence. Sex, for fox women, had a very specific purpose: yang cultivation for ascendence toward immortality. Compared to Lillian, Liana was not just any vulpine enchantress, she was almost huxian, a transcendent: an eight-tailed fox spirit on her eighth life masquerading as a human. One more cycle of gathering life essence before she emerged as an immortal transcendent— nine lives, nine tails.

Lillian, on the other hand, was the embodiment of yin: a female ghost who died young. It was common knowledge that the ghosts of young unmarried women were dangerous because they lacked progeny, falling away from the ancestral line. All the unfulfilled longing they experienced in life manifested into sexual insatiability as ghosts. Their living lovers often died from yin poisoning. (This was all according to the classical stories of the strange, the zhiguai and chuanqi. There weren't many stories of women with interiority coupling with charming ghosts, of course— most consisted of this tedious heterosexual tale between a grown man and beautiful melancholy ghost girl—nine times out of ten, she was a teen virgin.)

By this point, Lillian had practically dematerialized, her head hanging in shame, her body covered in Sang's comforter, as Sang pleaded some nonsense Liana couldn't make out.

"I am disgusting, I am foul, you're right. All I do is pollute him," the ghost whispered.

As Sang prattled on, Liana began to recognize what she and Lillian were—two feminine creatures, one human and one not, one living and one not, squaring off over a person whose only virtue was that he was both human and living. That night, Liana broke up with Sang and moved out of the apartment, letting him grow ill and emaciated from fornicating with a ghost. Soon, Lillian followed suit.

. . . . .

It was true that they perhaps should have despised one another. But when Lillian showed up at her apartment two months later, begging to make it up to her, Liana considered their circumstances.

"I know what you're thinking. How could you trust me?" Lillian said. "But I don't harbor ulterior motives. I owe you a debt, and I intend to pay it. Ever since I died, I've been floating in this world like a piece of driftwood, but now I have a mission, a purpose: to right my wrong." She tugged at her sleeve, choking back sobs.

"Stop it. You're okay. Stop crying." Awkwardly, Liana stroked the top of the ghost's head, now tousled.

In the end, Liana had to give it up to her: Lillian was right. She had nowhere else to go. You would think that the scourge of gender politics would not bleed into the spiritual realm, but there it was, sneering: arbitrary rules and roles for feminine monsters, whether they were ghosts or shape-shifting foxes—the absurd routines, the mortifying and debilitating cycle of seduction and deceit, the ridicule, the ostracization, the vitriol.

Also, what kind of grudge was worth harboring for the sake of Sang? Sang came on to *her*, but it was *Liana* who had to assume all the domestic duties once they lived together. *She* was the one forced to constantly cater to his emotional and physical needs, babying him, healing him when he was sick, yet it was *she* who was also considered the sexual parasite, the alien. She'd humored his every sexual fantasy, by assuming the shape of various actresses, supermodels, and celebrities, even the historical beauties of China like Xi Shi and Wang Zhaojun. She had been anything he wanted her to be, and he had still betrayed her.

And so Liana admitted to Lillian that she had been a bit unfair earlier. "I think we both lost ourselves in that person," she said. It had been wrong to distinguish herself too much from ghosts, at Lillian's expense. At the end of the day, both ghosts and foxes were regarded as sexually insatiable, dangerous women.

And Sang, who seemed so sincere in the beginning, was no different from any other man she'd met—and in her eight lives, Liana had seen them all: the Tang Dynasty suitor who had pummeled his own penis with a mallet to prove his virility. The Ming Dynasty suitor who had tried to wrangle her into a glass bottle. The Qing Dynasty suitor who had hired an exorcist to break up with her. Now Liana found she was ready to take an indefinite break. After a few centuries, the art of seduction had gotten boring. The search had lost its marvel, as had the prospect of a human domicile, assimilation into some human form of family or order. She was tired of the role of the responsible healer, protective fox spirit. She was eager to go back to her wilder ways—the ways of a poltergeist, an imp-like vixen, who played games, who tricked people instead of taking care of them. A prankster, a force of chaos.

"I want you to haunt this city with me, so we regain our power," said Liana. She asked Lillian to move in with her when spring arrived, so they could frolic together.

In Lillian, Liana finally found a common ground with another alien, someone who understood this marginal existence. In their liminal household, no one would be the parasite.

Two weeks after move-in day, black water began leaking out from the ceiling. A clog in the drainage pipes from the apartment upstairs had caused the water to come flooding down, the super said. It would take at least a week to fix.

It was the last chill of spring: The gas heaters were radiant with noise. The drip soon transformed into a syrup of dark sedimental liquid, now spilling from the faucets, the showerheads, its stench unmistakable. Liana tried to fix the place up with her illusions: she tried to mask the smell with a lotus scent and musk she'd acquired with her experiments with perfumes. Bemoaning her choice of apartment, she began to look for an exit plan.

"Don't worry, we'll find somewhere else to live," said Lillian. "We're resourceful." City ghosts and city foxes could only go so long without a new place or person to haunt—it was only a matter of time before they would be forced to move on, anyway.

The two of them scanned through Zillow and StreetEasy looking for vacant apartments, condos, lofts. Sometimes they wandered through the city together for hours, gawking at all the newly constructed skyscrapers muddling Midtown and Hudson Yards. At first they were careful to select places that looked long-empty or abandoned, but gradually, they grew braver and bolder as the weather thawed and the city came back to life. Forget propriety; they threw caution to the wind. They vacated the space in Chinatown, skulked every place in the city they fancied.

The small heists usually began with a spontaneous invasion: Lillian would materialize into some empty gut-renovated apartment, and then she'd open the windows or doors for Liana to climb inside. They found their way into empty hotel rooms in the Waldorf Astoria. They found the French country–style mansion of Liana's landlord upstate in the Catskills and ate his whole batch of chanterelle mushrooms, drank the oldest bottles in his wine cellar. They bounced on California king mattresses in the penthouse apartments on Billionaires' Row owned by shipping magnates. They went on joyrides in an Aston Martin DBS 770, blasting reed flute songs from other lives on the stereos. They broke into Sotheby's and stole the opal collections of deceased heiresses. They tried on the sumptuous satin gowns at Bergdorf's and exited camouflaged as mannequins. After the cleaners finished sweeping and the lights were turned off, they read the tomes of Qing scholars from the rare collections at the New York Public Library Rose Main Reading Room. At midnight, they shared pots of Pu'er and Longjing teas at the Astor Chinese Garden Court at the Metropolitan Museum of Art. They touched the moonlit taihu rocks and ginkgo latticework, basking in the artifice of a remote home they both could barely remember. They lived like nomads: every few nights, they moved to avoid detection.

"Rich people have limited taste," Lillian said one day, as she surveyed the eighteenth century rococo trousseau in the primary bedroom of the six-story limestone mansion overlooking Central Park that they were squatting in for the week. It was late afternoon, and light spilled in from the Palladian windows. The cupboards and refrigerators were filled, although the family was reportedly vacationing in Bali.

For dinner, Liana chopped scallions and ginger in the chef's kitchen to make a brothy soup. She unwrapped some frozen oxtails and set to cooking. Lillian had her phone and was swiping on dating apps.

"You're really dating again?" asked Liana, curious. "How do you intend to explain to these suitors that you're no longer living?" She set down bowls of marrow soup with oxtails on the carved satinwood dining table.

"I don't have to, because I'm only swiping for shits and giggles. I will not actually go see any of them," said Lillian as she took a spoonful. "Delicious. Best home-cooked meal since I died." Lillian's ghost smile was unnervingly charming.

Amused, Liana started swiping, too. After they lurked on the apps for a while, the two made a list of the preferences written on the profiles of these men. Lillian wrote out the first few on the whiteboard hung on the refrigerator:

- Must be easygoing, chill, drama-free.
- Knows how to lighten up and have fun, must be classy yet sexy.
- Kinky, beautiful, happy, smart, sexy, and passionate.
- Prefer Chinese girls under 70 kg.
- Must know how to take care of her man and spoil him. Loyalty is key.

"My god," said Lillian. "I'm glad I died a virgin if *this* is the pool that's out there. . . ."

Liana laughed. "Our heists are way more fun than dating," she said, and really meant it. A year and a half ago, before Sang, Liana had created her first profile on a dating app. Trying to date in twenty-first century New York as a fox woman—how bad could it be? Soon she experienced the full extent: the date where, after one drink, the man compared her to a "vulnerable and succulent oyster" that he wanted to suck from the shell. The date where the man Venmo requested her for the bill after she politely turned down his request to go home with him. The date where the man, upon successfully getting her to go home with him, couldn't get excited and so instead she spent an hour listening to him complain about all the women on the app who rejected him.

By contrast, Lillian was a fearless specter, unexpectedly wily and enterprising for a female ghost, in a way that Liana had always avoided, careful to evade the vulpine stereotype. The Lillian

who had wept in Sang's bed in the beginning felt remote. Now
their laughter spilled freely, carrying over the view from the fifth
story of the town house, the treetops of Central Park, canopies
crowned with dusky yellow seedpods, leaves as big as saucers.

Lillian stopped swiping, breaking their spell. "Hey, I recognize
someone. This guy." On the app, the face of a man. Bearded, bespectacled.

"Was he . . ." When Liana saw him, she understood. It was the
professor they both knew, the one from whose office window Lillian had leapt.

"Yes, he was." Lillian didn't seem to want to talk about it.
Without her divulging, Liana knew what this person had done.

"Why didn't you tell me before? Also, why is he on a dating
app? I thought he was married."

Liana's mind raced with ways to haunt him: Pelting him with
bricks or roof tiles. Pelting him with crockery, smashing his china
collection. Mixing filth into his coffee. Scaring his daughters,
possessing them. Shaving what hair was left from his head while
he's sleeping.

"Want to get even?" Liana asked. "We could find him, easily."

To Liana's awe, Lillian simply shrugged and said, "No. What's
the point?"

Liana was really impressed. Even though this woman was a
female ghost, even though she had studied vengeful, bloodthirsty
female criminals of Meiji-era Japan during her very short life, she
herself felt no desire for revenge.

If it were Liana, she would not be nearly as noble. Sometimes
she still kept tabs on the fates of people from past lives who had
wronged her—that Qing Dynasty man who tried to exorcize her,
for example, fell into a rainy ditch on his way to the Daoist tem-

ple. The Ming Dynasty man who trapped her in a glass bottle bit into a fat plum spiked with a blister beetle's poisonous eggs. The Tang Dynasty man who beat his penis with a mallet had cheated on Liana with one of his family maids, so he ended up mad after his member shriveled up into the size of a silkworm. There was a whole pantheon of such unfortunate souls, and Liana smiled when she remembered all the fruits of karmic retribution.

Sang called them constantly. He left voice mails, text messages, emails. He seemed to know they were living with one another; in all his voice mails, he implored them to come back. The stoic, mild-mannered façade was gone: The messages were steeped in flaccid, self-centered apologies. Listening to them, Liana realized that Sang's objective was not their reconciliation, but reassurance that he was a good man—or, if not a good man, at least that he was not a bad man. It was almost amusing how desperate he was to hear them say it.

"He seems sincerely sorry," said Lillian. "Are you going to keep ignoring him? What if he honestly wants to make amends?" She paused uncertainly, and then added, "I promise I won't interfere if you want to get back together with him."

"I'm not interested in amends," said Liana. "And I'm done with him." The thing about these situations—and she'd experienced them over and over—was that even though she had been the one wronged, even though she had tried to do right by him, somehow it always amounted to her being the one to feel sorry for him.

"I don't know," said Lillian. "I feel like he can't be lying if he's willing to grovel like that. Why deny yourself true love?"

"Love, darling, is that something you want?" Liana asked.

"Well, yes," said Lillian. "I'd always wanted it, even though I never knew what it was. Never could find it while I was still alive." Her eyes were shimmering, fertile with dangerous dreams.

"Love has other purposes for me," said Liana. "I need a man's love in order to extract his essence. But he needs to understand that I cannot stay. I will always have to depart."

Maybe this time Liana wouldn't secure a human host. Maybe she'd fail in her vulpine duties, be forced to circle the sun eighty times again before becoming a celestial fox, but she was okay with that if it meant getting to live this one life on her own terms, this time with Lillian by her side so she wouldn't feel lonely. They would turn this world hospitable together.

If only.

After a decadent spring and summer, trouble finally caught up to them. Around seven o'clock in the evening on a crisp September day, Liana came home to find a stranger in the house. He was naked, lying on his side with his face down on top of the shag rug.

A dead man.

Lillian was bent over him, trying to resuscitate him and failing. On impulse, Liana ran over, swatting Lillian away. "Is this . . . is this *Sang*?" she shouted.

"I didn't mean to kill him! I only meant to haunt," moaned Lillian. "He had a planchette and was trying a séance and the next thing you know, I . . ."

"Oh my *god*," said Liana. "Don't tell me."

"I never thought that just *one* roll in the hay would kill him!"

"We have to do something about this!" cried Liana, surveying the mess: bottles of champagne on the floor, mirroring the moments before her first encounter with Lillian. "How could this have happened?"

"I'm so sorry, you know, he came back all apologetic, and he sweet-talked me, made me believe we could be a family, with you included. . . ."

"And you believed him?" Liana spat. A pang shot through her. It had never occurred to Liana that Lillian would revert back to her romantic illusions, at the expense of both of them.

Liana knelt down to Sang's mouth and opened it with her fingers. One whiff of his scallion breath informed her that he was still alive. She kicked him. Once, then another time, then another. With a violent jerk, Sang finally moaned, turning around and revealing a swollen growth on his chest. He was on the edge of dying.

For a moment Liana considered it: Was it worth saving him, yet another time? This time the cost would be much more dire. Another life dreamed, another life wasted. Then she looked at Lillian, on the floor, inconsolable, her panicked croaks spilling in all directions. An unexpected warmth took hold of Liana.

Gently, Liana took off her cinnabar bracelet and placed it on Sang's growth. Then she crumpled into herself, heaving a little, making herself as small as possible. She coughed up a red object. From her throat it emerged, covered in phlegm and marbled streaks of blood—a pearl, a pill, an elixir. The essence she'd cultivated for all these years. She pressed it to his wound. Slowly, the breath returned from her mouth to his. Hot tears emerged through her ducts. As a fox spirit, she didn't want to give back her breath. She needed his breath, his life force, to ascend beyond this wild nightmare of a world. She released it and all that she had worked for, all that she desired—the palace of peace, freedom from the vicissitudes of human emotions—retreated beyond her line of vision until it was no more than a cloud bank in the sky of bare illusion. She heard a voice, distant: "Liana, no! Liana, I'm so sorry! I was weak, I won't betray you again!" The sobs gained traction until they reached a crescendo, washing over Liana like water from a hot spring. She shook her head, tried to speak. She wanted to say: *There is nothing to forgive.*

Liana understood now: their shenanigans had always had to reach a terminus. Female ghosts wanted romantic love, the safety of family to remember them in their afterlives. At the end of the day, Lillian was still a human. Her desires all belonged here; condemned to only this earth, she would wander here forever. Lillian wanted love, but love was not enough for Liana. Liana wanted escape: She wanted transcendence, didn't she? She wanted to end her stint as a guest on this earth. And there was a way, Liana now knew, to get what they both desired.

Lillian gathered her friend's slumped form into her arms, the ropy flesh of Liana's limbs slowly giving way to the shape of furred skin and bones, hollow and limp, heavy. In a matter of minutes Liana's body had degenerated into a carcass of an exquisite red fox, pungent with wounds.

Was she gone?

Beside herself at the thought, Lillian let out a cry, alarming like the screams of foxes. She cried and wept and screamed so much she terrified Sang, now awake, who tried to console her. She pushed him away, already far afield.

First she fell into memory. It was late spring, two years ago. They were in that class together, English 401, the professor had assigned the book *Nine Stories* by J. D. Salinger. The professor had assigned them to the same discussion group, analyzing the story "The Laughing Man," in which Salinger imagined a fabulous version of China. The story followed an American protagonist, the child of missionaries who lived in China, near an imaginary border with Paris. He was kidnapped by mercenaries who injured his face by compressing it in a vise, disfiguring his mouth into a permanent smile. A troupe of Chinese freaks followed the American protagonist blindly on his hijinks. The other students had loved the story because it was a version of an even older novel by Victor Hugo called *The Man Who Laughs*, and these stories eventually coagulated into the character of the Joker, from *Batman*, a face they recognized, a face they knew well.

Liana had hated the story ("Imagine," she had said, miffed at the curriculum. "A Paris-Chinese border. This sure is some fucked-up imperialistic fantasy!"). Lillian, too, had hated the professor, who had often leered at her not-so-clandestinely during office hours. Still, this part of his lecture came to her now, in her afterlife.

"Stories and characters have so many lives," the professor had said. "The same fates, the same lives, get repeated in a cycle, over and over, until the story is perfected. We may not live to see the perfect version, but you will recognize it when you do."

Thinking of this, Lillian ululated, and her cries were so powerful she began to dream. A field, a parallel place—not earth. Deracinated, she lost her shape. Her insides emerged: blood and guts and worms. Flowers, too, and tiny poison mushrooms, their feathery jeweled gills. All this organic material she never knew a ghost could harbor. She wept, and as she wept she transgressed, all boundaries were broken now, she was crossing into an illusion, a phantasmagoria. She took a deep breath, and it was something more than air she inhaled. Ferns, heather, fields of lupine. Was that Liana, running forward in the grass, the copse of trees beyond where she stood? Lillian's heart leapt. Her own desires lost materiality as she chased her friend toward god knows where, all her entrails strange and loose. Past the pastures, the misshapen pines, she saw a lush primeval sea. Her body, left behind. And her friend, now a fata morgana against the winking crepuscule. Ahead, the low thunder rolling.

Midnight struck, and Lillian came to with an ache throbbing wildly in her chest. And a bolt of—was that *pain*? And how? Did she have nerves again? Rising, she felt the smooth skin of her arms against the linen duvet, the bones underneath. Tight braids of veins and vessels. The movements of bowels. She pulled at the foreign hair growing from her scalp. A white hair curled around her finger, and when she extracted it, a pang flicked through her head. Breath moved in her lungs, her rib cage contracting. A lump sat in her throat.

Sang had long since left. His string of texts she didn't bother to read. Instead, she turned to where Liana's body was supposed to have lain, but it was gone. The red fox corpse was gone—and she, Lillian, was fully, shockingly alive again. She got up from the bed and ran through the house's many halls looking for the bathroom. In front of the mirror, she saw the face of someone dear to her, and then she finally understood what Liana had done, who her sacrifice had been for.

A year passed. Lillian re-enrolled in their school to complete her degree and moved back into their first shared apartment in Chinatown, signing a two-year lease. One afternoon, she was browsing at McNally Jackson when she spotted a novel: *Lotus Stench*, by Sang Xiao. She had not thought of him since Liana's death. So, he had miraculously sold and published his novel. She was impressed that he'd actually made it to the end of his draft.

The novel was the story of Liana, Sang, and Lillian, fictionalized with an ending that Sang wrote in place of what had transpired. In the happy ending, they lived on together, a ménage à trois, in harmony despite all the misgivings and jealousies in the beginning, which the protagonist-Sang dismissed as women's excessive "emotions." Whenever protagonist-Sang found himself enjoying too much sex, Liana and Lillian took turns nursing him back to health, making him drink their saliva to treat his yin-sickness. Lillian is eventually reborn in the body of a teenage girl, who runs away from her family to live with protagonist-Sang. Liana gets pregnant with his child. After the birth of her fox son, Liana falls ill and dies, and her corpse returns into the form of a fox. The revenant Lillian and Sang weep for her, visiting her grave every year thereafter. Years later, Liana, too, is reborn as a human (teen) girl, and the three of them reunite and continue to live a happy life together.

Finishing the novel, she whooped at his audacity. Sang had described Liana's breasts as "juicy little kumquats," and Lillian's sex parts as "lagoons of unadulterated ecstasy." He described all their sexual encounters in excessive, lurid detail. Lillian imagined Liana's reaction: *I'd rather be dead than alive and in someone else's postpubescent body!* At the thought that Liana was not around to read this travesty of a novel, Lillian felt a wrenching ache spear her spine.

The next day, Lillian placed the book in the "Free" bin next to the English Department's offices. As she set it down, the professor appeared. He was exiting his office and tilted his head, glancing at her. His bloodshot blue eyes twitched slightly, averting her gaze. The flesh on his face pinkened, and he began to tremble, agitated. She walked up really close to him, felt him recoil.

"*Boo!*" she barked.

The professor coughed violently, dropping his tumbler of coffee. Hot liquid stained his wing-tipped shoes, sizzling the threads of the midnight-blue carpet.

"Are you okay?" a passerby shouted, holding the professor's arm steady. There was a commotion now, the people in the vicinity surrounding him. He was sinking now, kneeling into the spilled coffee.

When Lillian was a ghost, she never wanted revenge: too much sorrow steeped it with an unappetizing bitterness. But now that she was alive again, the idea didn't seem half-bad.

The Crush

Morgan first saw the stone when she was waiting at the Kitano izakaya. It had just begun to rain, and Irving Street had taken on an otherworldly color—gray-blue, like the plumage of a heron. She was sitting under the outdoor awning and something glinting on the street caught her eye.

It was barely noticeable at first—an iridescent sliver, this tiny rock on the ground. It reflected the light of neon signs: argon for lavender, xenon for blue, helium for orange. It reminded her of abalone shells she used to buy with her mother at the fish market on Castro Street back when they lived in Mountain View. It cast a brilliant effulgence no matter where Morgan looked, calling to her. Morgan got up from her table and pocketed the stone. When she sat back down, a waitress brought out a pine tray with a hot towel and barley tea, and she savored the feeling—the smoothness of the stone under the rough towel, the heat in her hands.

She sipped the lukewarm tea until he arrived, apologetic. He was carrying a helmet, having parked his scooter across the street. He grinned at her. "I'm Dean," he said. "Dean Wu."

"Pleased to meet you. I'm Morgan Zhang."

He was about three inches taller than her, with a flat nose and large, heavy-lidded eyes, his jaw curved against his damp hair, which was long, nearly chin-length. Handsome, Morgan noted, without being overwhelming. A few strands were stuck to his face, and he peeled them off as he took his seat.

They had been introduced by her friend Hazel Lin for an upcoming fundraiser Morgan was hosting for the Lunar New Year Cultural Festival, coming up in about four months. Morgan worked at a Chinatown advocacy nonprofit, and the other organizers wanted to find a cohost from outside their organization. Enter Dean, a performance artist Hazel had collaborated with for their MoMa PS1 show last spring. Before their meeting, Morgan had Googled their show and found videos of Hazel, Dean, and a bunch of other dancers writhing through the wings of the museum, with onlookers amused or engrossed or woefully unsure of where to place their bodies.

"I'm excited to host this gala together," said Dean. "I heard about your work on a podcast. Your book, I mean."

Morgan found herself flushing. The idea that this man could have spent a whole half hour listening to her ramble about her novel was both exciting and unbearable. "I haven't listened to it yet, even though it was from six years ago! Hearing my own voice makes me uncomfortable."

"I get that feeling," he said. "I'm used to being recorded, but what comes out of my mouth is mortifying." He smiled, revealing a crooked incisor and one right dimple. His smile put Morgan at ease.

The waitress came, and Dean ordered for them, making sure that Morgan got what she wanted. He ordered a bento box with rice, mackerel, and chawanmushi; she got fried tofu and soba noodles. To share, he ordered hamachi, bluefin, raw oysters with cod roe. He even ordered the special: sea urchin. Then he excused himself to wash his hands.

Morgan smiled. Though the place Dean had picked was casual, his order gave her the impression that he was trying to impress her. Then she caught herself: *This is a work function, not a date.* As she shifted in her seat, the stone in her pocket tumbled out. She reached down to grab it and when she opened her palm, she was shocked to discover the stone had grown. It had sprouted a glassy translucent layer, like the lava glass she used to bargain for at flea markets. As a child she had quite a collection of rocks and shells, gathered anywhere from neighbors' yards to China Beach to the shops at Pier 39.

When Dean returned, the food came, and Morgan noted that before he took a bite of anything, he would spoon food onto her plate unprompted. An orange slice, a piece of charbroiled mackerel, a spoonful of steamed egg, the largest piece of uni. It reminded her of Lunar New Year dinners at which her parents placed everything on her plate, the plumpest prawns, the best cut of ribeye. Dean was a caretaker.

Their conversation took off, lasting for the better part of four hours. It ran the gamut of everything except the gala: their favorite filmmakers, musicians, philosophers, and poets; their childhoods; their pariah status in their traditional diasporic Chinese families; their time spent lost and wandering in their university years and beyond; their ancestral migration patterns. (His people emigrated from the Pearl River Delta to Indonesia in the 1940s, then America in the 1960s; her people stuck around in Suzhou and Shanghai until her parents moved to America in the 1990s, when she was only four.) Dean loved Agnes Martin and Alice Neely; he also spent time in Mexico City before making large-scale murals in the Dogpatch and Bayside neighborhoods. They discovered they read the same book last month, Eileen Chang's *Love in a Fallen City*.

In the span of those hours, Morgan's thoughts became speculative, tentacular. Between bites of soba, she saw the two of them walking at Lands End or the Presidio. In between laughs, she saw them spending holidays together. She imagined introducing Dean to her eighty-four-year-old grandmother. Slurping her uni, Morgan saw the look on her grandmother's face, the delight and relief that her thirty-three-year-old granddaughter was not a lonely witch who, with her lack of luck in the romance department, would collapse their whole ancestral line.

It was so rare for Morgan to get over her shyness that quickly that she realized she'd been holding her bladder for hours. In the bathroom, under the light of the halogen lamp, she checked the mirror. Her face was flushed pink, and her hair was unusually soft, bouncy. Where did her limp hair suddenly find curls? The face that stared back was pretty, she decided, even though her brows weren't trimmed and her lipstick was smudged. When she reached into her pocket to reapply lipstick, she felt the rondure of the stone. It felt alive, almost pulsing. She resisted the temptation to pull it out again and went back to join Dean for sake.

When she arrived back home, it was past midnight. Morgan lived in a four-bedroom apartment partitioned in a run-down Victorian with three roommates in Hayes Valley. It was her first and only grown-up apartment. A decade ago, she had graduated and moved in after starting her first office job at a tech start-up.

With the aftermath of the market crash and the star of *The Terminator* as governor, she felt lucky to have found work at all, though she barely lasted a year. Thankfully, the apartment was rent-stabilized, but rumors surfaced that after this wildfire season, the owners planned to sell it and move to Alaska, away from this combustible Golden State. Morgan didn't know where she'd go if she had to move.

She set her purse down. The house was silent except for the hushed laughter of her housemate and his boyfriend in his room, a thread of orange light leaking onto the kitchen tiles. Her other housemates were not home, probably with their partners. Turning on the lamp, Morgan examined her new friend, the stone. It had grown again a couple of sizes, about the width and shape of a cherry tomato, lustrous like an opal. In the dim light, it looked alien, like it didn't belong in this world, so motley its colors and heavy its weight. How it shone, unapologetic in its candescence. In the span of a few hours, it had transformed from a sliver to a solid object, a pebble smoothed as if by a river. Though she was bewildered, the heft of it comforted her.

The rock had witnessed her whole night—the banter, the jokes, the way Dean's hand brushed hers when he reached for the check. He had paid, which meant it had to have been a date. And if dinner didn't prove this, then what followed did. He'd offered to give her a ride home on his scooter, handing her the extra helmet in his seat, and then taken the long way around. They'd crisscrossed up Eighteenth Avenue and into the Golden Gate Park, with its mossy dankness, passing the Botanical Garden, the memorial groves, then onto Oak Street, where they could see the Haight at night, people swarming around smoke shops and secondhand stores. They'd navigated up and down the steep side streets approaching Alamo Square, the Painted Ladies. Morgan couldn't help loving the lights of the city, how transcendent they looked from the back of his bike. They'd sped down a hill and her stomach free-fell as she smelled him through his polyurethane leather jacket. She'd pressed her hands against his front where his shirt was warm, and then, before she was ready, it was over, and he parked in front of her house. She'd hugged him goodbye, brief and sheepish. At her kitchen table, she lost herself recounting every detail of this encounter, how her wrists were wet with residual rain, still a little shaky.

She creaked up the stairs and slipped into her room, wide awake. Her corner bedroom had bay windows overlooking a laundromat, a boba and shaved ice shop, and a convenience store. It was the smallest room in the house, but it had the biggest windows, which she covered at night with heavy blackout curtains.

She opened her laptop, putting on a live stream of the news. Today was the first rain they'd experienced in four months, and even that was not enough to put out the fires raging across California, swallowing up thousands of acres in Napa and Mendocino Counties. The video showed a whole valley on fire, the flame licks resembling a superbloom, fields upon fields of golden poppies. Wine country and vineyards were at risk, and the governor ordered a mass exodus. According to the reporter, it was normal for dry grassy fields to burn, but conflagrations of coniferous forests, redwoods, and Joshua trees signaled that something was very wrong. Tall sequoias older than this nation were splintering into spumes, their insides molten red as if full of blood.

On Saturday, Morgan went to meet Hazel at a gallery space on Valencia Street. Hazel was performing in a group show called

Future Losses. When Morgan showed up, she couldn't find Hazel in the group of performers in head-to-toe hazmat suits, which were acquired from a hospital ward that was recently shut down.

In the gallery, she sensed Dean's presence and a prickly sensation on her neck startled her. With her peripheral vision, she had a sense of exactly where he was in the room without having to look for him. They'd been texting on and off since their meeting, but he was inconsistent with his responses, and their conversation had petered off after Thursday. She wanted to see him again, if only to remind him of the connection she was certain they had shared in person, but she didn't want to seem too eager. Instead, she searched for Hazel in the crowd, surveying paintings of various apocalyptic scenes.

"Hey! Thanks for coming!" a hazmat-clad person said, patting Morgan on the shoulder. Hazel shook off their mask, revealing half a mane of long black hair. Earlier that year, Hazel had shaved off half their silver-dyed hair and come out as nonbinary.

The two of them had been friends for eight years. Hazel was two years younger. Back in the day, they'd studied at the California College of the Arts. In 2012, they'd reached out to Morgan for an interview about her first novel for CCA's literary magazine. Since then, the two of them had kept in touch, with Morgan picking up and dropping off Hazel at SFO until she totaled her car in 2016. In eight years, Morgan had never stopped feeling a little awed to be in Hazel's presence, with their tattoos and loose tank tops, their spitting laugh, their knees that were always elegantly scraped from cycling around the city on a fixie they called their "bad girl." Soon after graduation Hazel began working at a nonprofit in the city that brought artists to host storytelling hours at public schools, and a few years into this job, Hazel began showing their own work around the Bay Area, and then a few years later in other cities around the country.

Hazel darted forward, grabbing Morgan and dragging her outside, into the small courtyard in the back.

"Don't look, I know he's here," Hazel whispered.

"Who? Glen?"

"Yeah." Hazel had been in an on-and-off relationship with Glen, the lead singer in the alt-rock indie band Turnstile Chasers, for seven years, but last spring they'd broken up for good before he went on his first big tour. Fresh out of college, Hazel had taken Morgan to see the Turnstile Chasers open for MGMT at the Great American Music Hall, and for many years after it was Morgan who held Hazel's shoulders up every time Glen blew them off during their relationship. Morgan thought Hazel was better off without him.

Back in the gallery, the handlers had installed stepladders all over the space between paintings, and they went back inside. Hazel, along with six others, began scaling the walls, ducking under or over the paintings, stepping on the ladders, moving their arms in circles without touching one another. *The story of a near-future pandemic*, the description on the wall read, *where no one is allowed to touch ever again*.

The music began, and it was a sharp, eerie harmonica. The hazmat suits moved from the walls to the center of the room, where they formed pairs. Morgan couldn't tell which one was Hazel. Each pair made a sort of seesaw motion where one dancer reached toward the other dancer but the other ducked, and so on and so forth until the end, when everyone collapsed on the floor.

As the audience clapped, someone gripped Morgan's arm

below her elbow. She swung around, and it was Dean. Here she was thinking he hadn't seen or noticed her. Her throat caught.

In his warm gaze, Morgan felt unmoored. Try as she might, she could not censor her own thoughts from spiraling out of control—their possible future was a reel that played over and over, in which they went to art shows like this all the time, together. Something in her tote began vibrating, and she thought it was her cell phone, but when she felt inside her bag, she realized it was the rock. It had grown again, softening in her hand like a fleshy organ.

"What's your next stop?" Dean asked.

"Um . . . I'm not sure. I don't have any plans," Morgan lied. She was supposed to get dinner with Hazel, but Hazel was standing outside the gallery with Glen, smoking. Based on how Hazel looked at him, Morgan concluded that their dinner plans were probably on hold.

"I'm headed to a poetry reading. It's close, only a few blocks from here. Do you want to come with?" Dean checked his watch. "Actually, it doesn't start for two hours. Maybe we can grab a bite?"

As soon as they stepped out, the ash assailed them. Outside, the air felt thick and smoky—the ashes from Napa's burning mixed with the fog to create an alien pallor. Silently they walked down Valencia and turned right on Nineteenth to get tacos at Taqueria Cancún. The sun was descending over the palm trees, but the haze in the sky obscured its motion.

They crossed the street to Mission Dolores Park, where they climbed to the very top of the hill, under a flowering ash tree. In the waning light, teenagers huddled like flocks of pigeons, smoking and chatting. Children played on monkey bars, inhaling the ash and marijuana smoke. Behind them, church bells clanged.

"What did you think of the performance?" asked Morgan.

"Well, I wouldn't be surprised if a pandemic actually happened," said Dean. "It's not hard to imagine. . . . I mean, California is already on fire, and they are forcing incarcerated people to fight the blaze."

As they ate their burritos, the sun had already set, but the sky was still covered in the strange haze, as if the day were suspended, time trapped, thwarted from passing.

"My uncle lives in Vacaville, and his family had to evacuate from their home," Morgan said.

"I'm sorry to hear," said Dean. "Are they safe?" He brushed a glob of rice off her hair, his tenderness taking her by surprise.

"Yes, for now they're staying with my parents in Mountain View."

"Thank god for that." He paused. "My brother's in prison. They sent him off to fight the fires about a week ago."

Stunned, Morgan stopped eating. This seemed like a big admission, and she savored the fact that he was comfortable enough to share it with her. She wanted to know more but was afraid to pry. "I'm sorry to hear that," was all she could muster.

"They're called fire camps, as if the inmates are all on one big camping trip! The one my brother's at, it's way up north. It's literally called Devil's Garden Conservation Camp."

"Who got hired to name these shitholes? Dante's ghost?"

He laughed softly, with a sadness that pierced her like a needle. "I've been wanting to create a piece about my brother, a choreography. But what kind of dance can capture the hell he's in right now? It feels wrong sometimes. Do you struggle with that when you write?"

Morgan noted how much thought Dean put into his artistic work, and that he respected her enough to ask for her input. "Yeah, I do," she said. "I haven't been able to write since my book came out years ago, and don't know if I ever could again. Back then, I was younger and more fearless."

They sat in silence, taking in the last shreds of the delayed sunset until it was finally dark. At eight, they headed to the event. The poetry reading was set in the basement of a bar on Twenty-Second Street. A sign for the event was drawn out on the chalkboard in curly lettering. There were four poets reading. Morgan recognized some of the names, but she knew none of them personally. As soon as they entered, a crowd turned and shouted Dean's name. He greeted a few young men who slapped him on the back. A woman, one of the poets, ran up to Dean and hugged him. Under the oily basement lights, Morgan noticed her glittery eye shadow, the thick black lashes that could be real or fake, it was hard to tell. It was criminal that this poet could pull off wearing hot pants and a tulle skirt without seeming excessive or tacky. In Dean's group, the rapport was obvious, and as an outsider, Morgan felt self-conscious.

Dean called Morgan over, introducing her to them. His friends, his collaborators, and his pupils. He coached a dance team and they were all in it, including the poet, whose name was Lara. She smiled at Morgan in a clipped sort of way, then said, "Well, gotta get ready for my set."

The poets went on, one after the other, until the air in the room began to stifle Morgan. Love poems, love poems, love poems. She was on the verge of excusing herself to go home when the organizer announced that the next one up on the open mic was Dean.

Onstage, he transformed. With the mic, his pitch dramatically rose. "Lately, all I think about is my older brother. From the time we were kids, if I stole cookies or did something stupid, he would always claim responsibility, and I let him do it. At the time, I didn't understand how wrong it was, to let our parents think he was the problem child. He got sent away to the army when he turned eighteen, while I went to Berkeley. I've been the selfish one, the asshole."

Morgan peeked at his friends, who were engrossed, nodding as if they approved of this self-evaluation.

"And then one day two years ago, my brother got in a car accident. He was driving, and he had had maybe two drinks, and his passenger was our younger sister Marie. Took a sharp turn on a mountain road, and bam. Crashed into a tree, totaled the car."

Dean continued: "My brother suffered a concussion and broken bones but survived. Our sister? Not so lucky. She died on the way to the hospital. And my brother, because he was the responsible one, requested the maximum sentence of ten years. Today he's fighting the fires that are making our skies so red."

When Dean spoke, he seemed to look directly at her. It was as if everyone else in the room who had caused her so much anxiety before vanished in his focus. She memorized this moment, this room: the harlequin-patterned armchair behind him, the red velvet curtain, the Wurlitzer jukebox, the two of them, alone in this dive bar at the end of the world. Only in an apocalyptic ruin could they both work up the courage to say what they wanted to say.

At this point Dean choked a little, his voice breaking.

"I wish I could just take back some of that responsibility, I wish I could just take it all back," said Dean.

Morgan saw herself supporting him through this struggle. Five years into the future, she would drive up to the fire camp with Dean to take his brother home. She imagined the look on his face, their hands clasped together as they pull into the parking lot. Reaching inside her heavy bag, Morgan touched her stone. Its surface felt electric, warm like freshly vulcanized lava. Then she touched a new sharp corner and stifled a yelp. Pain seared her hand. Opening her palm, she noticed two deep cuts on her index finger—paper-thin red lines, like an equal sign. The warning, in blood, startled her out of her reverie. Seconds later, the whole room drowned in applause.

Over the next two weeks, Dean and Morgan texted for hours every night. Morgan would half fall asleep, and he would send her another image of a lake, or an Alexander Chee essay, or a menu of a new pop-up restaurant, or an interview with an up-and-coming dancer, and she would wake herself up just to read, listen, watch everything he sent. Once, he stayed up all night reading a book she recommended. Another time, he fell on his motorbike and texted her a photo of his bruise. Morgan was not grossed out—in fact, on his leg it resembled the shape of an island she had once visited, and when she told him, he said they should go together someday. They even shared a Spotify playlist, waxing nostalgic about sappy Chinese ballads, Jay Chou and Teresa Teng, songs she grew up listening to at family gatherings. When he sent her a cover of Jay Chou's "Hair Like Snow" she listened to it on repeat until it was stuck in her head for days, awake or dreaming.

They followed each other on social media, and she scrolled

down his entire Instagram feed in the span of one afternoon, all 1,472 posts dating back to 2013. She noticed that he had quite a few pictures with the poet girl from the open mic night, but their poses were not intimate, even a bit standoffish, so Morgan couldn't tell whether their relationship was romantic. She clicked to Lara's profile, and predictably the poet had over sixty thousand followers, and her posts were all professionally edited photos of her traveling, lounging in Adirondack chairs in Big Sur or beside infinity pools in Palm Springs resorts. She captioned the posts with her poems, but Morgan noticed that the words were distinctly not the focal point.

Meanwhile, Morgan's stone transformed into a rock the size of a boot—a week ago she had no longer been able to carry it around the city in her pocket, but now she could not even fit it inside her purse. It became an ornamental object in her room, and every so often she saw something inside its iridescence. A future took shape, but this time it felt attainable—her desire manifested an imaginary Dean, trapped inside the rock like a jewel beetle suspended in amber, waiting for her to free him, for her to shoulder some of his burdens. This Dean made his feelings known, this Dean was passionate and caring, and, most importantly, this Dean desired her. Morgan began confusing this Dean with the real Dean. As September turned to October, San Francisco cooled down at night, but the fires were still uncontained. The clouds of dust were easy to choke on, and people began wearing N95 masks. The air quality was worse than Beijing's, where Morgan and Dean had overlapped for a week in 2017, Morgan at a writer's residency and Dean visiting family. They hadn't known each other then, but Morgan imagined the times they might have passed each other on the street—in Sanlitun at three a.m., drunk at the club, gnawing at lamb skewers mere yards apart.

The first time Morgan saw Dean dance, it was at a theater in SoMa. He had comped her a last-minute ticket in the third row, a prime seat. She hadn't expected to recognize meanings in the choreography, read the shape of his muscle cast against the harsh shadows, but she did—Dean's arms spun on a sinuous axis that made his entire body a soaring planet. In his body she saw all his thoughts and cultural influences—the balancing acts and rapid-fire swan dives of Chinese acrobats, the angular techniques of traditional Balinese dance. It thrilled Morgan to truly witness Dean in his most elemental form. He looked at her from the stage, just like at his open mic.

At the end of the show, the other choreographer announced that their dance group would go on a nationwide tour. They had applied for a grant and gotten off the wait list for funding. Stunned, Morgan glanced at Dean, who kept his gaze focused on her. Later that evening, after the show, Dean told her he was leaving in two weeks, and she tried her best to hide her dismay. He promised her to keep in touch, but her doubts simmered. The inchoate future she'd dreamt for them began to splinter.

The next evening, Morgan met Hazel for dinner in the Haight. They slid into the cool booth of a Burmese restaurant, ordering the tea leaf salad.

"You ditched me the other week," Hazel said. "Tell me it was worth it." When Morgan finally gave the update, Hazel raised their eyes in a half grimace and sighed.

"I'm sorry for the role I played in this. I feel responsible."

Morgan rolled her eyes. "It's just a crush. No biggie."

"A small percentage of crushes need exorcism."

"What do you mean?"

Hazel sighed dramatically. "Do you have a rock?"

"What are you talking about?"

"I want to show you something."

Morgan paid the bill and the two of them walked around the corner to Hazel's art studio, which was a huge loft space they shared with four other sculptors and painters. In their corner, a boulder around the size of a small fir tree towered over most of their pieces. One could mistake it for an actual sculpture, it was so beautiful—it reminded Morgan of scholars' rocks in the Lion Grove Garden in Suzhou. Parts of this boulder were spray-painted with phrases like I LOVE MYSELF and DUMP THAT BASTARD.

"This is my rock. I've been needing to get rid of it for years. I've done extensive Google research—basically a tiny percentage of hopeless crushes manifest as rocks. It's like a rare external disease."

Morgan was floored. She had been to Hazel's studio before, but she had never noticed the boulder. She thought back to her stone, which had already grown to the size of a toddler. Soon it could overtake the tiny space in her room.

Before Morgan could ask, Hazel said, "It's Glen."

"But y'all were in a long-term relationship. Can you call it a crush?"

"What's a crush, anyway? Projections. Middle school delusions."

"Elevated misery." Morgan paused. "It feels worse than regular misery, but at least it's more exciting."

"Exactly like my relationship with Glen. He never made me feel secure even when we were together. It was euphoric misery."

"I still found myself envious," Morgan admitted. "Whenever I ended things with my short-term lovers, I always blocked all of them."

"So you wasted a lot less time than I did. I used to think love was this sinking feeling at the pit of your stomach, an emotional *Titanic*, a weird sexual gravity. But now I think love is just prolonged attention." Hazel wiped dirt off their stone with the sleeve of their shirt. "No wonder this never went away."

Morgan felt herself growing lightheaded as Hazel continued: "I've read all the Reddit threads. I've done all the meditations. I've gotten my *I Ching* read, I went to a priestess and a fortune-teller in Taiwan, even went to a vulpine shaman in Harbin. I thought I'd tried everything, but recently I finally figured out how to get rid of it."

"How could you get rid of something that large?"

"The best way to exorcise a crush is to seek the truth. And if you get heartbroken in the process and still can't let go, then there's always Ghost Canyon." Hazel shrugged, squeezing the water out of a brush with their fingers.

"Ghost Canyon?"

"I read about it recently," said Hazel. "It's a surface rupture in the San Andreas that opened up about two years ago. The mystery of it eludes geologists: when it appeared it was quiet, there were no earthquakes whatsoever, and a chasm of that size is usually the result of a tectonic shift."

"So it just randomly appeared?"

"Yeah. People have been driving their boulders down this canyon since it opened. It's a place you can let go of the stones that encumber you."

"I had no idea. And I don't know if I'm ready for that yet."

Morgan felt pulled the other way. The rock had become, for her, a center of gravity. Her most intense crushes in her teens and twenties never amounted to anything—but this time around, she felt hope. She and Dean had a real connection, she was sure of it. She was desperate to prove to Hazel and herself that this time, things would be different. She just had to get rid of her anxiety. She thought of the book both she and Dean read, Eileen Chang's *Love in a Fallen City*, in which the protagonist was driven by intense anxieties about her relationship with her beloved, until suddenly, in the last ten pages, Hong Kong was bombed during the Japanese occupation. External chaos replaced internal chaos, and suddenly the characters could get together because now their main fear was not love, but death.

To Morgan, 2020 San Francisco didn't seem that different from 1940s Shanghai and Hong Kong. Just as the rich people escaped and left the rest of Hong Kong to burn, tech billionaires were building luxury doomsday bunkers in the deserts of California, stockpiling and hoarding resources for the oncoming climate apocalypse. The fires in Mendocino were inching closer and closer to the city. Some billionaires moonlighting as survivalists had already fled the city based on the evidence in the sky. These were the same people she sought donations from for her job, and the prospect of this indefinite existence pelted her with a new fatalism. Any time now, Morgan thought. She didn't have to wait for the cataclysm. Soon all her uncertainty and inner turmoil would disappear, and she would be loved. If she could, she would trade that for the end of the world.

On Saturday, Morgan woke up to an infernal haze. It shocked her out of her sleep, the mock-orange sky, dousing all of California in lighter fluid. The bay windows cast that hellfire-orange onto her bed and her skin, exaggerating every shadow. The knots in her stomach tightened. Her stone had morphed into the size of an adult human and clamped down on her bed. The very air felt heavy against her skin and bones. Was this a sign? Was the world burning down once and for all?

She logged on to Twitter, and everyone was posting photos of the orange haze. The Bay Bridge, the Sutro Baths, the Palace of Fine Arts, all cloaked in the same infernal filter. An article from the *Chronicle* explained that this was the result of scorched dust and San Francisco fog, the smoke particles and airborne ash from the fires scattering light across the sky.

Text messages appeared on her phone. Are we in hell? Hazel texted, with a photo of the red sky from their window.

Cover your face today, her mom texted. Don't spend too much time outside.

Then Dean texted. They had vague plans to hang out that day. Perhaps they could meet at Crissy Field in the afternoon? He had a camera, he wanted to take photos of the orange haze.

As she waited for Dean on the beach, the color did not let up. Sitting on a rotten log, she watched the orange haze lapping against the sea as she gulped down a cup of coffee. It tasted strange, as if she were drinking a stranger's ashes. It really felt like the end of the world. This was as good a time as any to confess. Even the sky was telling her to do it. High above the bridge, a helicopter circled around like a seagull, dragging a banner: BE BRAVE BE BRAVE BE BRAVE. It was an advertisement for windsurfing.

After ten minutes, Dean showed up with a Canon EOS Rebel.

In the orange air, he looked fictional, almost feral. They sat on the log in silence, him snapping photos of the deserted beach, the thin threads of the Golden Gate Bridge. She needed to get it off her chest, but in his presence, her crush on him suddenly felt silly and unreal, all the fantasies of them together crumpling into Magic Marker stick figures. Perhaps a few moments of someone's attention in the desert of her love life had caused her to feel a phantom intimacy. But then somehow, against the onslaught of her uncertainties, Dean's smile managed to disarm her, always— his one dimple like bait.

"Let me take your portrait," Dean said, aiming the camera at her.

"Oh no, I'm not prepared." She didn't want to further embarrass herself by letting him capture how she felt on camera.

"Don't worry. You're doing great. I'm just going to focus my lens. . . ." His coaxing was gentle, unharried. He clicked his camera a few times, and Morgan turned her face toward the sea. Underneath the flaming red sky, the ocean looked mysteriously motionless, as if the sun and moon's gravitational forces had come to a standstill. They could either be in Dante's Inferno or a lakeside beach on Titan, Jupiter's moon.

"Wow, these are amazing," he said, and when he showed her, she was shocked that, indeed, the photos were gorgeous.

"You look really beautiful," he said.

He was leaving in three days. Above his head, the same helicopter, circling around and around. BE BRAVE BE BRAVE BE BRAVE. The sky, the coffee, the orange—nausea overtook her again, suddenly coming up her throat, fever-pitched. The swollen thing inside her burst. If she didn't tell him then, she knew she never would.

"I don't know how to say this, but . . ." She hesitated. She didn't want to look at him, so she focused on the Golden Gate Bridge. *I like you.* Why couldn't she say it? She remembered reading somewhere that every two weeks, someone tried to jump off that bridge. The article mentioned that those who jumped chose the Golden Gate because of its glory, and its views: Angel Island to the left, Alcatraz ahead.

"I like you. I like you a lot, and not just as a friend." She exhaled, finally emptied.

Dean stopped clicking his camera and held it, looking at the sea or Alcatraz. The silence that followed was thick. Morgan couldn't stand it. With every silent second, something evaporated inside her, a crescendo fast plummeting. The orange alien smoke now seemed to suffuse her very windpipes, her lungs, her blood vessels. It occurred to her at that moment that they were witnessing and breathing in the charred remains of California.

"Well, I'm . . . flattered," he finally said. "But, like, I'm dating someone else right now."

Her moving parts, moving again, great, back to normal. This phantom Dean who loved her was a plea carved in the sand—erased within seconds by the next tide. Like so many of her dreams of romance.

She felt him put his hand on her shoulder. His grasp was firm, holding all her moving parts together. "Are you okay?" he asked after a long moment. "Maybe we should go inside?"

"I'm okay," she lied. She didn't want to go inside. She didn't know if she could. Silently she thanked the infernal haze for masking the flush in her cheeks, the humiliation of her pounding heart. Dean narrowed his eyes, loosening his grip on her shoulder. *Don't let go of me*, Morgan wanted to say.

"I'm sorry I led you to think . . ."

"Oh no, you didn't lead me anywhere, I'm sorry for bringing this up," said Morgan. "It's good to clear, you know, the air around this. No pun intended. I just felt . . . a connection with you. Like every time I saw you, I felt . . . tender." Her eyes watered. The more she was rejected, the more she exposed herself, her insides ripped open for the pecking. A habit that she'd hated since childhood.

Dean chuckled nervously, putting his camera back in the bag. "I should have mentioned the fact that I wasn't single sooner. I don't know what I was thinking." He shook his head, massaging the bridge between his eyes. "This is awkward. I'm sorry."

"You can go, if you like." She didn't mean it, she didn't want him to go, but now she could think of nothing else to say.

He shrugged. "Okay." With that, he walked away without looking back.

Harmony in the heart, calm in the thoughts, Morgan repeated to herself. *Breathe*, she thought. *Big breaths.* She breathed in the hot orange air and sputtered, coughing. None of it worked. Her heart was plunging into her guts. To calm herself, Morgan walked across the sand to where the edge of the sea began, took off both her shoes, and sank her feet under. The freezing salt water shocked her out of her senses, for she was expecting it to be hot, like lava; she was expecting it to boil her alive.

When Morgan got home, it was past sunset. She fell onto her bed, and to her dismay her stone had grown larger instead of smaller like she'd hoped. It was now practically a boulder, taking up most of the bed, taking up most of the space of her tiny room, and she cursed it as she finally allowed the tears to fall from her waterline.

How desperately she wished she lived in a world where the desire for love didn't have to be so humiliating. When she sought human warmth that did not, could not exist, she found it in the stone. For all the rock's bulkiness and encumbrance, its warmth had become a sort of hearth for her nights, where it got cooler and drier in the evenings and the smoke particles clung to every exposed inch of flesh. She folded herself against the stone and, pressing her ear to its heat source, she detected a faint, thrilling thrum: Dare she say it was a heartbeat? Or was it just a trill of her invention? She buried herself in her bed and kissed the stone's smooth surface absently. She reached around the stone, spooning it like a lover, and stared into her own face, barely reflected. She saw Dean going home to the apartment she had been in, except now with his girlfriend, whom Morgan realized was the poet girl, of course. *Where have you been?* she would ask, and Dean would say, *Oh god, baby this terrible thing happened today, I don't even want to talk about it. Let's just go to bed.*

And then she imagined him there, as real as anyone can be, hovering over her. To fantasize about this at this moment—thank god she was completely alone, with no one watching! She could smell him, his sweat, a hint of amber, like the night of the scooter ride when she clung to his damp T-shirt. Soon she was touching herself against the rock, imagining his hands, cold and wet, in place of her own.

Then, as she came, a line from a poem somewhere flashed through her mind, about drawing water from a stone. The poetry reading they attended together. The lovely poet, Lara, reading aloud lines that had made her brim with anxiety. *Hope harmed me with its breath*, she'd sung out. *I breathed it in and then I was lost in a dream I could not repair.*

. . . . .

Morgan rented the moving truck on the Sunday before Halloween. By then the autumn spells of heat had begun to abate, but the fires still raged—the hills still burning.

Hazel had spent the night at her place and between the two of them it took some wrangling to maneuver the rock down the stairs of the rickety Victorian. At the art studio, the two of them managed to transport Hazel's boulder onto a hand trolley that was inherited from a studio-mate.

Once they hauled everything into the truck, Hazel said they had to make one more run. Waiting in the parking lot, Morgan marveled at the sky. The orange had thinned somewhat, not the infernal red it was before. When Hazel returned with a photo of Morgan, one of those that Dean had taken, Morgan didn't know how to react.

"You're throwing this down, too, with the rock," said Hazel. They hugged each other. When they finally broke their embrace, they were both crying.

Morgan and Hazel took turns driving the four hours to Ghost Canyon. The whole drive, they watched the smoke plumes from the conflagrations peek out behind the miles of vineyards and orchards, the parched chaparral beyond. At some point they made a sharp turn, and the pavement became gravel, then dirt. When they finally arrived at the spot where the canyon was supposed to be, they noticed all the parked cars with loose bungee cords on top. Deeper into the path, Morgan saw the people struggling. There must have been dozens of them—the young and old, all carrying or pushing something heavy up the path.

Some tied their boulders onto bobsleds. Some put their boulders inside shopping carts stolen from Safeway. Some had smaller rocks that they carried in their arms. The hand trolley narrowly accommodated both of their boulders. Their rocks vertically leaned against the titanium poles in a precarious dance. Hazel began to slide the trolley into the dirt. Together, they joined what appeared to be a procession. Slogging alongside everyone, Morgan felt a strange communion. There was safety in numbers. One woman with a football-sized stone and a megaphone shouted, "Wonderful job! You're all doing great! You're all amazing! You're all gonna be okay! We're gonna be okay!"

Once Morgan and Hazel reached the summit, a sharp canyon gaped at them. Beyond a blanket of haze, they could make out a dried-out river filled with salt. It was burning. There were fires in the valley, whose plumes mysteriously did not emit any smells. The hazards were clear. One wrong move, and the result could be dire. Some struggled against their boulders in what looked like a futile duel: wild, unkempt, they risked being crushed or slipping down the canyon to their deaths. Some surrendered, buckling under the weight, so they left their boulders on the edges without pushing them down. Some changed their minds at the very last second and tumbled with their boulders down into that foggy abyss of salt and fire. Morgan felt awed to be among them: these gorgeous superhuman beings, how their sheer lack of insouciance made them beautiful, how their desperation made the sweat running down their temples glint in the heat of the smoked-out sun, how alive they all were at that moment with their collective hysterical strength, clawing for their dignity, pushing their boulders into the canyon in exchange for their peace.

At the ledge, the two of them summoned their breath. "Are you ready?" asked Morgan, dazed from the sun. "On the count of three."

"One," huffed Hazel, gently pushing their hand trolley closer to the edge.

"Two," cried Morgan, as rocks crumbled under her feet. Suddenly she felt vertiginous, as if one shudder could send her crashing down. So she ambled up beside Hazel, wanting to give the stone one last embrace. She lifted it against her chest, the stone heating up like a body. But then she let go, shoving it back against the pole of the hand trolley, which dangled precariously in slow motion like a roller-coaster train about to plunge. Down in the canyon, the discarded rocks seemed to glitter all at once, in unison, casting an obscene polychromatic light out of the sediment of broken infatuations. They were alone again now, at the edge of the world where anything was possible. They clasped hands, and then, together, they pushed.

The Haunting of
Angel Island

DEPARTURE

9

On muggy days, the sounds of the fog bells from Point Knox moaned from the distance. Ever since she'd arrived at this post, Tye had marveled at the scrim of fog that covered this island. How different it looked from this vantage point—how the grasses on this island shone yellow like a little church girl's hair, their spectral stirrings alive against the fog. If she squinted, sometimes she could make out the cannons of Alcatraz against the shapes of distant ships.

It was March 1913. By this time, Tye had worked at Angel Island for almost three years, and so much had changed. The year before, she'd landed on the front page of the *San Francisco Exam-*

iner for casting a vote at the polling place at Powell and Pacific. California was the sixth state to grant women suffrage, and Tye thought it deliciously ironic that she should be among the first group of women to vote, before white women in other states could. The article described her as a "pretty little Chinese maiden," and its headline read "Pretty Celestial Maid of 21 Casts Ballot Here; Epoch in the Sex's Emancipation." The author did not mention that Tye was employed by the U.S. government, declaring her one vote as the signal to "an epoch in the history of the world's progress," "the latest achievement in the great American work of amalgamating and lifting up all the races of the earth."

Never mind what she actually witnessed day by day: immigrants caged on Angel Island against their will, forced to eat and bathe together in conditions befitting chickens or livestock. Never mind that the Chinese Exclusion Act was still being enforced in full swing and prevented any Chinese immigrants from ever being naturalized. The idea that her lone vote could mean something to all the paper sons and daughters who lived in fear and precarity every day seemed absurd.

Despite Tye's misgivings about the article, Donaldina Cameron framed it and put it on the wall above the entrance to the missionary home. Tye did not protest.

She had other things to think about. For one, she'd met someone. The man she'd spotted on her first day, the red-haired immigration inspector. She learned his name was Charles Schulze, and he was a Scottish-born immigrant himself. She learned that he was the most desired inspector among the Chinese women, reputed to be the most lenient. Merciful. And, indeed, Tye found him pleasant to work with, unlike some of the other, bullish inspectors who regarded her with unconcealed disdain. He was patient. Never talked down at her. He cracked dumb jokes to make the immigrants feel more at ease, jokes that she translated with care.

One evening last September, she saw him step off the same ferry but from the whites-only deck. She waved at him; he waved back. To her surprise, he lingered until she could get off the ferry. He took her to a discreet watering hole near the pier, a near-empty saloon—they sat in a polished wooden booth facing a huge window that framed a view of the cobalt-blue sea. Above, the seagulls cried, circling the shipyard at dusk.

"Do you ever feel sad when they go?" he asked. "Do you get attached to them?"

"Yes," she said, sipping the drink he had bought her. Its taste stung her tongue, acrid and salty, like the sea.

"What do you do with that?"

"I don't do anything. I keep my head down. I wish them well."

"Do you have any regrets? I mean, with the women there," he said. At that moment, it felt like he was interrogating her, and it rattled Tye. His voice a slow and husky drawl, the twang of formality he used with the interview subjects. Any series of questions, even innocent ones, triggered a defensive reaction in Tye, and she found herself adopting the same expressions she'd seen her detainees make. His last question most jarred her. Because she would not dare answer honestly.

Yes, she'd made errors of judgment. There was the time Tye caught a woman with a package full of coaching notes and Tye turned her in to her supervisor, a move that eventually caused the woman's deportation. There was the time Tye broke the news that a beloved older woman was going to be deported, and several detainees spat at her. There was the time Tye hired an envoy surreptitiously so that a recently released young pregnant woman could procure an abortion. The woman never asked her husband for permission to terminate the pregnancy, and then the rumors reached him and he denied their relationship had ever existed. Donaldina admitted the girl into their missionary home, for now that she was freed of her husband she had nowhere else to go. The girl entered into a trance, sick with fevers and fits for several months. In the end, Tye questioned whether it was the right decision, to give her what she had wanted.

Then there was the time another woman vanished right under Tye's nose. Poof, overnight she was gone, and the other detainees whispered that it was because the missing woman had been a shape-shifter, a fox spirit. A shape-shifter? Tye wanted to laugh. God did not make women "shape-shifters"—if it were true, then no woman would stay a woman, least of all a Chinese woman. Still, nothing else could explain the woman's disappearance—just as nothing else could explain her reappearance, a year later. Tye had not been prepared for the moment she walked into the newly rebuilt Palace Hotel and recognized that woman, sporting fox fur and the marcelled hairstyle popular at the time, which Tye understood involved a painful hot iron, sitting at the bar on the arm of a man who was clearly not the husband she had claimed in her papers. One of those oil barons with a mansion on Nob Hill? Brazen, thought Tye. Just brazen.

"I have many regrets," Tye said, finally. Charles asked her if she wanted another drink, though she had not yet finished her first. The night had descended full force, and without the reign of sun and purple oilskin sky, the seabirds hushed. She told him she really had to get going, and he asked if he could see her again. "Of course I'll see you again," she said. "Tomorrow, when we work."

"I meant outside of work. You know. Like, the way we are right now."

"Maybe. We shall see." She trotted off, leaving him and her half-finished drink alone with the moon. Then the next day they returned to their post. Avoiding each other at work, and then converging again at their window in the watering hole at dusk. Again, then again, then again.

There was the time Tye interpreted for the interrogation of a twenty-five-year-old woman believed to be a "daughter of joy." It was a euphemism that Tye learned from Donaldina Cameron when they used to raid brothels together in Chinatown. When Tye was younger, making the rounds with Donaldina energized her. Every time the impressive white woman hacked a window open with her hatchet, Tye felt a rush inside her, a satisfaction. When they broke into buildings, boardinghouses, gambling parlors, general stores, Tye loved the simultaneous feeling of transgression and heroism, though what they were doing was neither. She loved the giddy routine of entrance, rescue, and escape—she loved seeing the expressions of the slave girls transform. Fear to gratitude. Suspicion to joy. That rush, that feeling, Tye realized, would never be replaced, least of all in that Angel Island interrogation room, where instead of broken glass, there was a caged window facing the sea.

Instead of joy, the sullen woman in front of her gave her a look so hateful that Tye felt apologetic. She made sure to choose her words carefully, massaging them a little to sound gentler than the words the inspector used. That was the best she could do. Even though she often merely parroted the words of the inspector, even though she didn't have a vote on this woman's fate, Tye felt responsible in a way that the white people in that room probably never did. Once upon a time, Tye had made it her mission to rescue girls like these, but now her job was to send them to the dogs back home. The woman had looked at her with such a specific spite, Tye knew it was reserved only for her. Because betrayal was a worse offense than misunderstanding, even hate.

A couple days after the interrogation, the woman confronted Tye in the dormitory. It was the women's recreation time, and Tye was smoking a cigarette under the giant sycamore. The woman came up to her, malevolence still in her eyes. "Do you think you're better than us?" she asked.

"Quite the contrary," said Tye.

It had been a long day. Tye had just finished interpreting for the other interrogation on this girl's case. The woman's "husband" had shown up in a nice suit and cuff links, but Tye had immediately known he was really her pimp. An American-born Chinese, he had a reputation in Chinatown. He had already "fathered" eight children, most of them girls, whose mothers were unknown or still living in China. Tye recognized the man from all her trips with Donaldina Cameron. The inspector asked him a total of 180 questions, and his answers did not align with hers. It was clear the woman had not studied her coaching book.

"I saw your picture in the newspapers. You do think you're better than us," she sneered. "You think you're truly American? With your fancy papers and job and clothes? Let me remind you what you look like—just like the rest of us. You look down on me because you think I'm a whore from China? I guarantee you it only takes one misfortune for you to come crashing down from your pedestal. And we Chinese will never take you back in."

A few days later, the results were as expected: That woman failed her interrogation, and for the first time in her short time at Angel Island, Tye took pleasure in the news of someone's deportation. But immediately she caught herself, feeling ashamed. Was it pleasure, or was it relief? Or were they the same? In the span of two years, had Tye already let herself grow vengeful, full of the same rancor that drove that lady's fuming resentment? Had Tye internalized those accusations?

Despite her misgivings, Tye found it hard not to get attached to the women of Angel Island. They didn't all treat her that way. The morning that Xiaocui arrived from Toishan, she mistook Tye as a fellow immigrant and offered her a bag of snacks—dried hot bean curd. Tye allowed herself a taste: slick and tantalizing, that hot chili oil an unusual taste, spicier than the dishes she knew in Chinatown restaurants. Afterward, her fingers were sticky, but it was worth it.

Xiaocui was a slender, saucer-eyed young woman around Tye's age who said she was on her way to join her father and her brother, who started a business south of San Jose growing chrysanthemums. "When they're in bloom, it's like nothing you've seen before," said Xiaocui. "I'm sure you've seen them before, right? In your hometown in China?"

When Tye told her that she was not native to China, that as a matter of fact she was an interpreter for Angel Island and she had personally never been to China, Xiaocui didn't even bat an eyelash. This information usually caused the Chinese women to keep their distance, or to adopt an overly formal tone, but not Xiaocui. Xiaocui wanted to know everything. What was it like growing up in San Francisco? What were Tye's impressions of China? Did Tye feel like a foreigner, though technically she was a native? Did Tye ever want to go to China? What groups of women on Angel Island most interested her? Did she love or hate her job?

Such questions usually caused Tye to shut down. But in this case, perhaps because Xiaocui seemed so curious and guileless, they didn't bother her. Tye didn't have a straight answer for some of them. She didn't know if she loved or hated her job. Some days it felt like a real honor: to work for the government, to have the kind of respectable job post that her parents never imagined or envisioned for her. Tye had surpassed the expectations of almost everyone in her life.

"Why aren't you prouder of your work?" Xiaocui asked her, and Tye wondered. Why wasn't she? If she were a schoolteacher, or a deaconess, would she be prouder? If she ran a newspaper, or a brothel, would she be prouder?

Most days, Angel Island was hard to bear. The poems on the bathroom walls, words crawling over stalls in every imaginable form—carved with a knife or written in ink, flowery or plaintive, calligraphy or scrawl. All the women's grief spilling from walls, threatening to flood. Even when the maintenance staff came over to cover the writing with putty and then paint, sometimes Tye could still *hear* the poems. Disembodied, floating in smoke or vents, a poem could surface at any time, its syllables shimmering, *pain, pain, pain.*

Were they true? Were they false? Sometimes a presence clawed inside the lavatory pipes. She'd heard rumors of ghosts, or fox spirits haunting the empty rooms, the broom closets that doubled sometimes as solitary confinement spaces for children who misbehaved. According to the matron, most of the women never went to the lavatory alone—they needed to go as a unit so they would not be outnumbered by ghosts. The haunted lavatories, the frightened women, the rumored fox spirits, all sealed in that building and unable to escape. How some women waited for over a year for their appeals to process, slipping slowly into hysteria. A few even died by suicide. These were the things she didn't have the heart to tell Xiaocui about. The girl would have to find out on her own.

On top of all this, Tye knew that if she continued to see Charles, soon it may not be a secret anymore, and both of their livelihoods would be on the line. Tye had to make a decision—and fast. She turned to face Xiaocui. The ferry had anchored—they'd arrived at last. Xiaocui grabbed Tye by both her shoulders and shook them in excitement. "Wow, Tye—look!" Tye whipped her head around but saw nothing of note.

"I thought I just saw a fox!" said Xiaocui. "It was so beautiful!" That wonder on her face, that excitement, Tye wanted to remember. Because it would not last.

On the rooftop recreation area of the administrative building, the two of them watched the merchant junks crossing the San Francisco Bay. Every day, dozens of these ships passed Angel Island. Today was the women's weekly walk around the premises of Angel Island with the Deaconess Katherine Maurer, and the sky was a rare clear blue. Xiaocui, instead of congregating with the others, spent most of her free time with Tye. From where they stood, they had a view of the long wooden walkway, where a group of five Japanese men were waiting, clutching their hats to their heads. Their gestures were so anxious, Tye could practically smell the sweat on their necks and foreheads. They were there to meet their brides for the first time.

The deaconess ushered a group of Japanese women downstairs, and slowly, the women walked to their counterparts. The women were wearing beautiful kimonos in spring colors, their hair in the updos of married women.

"Picture brides," said Tye. "They cross an entire ocean to marry men they'd never met before. These men chose their brides based on a photograph, and the brides also only knew their husbands through the photo they were sent."

"You know, that all sounds really awkward."

"Oh, I've seen it many times. In fact, the matron tells me that many of the brides can barely contain their disappointment. Their new husbands don't look anything like their photos."

Xiaocui chuckled. "If it were me, I'd slap them! Oh god! The *deception*. Imagine crossing a whole ocean for a husband, and then . . ."

Tye went on, "It's such a shame. I've seen some photos, too. The photographs show these handsome young men, groomed at these photo studios, professional makeup and haircuts, and you know how photographers can touch up the final product. So guess what? Some of the women don't even recognize their husbands when they meet."

The two women laughed. In one pairing, a Japanese man in Western clothes, distinguished-looking, was talking to a woman in an elaborate lace dress. She was wearing her hair in a short wavy style covered by a velvet hat that looked luxuriously expensive. Based on his gesticulations, Tye could tell he had big plans for them.

"That woman's name is Kiyoko," said Tye. "The story is, her husband was recently divorced, and a year is required after an interlocutory divorce, where he cannot get remarried. She might have to be sent home."

The bride's expression remained blank, mostly silent, and she didn't even raise her eyes to look at him. At times she smiled at something he said, but her eyes remained on her own shoes, or their long shadows stretching out toward the sea.

Xiaocui asked suddenly, "Did you ever want to get married?"

Tye paused. "As a matter of fact, I do. Someday."

"I can't imagine that being easy in America," Xiaocui said. "What kind of potential husbands are there here?"

Tye took out a cigarette, lighting it with a match. "Chinese women are rare in this country. You won't have any trouble finding someone."

"*Please*," Xiaocui scoffed. "I come from a line of women who made vows they'd never marry. I want to be a comb sister, like my four aunts. They all work at a silk factory in Shunde."

Tye chuckled. Comb sisters were women who swore allegiance to their independence and remained single and celibate all their lives. She'd heard of women like that from the other detainees, their daily gossip about their villages back home. In fact, Tye had even privately considered herself a comb sister, before she started meeting with Charles.

Xiaocui continued, "What about you? Do you have someone you like?"

"That," said Tye, "is something I can't tell you. You and me, I think we have very different conceptions of love."

"I don't mean to offend you, I just want to know about your life, that's all."

"We're forgetting who we are to each other." Halfway through the cigarette, Tye extinguished it, stepping on it with her cloth shoe. This time, Xiaocui had asked her the wrong question.

"Don't tell anyone I smoked here. This whole island is a fire hazard."

After six months of meeting after work at the pier, Charles didn't want to keep their relationship a secret anymore.

"But . . . this can't work," said Tye. "The law prohibits it."

They were speaking in whispers, even in the near-empty saloon. He suggested that they travel across state borders, to Washington, where miscegenation was legal.

"But if we married there, and came back here where a marriage like ours is outlawed, then wouldn't we be illegitimate?" Tye asked. "And besides . . ." She trailed off. "I don't know if I'm ready." She did not know what a marriage between them could even look like. She'd never seen something like that before. There was no coaching book for this sort of thing.

"What would you rather do?" asked Charles.

"I have to consult a few people first," said Tye. "What's the rush?" She wondered what Donaldina would think. When she first applied for this job, she thought she would never marry. That the job would be the reason she would never need to.

"The rush is, I'm going mad," said Charles. "Pretending I don't know you. Pretending."

"Pretending doesn't bother me," said Tye. She was well versed.

So deep were they in their conversation that they didn't notice they were being watched. A cough, a smirk, an approach. The man, a burly stranger, his reek finding them before he could make their acquaintance.

"Haven't I seen you somewhere before, boy?" the man asked Charles, raising a stein of beer at him.

"I don't think so, sir," Charles said.

"Oh yes I have! Charlie, that your name? I knew your father." The stranger then fixed his eyes on Tye. She knew exactly the kind of gaze it was—she didn't have to even look at him. "Didn't know you had a taste for Chinks."

A pause. A break in the spell, a rip in their arrangement. Tye's neck and face burned from her whiskey. She could never hold liquor, not then, not now—why was she pretending? For him?

Finally, Charles said, "It's none of your business." His voice low and steady, calm like a lake, something broiling just beneath. "You have me mistaken for someone else. Now, if you would leave me alone, I'd appreciate that very much. I don't want any trouble."

Tye stared down at her hands, which bloomed red, little poppy fields, not daring to look at Charles. One moment he was intent on marrying her, the next he could not defend her from a word that at one point she had thought had lost its sting. But there it was, the spittle of *ch*, the curl and fling of tongue, the tail of *ink*, the hateful *k* sound, contorting itself just like a scorpion's tail. Once, Tye saw a scorpion in the wild in Chinatown, before she left her parents. She mistook it for a spider, but then realized what it was: brown like a blister, bent toward death. Must have escaped from one of the markets. So transfixed was she that she didn't notice the white girl, the tourist, staring at her from a parked wagon. Then she heard: "Chink! Chinky! Chinky! So many Chinks!" Tye could not locate where the voice was coming from, only a pair of dangling white legs. From that day on, she associated the word with a scorpion, as if it were that creature that had poisoned her with its stinger. Now the word filled the room, buried her view of the sea, of Charles, and she could no longer be there. The man had backed off after Charles's choice words, but Tye no longer felt safe. She had to get out. Despite his protests, she walked out of the saloon, its dim lighting disappearing behind her. She made a careful curve around the bend, took the shortcut back toward Sacramento Street. Back toward her mission home.

Donaldina was on a trip to visit her relatives in Santa Rosa. The only person Tye found who could listen to her was Axiu, the mad girl she brought home from Angel Island. Still woozy from drinking, Tye told her what had transpired, except for the incident with the stranger.

"I sense something fortuitous about this potential arrangement," Axiu said to Tye.

Axiu kept a cracked head of the goddess Taishan, an idol that Donaldina only tolerated because the girl denied ever worshipping the broken goddess, claiming it was a sentimental gift from her mother back in Canton. But Tye knew that Axiu had been making divinations behind the missionary woman's back, lighting incense and reading the smoke. After arriving at the missionary home, Axiu had spent two months sick and feverish in bed. According to Axiu, after her baby was ripped from her body, something else had replaced it. A gift. The illness gave her the powers of divination—and she could communicate with spirits and see the future.

Who was Tye not to believe her? Although she was a Christian, there were times Tye wondered whether God was testing the strength of her belief. The first days she visited Angel Island, Tye felt the presence of fox spirits everywhere: in the hallways, in the closets, in the spaces behind walls, in the poems and bathroom stalls. Did this contradict her belief in God? Tye never brought it up to Donaldina: she didn't feel the need to. Some experiences were beyond attempts at explanation.

"There are many ghosts here in this house," Axiu had said, when she first arrived at the missionary home. "But don't worry. They're not malignant."

At times, against her faith, Tye found herself wanting to consult Axiu for direction in her own life. Would it betray her God if Tye asked Axiu to divine her future? After all, many of her predictions did come true. That evening, she decided she would. She procured a match and a joss stick, and a fistful of plump, half-peeled longans from the markets, and Axiu set them on a plate in front of Mother Taishan's head. She then pressed her hands together, touching her face with ink.

Read the flame, then the smoke. Axiu began writing—beautiful calligraphy, Tye noted. The ideographs soaked in ink and smoke. Then Tye saw her: a girl with blunt-cut bangs, in the smoke. She was wearing a robe embroidered with an old-time brocade, and she was frowning. She looked so familiar. Who was she? Tye looked over at Axiu. "Do you see that?" she asked softly.

"See what?"

"That girl."

"All I see is your future. Perhaps she's your daughter?" said Axiu.

"She can't be. She's dressed in old clothes."

"Well, I see a big family. Prosperity. A real home. Progeny who will be grateful to you for all of your days. Marriage will not curse you." Axiu laughed. "Wow, I'm beginning to envy you. It's rare to see such a bright future, but the man who asked you might be sincere."

"What about the . . . differences between me and him?" Tye asked.

"An impediment, but just an impediment," said Axiu, a smile blooming on her face. The girl in the smoke laughed once and was gone.

The next Monday, Tye arrived on the island and didn't see Charles. His absence distracted her all morning. In the afternoon, Tye and Charles were scheduled to interview Xiaocui and her father, the chrysanthemum grower. Tye had pulled what strings she could, between Charles and her supervisor, to get Xiaocui assigned to his Board of Special Inquiry.

Taking Charles's place was Inspector Johnson, a ruddy-faced man with a bad leg and a mean streak. The women gave him a nickname: Rat-Smeller. The man had the pink skin of a hairless rat and prided himself on smelling vermin—his goal in each and every interview was to trip up and intimidate the detainees so that they were denied admission. Johnson specifically loved to flog and humiliate the women he interrogated, reserving the most invasive questions for the younger women. Tye had always tried to avoid being assigned to him, because she knew his habits didn't end at just the detainees. This didn't bode well for Xiaocui.

The interrogation lasted all afternoon. In the hot seat, Xiaocui looked visibly more meek than her usual bubbly self. Her shoulders were hunched over, she stumbled over her answers. Her normally clear singsong voice flattened. She was soft and meek, somnolent prey.

"How old are you?"

"Nineteen."

"The file says you're seventeen."

"It was in error. My age I count in the lunar calendar."

"What was the name of your village doctor?"

"I don't remember."

"When was the last time you saw him?"

"Last year, February."

"Are you pure?"

"Yes."

"Do you know what I mean by pure?"

"I think so."

"What bedding was used in your bedroom in Toishan?"

"I believe cotton."

"Where were the light fixtures?"

"I don't recall."

"What color were the tiles in the kitchen?"

"I don't recall."

The stenographer typed furiously as Xiaocui grew more and more crestfallen. Xiaocui's lips began quivering, and Tye whispered to her softly, *It's okay. Try to be composed. You'll be okay.*

By the end of the interrogation, the sun was setting and the ferry to San Francisco was filling with just-released detainees. Row by row, the newly admitted immigrants ascended the gangplanks. It was still February, and the San Francisco night brought a dank chill that made Tye shiver, even indoors. Everyone was bundled in thick coats, their breath warming the air. Xiaocui stared at them from the window as she gathered her things.

The next day, Xiaocui sought Tye out in the breezeway where they watched the other women play ball.

"You promised. You promised to help me," she said.

"I tried. It was settled. But yesterday, I had no control."

"When I walked into that room, I didn't expect to see the face of that *Rat-Smeller* instead of Schulze!"

"That was the plan! But he didn't show up to work yesterday, and . . . I had no choice but to let them assign you another inspector."

"And now my fate is sealed." Xiaocui sighed. "I'm sorry for acting like this, it's just I never expected to fail. To crash so hard—I got my own *age* wrong!"

"I really did try," said Tye. "I really am sorry."

"Well, if you're truly sorry, then can you please at least do this one thing? Can you relay this message to my brother? He lives in San Francisco, I think: 853 Post Street. Three years ago, that's the last time I heard from him. If I could get this to him, he could find me a lawyer—and . . . and I would find out if he was really out here."

Tye paused, straining. "I've already risked my job once for you," she said. "Now you want me to do it again? I cannot serve as an illegal intermediary. You do realize that I'm employed by this immigration station, don't you? That it's my job to keep women, including you, in line?"

"It might be your job," said Xiaocui. "But . . . don't you think that all of the Chinese here who pass through this place . . . don't you think our lives mean something? Don't you feel any type of loyalty towards us?"

Tye took off her glasses and rubbed her eyes. "Of course, of course I do. But . . ."

"But what? You told me before that you were born here, that you don't even know China. That just tells me that your allegiance will never be with the people from my country."

"That's not true."

"Then you must see that I'm not asking for much! I'm only asking to know whether my brother is alive or dead, you think that's a lot? You think that risks your job?"

"If I allow it this one time, what will be next? You want me to cheat for you? You want me to get you out of here?"

"You told me yourself, the Canadian and Russian women live in better conditions here than all the Chinese! I just want to feel like a human again!"

"Then you might be disappointed, on the mainland, if those are your expectations."

At this point, Xiaocui's eyes were wet. "You don't know the hell we're in, do you, even though you see it clear in front of your face? That's the only way I can explain why you do this. I thought I was your friend, but there are fences and rules and boundaries here everywhere. I should have understood what that meant."

Xiaocui began moving away, walking back toward the building. Tye tried to pursue her.

"Xiaocui, please! You're . . ." Tye reached out and grabbed her arm, but Xiaocui pushed her back with such force that Tye fell over backward, losing her balance and tumbling onto the ground. Dirt under her fingernails, dirt on her clothes. Cattails scratching her face, and ahead, that long, familiar pier. She whipped her head about. No one saw them, to her relief. For a moment, Tye sank into the grass. She rolled herself into a ball, a small one, so small no one would detect her. Coyote brush, cool earth, the scents of wild animals stalking the island.

Xiaocui and the other girls were right. What was Tye doing there? Perhaps her job—which she wanted to think of as a helpful one—only further alienated her from the celestial place she would never know, a kingdom and a people and a history whose specter followed her very existence, from the seat where she took a photo for the newspaper, to the saloon where that white man's poisonous word bent her spine into the shape of the shame he wanted, the shame he saw in her. And Charles: Why did he want to marry her? So he could be an exception? Was it to allay his own feelings of guilt, an inspector who judged and determined the fates of desperate strangers every day of his life, whose only crime he, too, committed: to be born in a different country?

And yet, Tye did not think there was anywhere else for her to go. She had Donaldina, she had Axiu and the other girls at the house. She had her siblings, whom she sometimes saw at the markets, the parlors, the fruit stores. She thought of Charles. How his absence reverberated that day like the fog bell, how consequences had so immediately arisen. How so many futures lay at his feet. Xiaocui's fate sealed because he didn't show up to work. It would be extraordinarily selfish, for the two of them to marry. It would cause an unknown amount of pain, if they resigned from their jobs just to love each other in the open. A cataclysm, and then a rift. There was no other woman who could interpret in Cantonese between the matron and the hundred or so Chinese women detained, no other intermediary, no other advocate, no other resort. And yet, Tye didn't know how much longer she would last there on the island.

The truth was, sometimes when she walked into the dining hall with the detainees, she would experience, momentarily, something like the opposite of déjà vu. Jamais vu, they called it: a peculiar disorientation—though she had been in that room every weekday for the past three years, she felt as if she were seeing it for the first time. White-hot fright sharpened her spine as she stood in a roomful of women who looked like her, with whom she had nothing else in common. It was the loneliest feeling, that alienation and bewilderment, as if she were the only one alive on that island, that the room was full of sad, vengeful ghosts ready to bite into her. At their sorrow and anguish she retained a kind of disgust. How embarrassing, all their gaping wounds carved onto the wooden walls, the bathroom stalls, for all to see. At such times, in the throes of jamais vu, Tye would have to catch herself and breathe—so she would get away from all those women, those embarrassing misfits, those pathetic vandals, and down the hall she would walk, her nails scratching each and every poem on the walls—down the hall, jade paint peeling, into the bathroom, where there was one cracked mirror, its edges all covered in poems, endless poems.

When she looked into the glass and saw a pretty stranger, there was the bliss, or comfort, of non-recognition. How marvelous: this pretty celestial maiden, her vulpine features, her long hair pulled tightly into a low chignon, how meaningless and constricting this hairstyle, this uniform. She let the pleasure wash over her. She unraveled the hair and it tumbled down the shoulders, then she unbuttoned the vest until her creamy satin blouse spilled out. When she removed the blouse, she shivered a little. In the reflection, the pale arms, the ribs, were stippled in gooseflesh. Then the face materialized in the mirror, the one with the blunt-cut bangs, smiling against the desperate poems of women long departed—the same girl she had seen in Axiu's smoke.

Perhaps this familiar stranger was a past life coming back to stay, perhaps she was the fox spirit. Perhaps she was the provenance of all the heartbroken poems. Perhaps she was her mother's mother, the princess of prospectors, arriving in San Francisco on a ship made of wood and sails, not iron and steam—who, in the dead space of that ship, in the steerage, drank bilge water believing it was fragrant cassia tea. The girl was only fifteen, her thick hair gathered up in a knot, secured with a sash. Only fifteen and she believed in the phantasms of other worlds. Alone in the dank, dismal steerage, she counted promises. Promise: a new life in Gold Mountain. Promise: a husband, a family, a job. Promise: comfort. Promise: perhaps even gold, a nugget or two, her entire worth fitting in the palm of her hand.

But when she arrived, there was no Gold Mountain: instead, as soon as she walked off the gangplank she was carted off in a horse-drawn wagon to a secret barracoon with a hundred other girls like her. Instead, the slave traders stripped her naked so she could be inspected and prodded by bidders for the price she could fetch on the auction block, which was called the Queen's Room— such a pleasant name, indeed very civilized, not a room but an outdoor paddock built to temporarily hold the unbought slave girls. Instead, men in strange Western suits put their fingers in her mouth, squeezed the flesh under her breasts, checked her "hymen" to determine her value. Instead, she was sold on the auction block of the Queen's Room for the price of two hundred silver dollars, signing with her one stained thumbprint a contract she could not read. Instead, she was then transported to a subterranean boardinghouse on Pacific Street, into a crawl space with no light, no sun, and her days and nights then blurred into waste, the Gold Mountain in her mind spinning its thread, tangling in her hair, her breath. Gold Mountain, the Queen's Room, the Palace of Degradation.

It was night she dreaded. Night meant the arrival of men. Their tongues like tongs stabbing her, hot with greed and stench.

The girls around her, painted red and brittle like dolls. One girl
prayed to the fox spirits to die, and she died. One girl ran down
the slopes of Jackson Street to the wharf, where she flung herself
into the freezing San Francisco Bay. One girl transformed into a
fox, slipping away in the cover of crepuscule. This girl wanted to
leave, too. Welts appeared, abscesses, too, up and down her body.
Unknown, terrifying ailments. A nightly searing pain, as she de-
ranged herself with dreams.

Perhaps she did leave. Perhaps the fox came to her one night in
the shape of a man. Perhaps it had a pearl in its mouth and gave
it to her as an offering. Perhaps she had seen this creature once as
a child, far away, the memory now buried—she might have rescued it from a pack of hunters or jackals back in her home by the
river, across the world. The fox's pearl, its grit and granule against
her teeth—the taste of sea, the taste of wild blood. Its spiritual
essence. Without it, the fox would die. *This will heal you*, it said.
Call it a karmic debt.

Are you sure? she might ask, uncertain her life was worth more
than the one of the ancient creature in front of her. She swallowed
the pearl and it cast an oily ray inside her, leaking into all corners
of her body until all the welts sealed up, all the parts of herself she
had lost to the passage. And then the strength materialized,
which gave her the will to defy her captors, escape her cage, and
flee to the hills, to Gold Mountain. The frontier, its violent excess:
Roaring rivers, endless sunlight, the thaw of spring. Poppies and
primrose everywhere. The wildflowers winking at her: *Congratulations, you've made it!*

But it was not Gold Mountain in front of her. It was another
mountain she'd forgotten altogether: the mountain in the storybooks from her childhood, Mount K'unlun, where the Palace of

the Immortals, marbled and blood-red like a lantern, rose from the edges of the rivers, thundering beyond this verdant valley. She had finally abandoned the sublunar realm of humans. She was finally free.

Before there was a Tye or a Donaldina Cameron, there was this girl, this slave girl, who had no name, no language, no life worth a damn, who learned early on what this world was, how ugly, how bleak—a life reduced to bodily functions, the oil in her lamp, the mat she curled on, where she dreamt of hogs and hounds and knives. How she was to be abandoned, no relatives to take care of her burial, no one in this country, no one.

Tye wept. Who was she? The girl shuddered, her bangs singed at the ends. *Better leave*, the girl said. *In the future, this place will burn down in a fire. All the poems eaten in flames, no traces left.*

It was time to say goodbye. The girl gave way to another face, and at first Tye could not recognize herself. The wire-rimmed glasses, the pink-rimmed eyes, the bangs cut asymmetrically against her temples, the gaunt collarbones. She didn't want to see herself. She did not like the woman in front of her. Dread overtook her as she tried to wipe herself away. Splashing water and lye on her tweed sleeve, she rubbed the mirror to clean it of its image.

And when that image vanished, it gave way to the image of Daji in a wedding gown—all lace, all fox-white crinoline. In verdure, somewhere in the Salinas Valley, Daji kneels next to a cold, shuddering creek, splashing water on her perfect face, licking pollen from her hands. No groom in sight except for herons and ospreys.

Axiu, perhaps a future Axiu, free of the Presbyterian mission home, holds a baby of her own, its face all purpled, all alive.

Mrs. Yee, silver-haired, lights incense for a fox shrine, with a stone Mother Taishan, intact, in an unknown village. She has set up a new shamanic practice and apothecary under her new name. Shorn of her old identity, she has gained a new following.

Fenglu wears a Beijing opera mask, the kind that distorts the wearer's face into its most exuberant, opulent expressions. She has landed the part of Consort Yu in *Farewell My Concubine*. Black streaks of glittering paint spill from her eyes as she contorts her arms into arcs onstage, brandishing a prop sword in front of an audience of hundreds. On Marchessault Street, in Los Angeles's Chinatown, at the Chinese Opera House, Fenglu has finally found a new face.

Mrs. Rong and Yingning, reunited with Mr. Rong, move into a small house on a cliff near the cannery where he labors. Every night, they hear the sounds of waves and shuck mussels. Yingning sells the jewelry she stole to a local pawnshop.

Mindy becomes a translator herself in San Francisco, working for a small printing press. Years later, Hanna surprises Mindy with a letter notifying her of a return. Hanna and Mindy move up the Oregon coast, crossing ghost town after ghost town until they reach the Puget Sound.

Xiaocui reunites with her brother and father south of San Jose, and every day she runs through fields of chrysanthemums.

The women who pass through here go elsewhere. This includes Tye. In the mirror, her face returns without fanfare. The foxes are mewling outside. They are in a hurry. They surround the whole immigration station. They swarm Angel Island. There are hundreds, of all ages and classifications: seductive vixens, the kind that transform into wanton women; nine-tailed foxes, the ones fabled to have achieved divinity; wise old foxes, generous with their wisdom; ordinary field foxes, who yowl at the moon for food; man-eating fox demons, who rip out hearts and tongues and livers. There are hulijing, there are kitsune, there are gumiho. Now it's an island of lustrous fur and marvelous women. They're singing, they're dancing, they're reciting poems. They signal Tye to collect what little is left of her belongings and go. It is dawn now, a gateway to morning. It is finally time.

Acknowledgments

A great many people, communities, and institutions have supported the completion of my debut collection. To Nidhi Pugalia, my editor, who helped shape these stories with me and understood them with a depth that I could not have imagined. To Clare Mao, my agent and champion, who believed in these stories from their beginning and helped me generate this collection and bring it out in the world. To the whole team at Penguin Books and Viking Books: quite literally a dream team, something I have only imagined from childhood.

In high school, I attended my first fiction workshop taught by Dave Eggers at 826 Valencia. Dave Eggers and Vendela Vida have been a source of support for over half my life: thank you so much. My gratitude to 826 Valencia for being a backbone to my writing life early on, as well as to Kundiman. My fiction mentor at Carnegie Mellon was Jane McCafferty—thank you. My gratitude to my poetry advisers and mentors, Alice Fulton, Terrance Hayes, and Lyrae Van Clief-Stefanon. Thank you to my students and mentees.

The New York Public Library Dorothy and Lewis B. Cullman Center for Scholars and Writers is where I first drafted these stories in 2016–2017—thank you to Lauren Goldenberg, Jean Strouse, and Paul Delaverdac for welcoming me to that unforgettable space, full of brilliant writers, scholars, and thinkers. I couldn't have imagined realizing these stories without the Cullman Center! As the Jenny McKean Moore Writer-in-Washington, I continued to work on this project, with advice from the incredible writer and mentor Edward P. Jones. The National Endowment for the Arts also supported this collection of stories, for which I received a (poetry) fellowship in 2021.

To those who read parts of this book and believed in it, lending their keen insight and words of support: C Pam Zhang, Ocean Vuong, Jane Wong, Cathy Linh Che, Thora Siemsen, Kyle Lucia Wu, Aisha Abdel Gawad, Alexandra Kleeman, Angela Flournoy, K-Ming Chang, Kelly Link, Gina Chung, Alexander Chee, and Vivian Hu. To Eugenia Leigh: I'm grateful for the lunch I had with you in September 2016, in which you encouraged me to write what would eventually become this book. To Karissa Chen for editing and publishing the first story in this collection in *Hyphen* magazine, to Soham Patel for editing and publishing "The Turtle Head Epidemic" in *The Georgia Review*. To Shelly Oria, who edited and published "The Fig Queen" for the anthology *I Know What's Best for You: Stories on Reproductive Freedom*.

Thank you to the residencies where I've worked on this collection, without which I would not have written these tales. At the Anderson Center in Red Wing, I wrote several of these stories. At the Black Mountain Institute in Las Vegas, I wrote the first draft of "The Haunting of Angel Island." At the Ucross Foundation residency, I finished my second-to-last round of edits. At Millay Arts, I worked on my next round of edits. The value of the time and space I found in those spaces is boundless.

I am grateful also to the researchers, translators, and writers of the following texts, which were instrumental to the writing of these stories:

Koro: Clinical and Historical Developments of the Culturally Defined Genital Retraction Disorder, by Arabinda Narayan Chowdhury

Alien Kind: Foxes and Late Imperial Chinese Narrative, by Rania Huntington

The Cult of the Fox: Power, Gender, and Popular Religion in Late Imperial and Modern China, by Xiaofei Kang

Foxes in Chinese Supernatural Tales, by Fatima Y. Wu (dissertation)

Strange Stories from a Chinese Studio, by Pu Songling, translated by John Minford

Angel Island: Immigrant Gateway to America, by Erika Lee and Judy Yung

The White Devil's Daughters: The Women Who Fought Slavery in San Francisco's Chinatown, by Julia Flynn Siler

Island: Poetry and History of Chinese Immigrants on Angel Island, 1910–1940, edited by Him Mark Lai, Genny Lim, and Judy Yung

And lastly, thank you to my family. To my grandmother, Juhua Wu, my father, Ming Mao, my mother, Hong Li, my cousin Ying

Mao, and my aunts. To my marvelous friends, near and far: thank you for the good times, the bad times, the laughs, the cries, the laugh-cries. To Bo: thank you for being here.

To you, my reader, I am grateful beyond language. Thank you for holding this book.